'Ch

1818

A lot of Christmas traditions, such as the Christmas tree with its decorations, Christmas cards, and Christmas crackers, were created by the Victorians. We wanted to know what Christmas was like in the Regency period, and the idea of twins separated in their childhood, brought together as adults, and finally sharing a Christmas with the men of their dreams seemed perfect. Each twin has her own story, first ROSABELLE, and then ANNABELLE, but rather than make you wait to link the stories together, we decided to publish both books at Christmas time. Sylvia Andrew has created two marvellously distinct women for the identical twins, the heroes are charismatic, and the Christmas detail comes cheerfully to life.

We hope you have a wonderful Christmas of your own and that you thoroughly enjoy reading about Rosabelle and Annabelle

~the **Christmas Belles**~

Sylvia Andrew taught modern languages for years, ending up as Vice-Principal of a sixth-form college. She lives in Somerset with two cats, a dog, and a husband who has a very necessary sense of humour, and a stern approach to punctuation. Sylvia has one daughter living in London, and they share a lively interest in the theatre. She describes herself as an 'unrepentant romantic'.

Recent titles by the same author:

ROSABELLE
FRANCESCA
SERAFINA

ANNABELLE

Volume Two

Sylvia Andrew

MILLS & BOON®

Extract from 'Past Three A Clock' by G R Woodward used with kind permission of The Society for Protecting Christian Knowledge (SPCK).

First published in Great Britain 1998
Harlequin Mills & Boon Limited,
Eton House, 18-24 Paradise Road, Richmond, Surrey TW9 1SR

© Sylvia Andrew 1998

ISBN 0 263 81259 6

Set in Times Roman 10 on 11½ pt.
04-9812-85453 C1

Printed and bound in Great Britain
by Caledonian International Book Manufacturing Ltd, Glasgow

Chapter One

London—May 1819

The carriage turned left into Park Lane at a spanking pace. Goss was doing what he could to make up for lost time. Annabelle Kelland held on to the strap and shut her eyes, but as soon as the carriage straightened its course she opened them again. This was an exciting moment, and she did not want to miss any part of it. The road was bustling with vehicles and people of every sort—gentlemen in curricles, on horseback, ladies in phaetons and barouches, street vendors with baskets and carts…the noise was deafening to ears accustomed to quiet country lanes. She was in London at last!

She gazed out at the busy, colourful scene. For these last few minutes she could still allow herself to be Annabelle Kelland, Rosabelle Ordway's identical twin, hardly able to contain her excitement at visiting London for the first time in her life. Just a few minutes longer. For, when the carriage finally drew up at Lady Ordway's house in Upper Brook Street, Annabelle Kelland would disappear and Lady Ordway's quiet daughter-in-law, Rosabelle, would emerge from the carriage—young Mrs Stephen Ordway, widowed but a year ago, returning to London after spending a month in Berkshire with her family.

Annabelle sat back against the cushions and tried to look calm. If she was to convince the people in Upper Brook Street that she was indeed her sister, then she would have to keep a tight rein on her feelings. No excessive curiosity, no amazement at the sights of the great city. Her sister Rosabelle had lived in London for the past sixteen years, ever since Lady Ordway, who was her godmother, had unofficially adopted her and brought her here to live. Rosabelle had ended up marrying the son of the house, and, as Lady Ordway's daughter-in-law, she must have become very familiar with fashionable life in London. There was nothing new or particularly intriguing for *her* in the Polite World going about its business.

So, for the next four or five weeks, while Rosabelle continued her convalescence in the tranquillity of Berkshire, independent, country-bred Annabelle would have to adopt her sister's graceful manners and quiet ways… She was confident that she could do it, though it wouldn't be easy. But—she leant forward again and gazed out of the carriage window— just for these last few moments she would be herself, Annabelle Kelland still, peering out uninhibitedly at the lively scene before her, admiring the fashionable crowds as they paraded in Hyde Park.

Another smart turn, this time to the right, a trot through a street lined with large houses…they had almost arrived! The carriage drew to a halt before one of the larger houses, and even before it stopped Goss had leapt out and was opening the door for her. This, then, was the Ordway residence in Upper Brook Street. The charade was about to begin…

Goss was looking worried as he helped her out, and kept throwing anxious glances at the windows.

'What is it, Goss?'

'Nothing, ma'am. Nothing at all. I expect the Colonel is inside.'

'The Colonel?'

'Colonel Stanton, ma'am. He's…he's a bit of a stickler for punctuality.'

'Indeed? An admirable quality,' Annabelle said as she went up the steps. Then she forgot Goss and concentrated on the task before her. Rosabelle's careful coaching was about to have its first test. The stately fellow coming towards her must be Lady Ordway's butler. She hesitated for only a second, then took a deep breath and moved forward.

'Good evening, Whitcroft. What a lovely day it has been!'

'Good evening, Mrs Ordway. Indeed it has. I trust you had a pleasant journey?' The butler's wrinkled face was wreathed in smiles, and Annabelle relaxed a little. The first hurdle had been successfully cleared. Whitcroft had been with the family for years—and had known Rosabelle since she had first come to London. To be accepted by him so unquestioningly was very encouraging.

She smiled back and said, 'Very pleasant, thank you. How is Lady Ordway?'

'Better, ma'am. Her ladyship is expecting you.'

Annabelle walked through the door, and gazed round her as if glad to be back. Yes, it was all as she had pictured. A spacious hall, paved in marble, with a handsome staircase winding its way up on the left. To the right a door, surrounded with a beautifully carved case. The dining room. In the shadows beyond the stairs the library. And at the top of the stairs the drawing room. Lady Ordway's room was another flight up… She turned to go up to it, but had only ascended a step or two when a voice came from along the hall.

'Whitcroft, get Goss for me, will you? Before he goes to the stables with the carriage. I want a word with him.'

The voice was brisk, but deep and attractive. The speaker had just emerged from the library. He was in shadow, but as he came forward and paused to speak to the butler, Annabelle stopped and caught her breath. A handsome man in his

thirties, tall, loose-limbed, clean-shaven, his black hair cut
fashionably short… Discipline and determination were evident in the firm mouth and the strong line of the jaw, but it
was a good face, with plenty of humour and intelligence in
it.

Was this…*could* this be the infamous Giles Stanton? The
monster whose brutally unsympathetic attitude to Rosabelle
had caused her breakdown? Whose harsh insistence that she
was to return to London today had resulted in Annabelle's
offer to come in her sister's place? Surely not!

Rosabelle's account of him had led her to picture a middle-
aged Colonel in the Duke of Wellington's service—a rigid
disciplinarian, coldly issuing his orders and his criticisms,
bullying poor Rosabelle till her nerves had been reduced to
tatters… She had been quite certain he would have a leathery,
weatherbeaten face, a soldier's face, complete with grey side-
whiskers and a military moustache. She hadn't imagined anything like this!

It was fortunate that the gentleman's attention was on
Whitcroft, for otherwise he must surely have wondered what
was wrong with her. But she was quite unable to move.
Fascinated, her hand on the newel post, one foot on the first
stair, her other on the second, she stared at this elegant man
of fashion, impeccably dressed for the evening. You couldn't
say he was a dandy, though he was obviously a man of
wealth. His beautifully fitted coat lay smoothly over the broad
shoulders, but the cut was plain, and though his linen was
snowy white, there was an absence of any fuss and frills, a
pleasing lack of ostentation. And she had to say that he didn't
appear to be a tyrant at first sight—his manner to Whitcroft
was authoritative, but easy, and that voice was very attractive…

Whitcroft went out and Giles Stanton turned his attention
to Annabelle. In spite of her raised position their eyes were

on a level. Hazel eyes, a curious mixture of tawny gold and green…

'Good evening, Rosabelle. I thought you'd be here before this. I sent the carriage early enough.'

The voice had changed—no warmth or flexibility in it for her.

'What's wrong? Have you left your tongue in Berkshire?' Annabelle swallowed and tried to think of something to say, but he sighed impatiently and went on without waiting. 'When you've finished staring at me as if I'd grown two heads, you had better visit Aunt Laura. She too has been expecting you for hours. Where the devil have you been?'

Annabelle suddenly came to her senses. Now that sounded *much* more like the creature of her imagination. For all his pleasing appearance she had not been so far out, after all! Overcoming a slight feeling of disappointment she surveyed him more calmly. So this was Giles Stanton, Stephen's cousin and heir, now in control of the enormous Ordway fortune. What a very ill-mannered way to greet his cousin's widow, newly returned after a month in the country! Resisting the temptation to reply in kind, she took a deep breath and said sweetly, 'Good evening, Giles. Thank you—I had a pleasant journey, and feel remarkably fresh. I enjoyed my stay at Temperley enormously. How are you?'

Hazel eyes looked at her coldly. 'We'll go through the niceties of conversation later—I have an appointment in ten minutes. Where *is* Goss?'

'May I have a word with you before you see Goss?' When he looked as if he might refuse, she added firmly, 'Please.'

'Very well.' He led the way to the room at the back—he didn't believe in wasting time, that was obvious. Though he was dressed to go out for the evening, the table was scattered with papers which he must have been studying until the carriage arrived. He ushered her in, then turned and waited. What a pity the expression on his face was so very disagreeable! Such a pity… Annabelle pulled herself together.

'If you are about to blame Goss for not being here earlier, you would be unjust.'

'What on earth do you mean? Goss had the express commission to see that you arrived in good time. He set off more than early enough this morning. You are an hour or more overdue. Of course he's to blame!'

His tone of impatient dismissal irritated her. 'I think your experiences in the Army may have prepared you ill for normal travel, Giles. This was not a military expedition, nor was Goss overseeing a baggage train! He did his best to do as you had…commanded. I am sure he is not an unkind man, but he was so anxious not to fail you, that he would have brought me to London—a journey of over forty miles—with no opportunity for rest or comfort on the way.'

'That cannot be so. I allowed plenty of time for stops!'

'That must be a matter of opinion. Five minutes or so to change the horses may be an estimable aim in Army life, but I assure you, it is not the norm in civilised society. Certainly not for me. Goss told me what you had ordered, but I insisted on adequate time for refreshment at every stop. He could do nothing about it.'

For the life of her Annabelle could not resist a slight note of satisfaction creeping in to her tone. Once Goss had told her of 'the Colonel's' orders, she had taken pleasure in spending much longer than necessary at the inns, determined to prove that 'the Colonel' could not order *her* about as he chose!

The satisfaction did not escape Giles's notice. His eyes narrowed, then his expression grew even more forbidding. Annabelle raised her chin and stared back at him bravely, but she was secretly puzzled by his reaction to her. He was not just simply annoyed. He quite clearly disliked his cousin's widow, but *why*? Rosabelle was such a gentle, inoffensive creature… Sooner or later, Annabelle promised herself, she would find out what lay behind this antagonism—and then she would make him pay for his treatment of her twin. He was still looking at her, as if debating whether to pursue the matter, but he eventually turned towards the door, simply saying as he went, 'You'd better see Aunt Laura.'

Annabelle stood her ground. 'Goss is not to blame!'

'Very well, very well. Let me deal with my servant in my own manner, if you please. You may spend as long as you like with Aunt Laura—I shall be out for the rest of the evening.'

'Thank you, Giles,' said Annabelle. At the irony in her voice he turned and she suffered another inspection from those cold, keen hazel eyes. But once again he decided to say nothing, and simply ushered her out. A few minutes later, as she was ascending the stairs, she heard Goss's anxious voice in the hall, followed by a brisk reply. She permitted herself a small smile at his words.

'Nonsense, Goss. You did surprisingly well. I had forgotten the allowances we have to make for the ladies. You'd better make sure the horses are seen to, I expect you've been pushing them. And now I'll have to hurry—the Duke doesn't like to be kept waiting any more than I do.'

Annabelle opened the door of what she hoped was Lady Ordway's bedchamber and went in. Heavy curtains were half-pulled across the window and the room was in semi-darkness, and she waited for a moment, letting her eyes accustom themselves to the dim light. The atmosphere was stifling. A maid-servant was remonstrating with a figure in a chair by the window, but was being ignored. Lady Ordway was getting up, arms stretched out in welcome.

'Rosa! You're back! My darling girl!'

'Aunt Laura!' Annabelle hesitated, for the first time feeling some qualms about her imposture. Her sister's mother-in-law had changed almost beyond recognition in the years since she had last seen her. It was cruel to deceive this frail, elderly woman, who was clearly so deeply moved at the thought of seeing her beloved daughter-in-law again. But she must do so, just for a few moments. To tell her the truth without warning would be equally cruel. She walked over to the window and gently embraced Lady Ordway. After a moment she was released, and the invalid settled back into her chair. Annabelle found she was being closely surveyed.

'You are looking well, my dear. Temperley has been good for you. Have you dined?'

'Not yet, though I had something on the way. I only arrived five minutes ago.'

'I know. I heard the carriage. I expect you would like to change after the journey, but we could have something to eat here together afterwards. Wilson will arrange it, won't you, Wilson?'

'Of course, my lady. Welcome back, Miss Rosabelle.' With a smile and a curtsy the maid disappeared.

There was a short silence then Lady Ordway said carefully, 'Do you know where your room is, my dear?'

'Yes, I… Aunt Laura! What do you mean? Of course I do—unless you've changed it.'

'Ah, yes. I suppose Rosa would have taught you all about the house and servants. Tell me—she…she isn't still ill, is she?'

Annabelle regarded Lady Ordway in amazement. 'You know! So soon? How?'

'You are so like her, Anna! But I knew the moment you touched me. How could I possibly not know? Rosa has been a daughter to me for the last sixteen years. We have always been very close—ever since I brought her here after your mother's death. And…and this last year has brought us even closer. Do tell me. Rosa *is* getting better, isn't she?'

'She's doing very well. But it was much too soon for her

to come back. I'd say she needs another month at least. She was so…fragile when she arrived—we were very worried about her. But Temperley is doing her so much good—it's peaceful there, and Becky spoils her shamefully!'

'I've worried about her, too. I…I wouldn't blame her if she never wanted to see this house again.'

'No, no! You mustn't say that. Rosa loves you. Indeed, she was so concerned for you that I had to work very hard to persuade her to stay in Berkshire and let me come in her place. She has written to you to explain.' Annabelle passed a letter to Lady Ordway, who opened it eagerly.

Annabelle smiled sympathetically and went on, 'Shall I leave you to read it, while I change? I feel rather travel-worn.'

'Thank you, my dear. And after you've changed you shall come back to dine with me so we can talk. Wilson will see that one of the new maids is sent to help you. Wilson will arrange it all—I rely on her for everything. And she is the soul of discretion. Off you go, my dear. Half an hour?'

'I'll be back as soon as I can. And…Lady Ordway…'

'Yes?'

'I'll do my best to be a substitute for Rosa.'

'Be yourself. That will be enough. Half an hour.'

Annabelle thought for a moment, then walked confidently along the landing to her room. She found Wilson already there.

'Your valises are here, Miss Rosabelle. Lily will be along in a minute or two, and she'll unpack them. She's new, but she seems to know what she's about, which is more than can be said for most of the young ones nowadays. She might suit you. I've had one of the dresses you left here freshly ironed. It's hanging in the closet. Now, if you'll excuse me, I'll see to her ladyship.'

'Wilson, how is Lady Ordway really? She still looks ill.'

'Oh, no! She is much better than she was. She was a little depressed after you went away, Miss Rosabelle. But the

Colonel…I mean the master, has spent a lot of time with her—he's been very kind.'

'He has?'

'Oh, yes. And truly, Miss Rosabelle, she is a lot stronger. But she…she needs to be taken out of herself.'

'We'll have to see what can be done.'

'I'm sure your return has done her good already, ma'am.'

'Thank you, Wilson.'

The new maid appeared as Wilson was leaving, and with her aid Annabelle changed the clothes she had travelled in for a pretty muslin dress in palest lilac. Lily was not a chatterer and Annabelle had plenty of time for reflection. It seemed to her that her stay in London could bring benefit to more than Rosabelle and herself. She thought that Lady Ordway had been immured for far too long in that dim, stuffy room, with nothing to think of but the sadnesses of the past. Fresh company and new thoughts might rouse her a little. Rosabelle had possibly been over-protective of her. It was a year since Stephen had died, and his mother should now be persuaded to take a greater part in the world. What better reason than that Annabelle wished to see something of London Society during her month in London?

When Annabelle presented herself for dinner she saw that a table had been set up for them in the middle of Lady Ordway's room.

'This is really very pleasant,' said Lady Ordway. 'I've been eating from a tray, either in bed or in my chair for so long.'

'You haven't begun dining downstairs yet?'

'I…I haven't managed to face it yet, Anna. I don't know if I ever shall.'

Annabelle eyed Lady Ordway. The last years had taken their toll, but she was still a pretty woman. 'I'm sure you will in time. And now I'm here, I'll help you. By the time Rosabelle comes back, you will both be ready to face the world again, I promise you.'

'I failed her so badly, Anna. I wouldn't blame her if she never came back.'

'I assure you, Rosabelle would be here this very moment if I hadn't persuaded her to stay in Berkshire.'

'But, Anna, I don't quite understand. It's very pleasant to have company, and I am delighted to see you again after all these years, but…why did Rosa feel it necessary to send you in her place? Why the deception? I am sure that Giles would have let her stay longer had she explained.'

'Rosa was quite sure he wouldn't! In fact, he said he would fetch her himself if she didn't come back today. She didn't think he would accept me as a substitute, either, so…we decided that I should pretend to be her.'

'But I hardly believe…' Lady Ordway paused for thought. 'He can be a little overbearing, I suppose…he always has such a clear idea of what he wants done, and he gets impatient with delay. I think he frightens Rosabelle. She's such a gentle creature.'

'And he's a bully!'

'No, no, my dear. You mustn't believe that! It's just that he's been so overworked this past year—he hasn't had time for niceties.'

Annabelle took time to reply to this. She would have rather said that Giles Stanton's attitude to Rosabelle revealed a chilling lack of humanity. Before being allowed to go to Berkshire, her poor sister had been harassed and bullied until she had given a promise to return exactly one month later. Giles had made it clear that, unless she did, he would refuse to pay Stephen's debts, and that she and Lady Ordway would consequently be faced with penury! Lack of nicety, indeed! He might have been bluffing, she supposed, but to someone in her sister's state it had been sheer cruelty!

However, though Annabelle was sorely tempted, she kept her thoughts to herself. It was obvious that Rosabelle had not told her mother-in-law of Giles Stanton's threats. And it was not for Annabelle to tell her, either. So she didn't pursue the matter, but said instead, 'This sole is delicious. Is Mrs Brook still here? I understand you have some new servants.'

'Yes. Wilson, Whitcroft and Mrs Brook are all that are left of our old staff. All the others went after…after Stephen died. But Giles has recently engaged a new housekeeper, and three new maids.'

'Personally?' asked Annabelle, surprised. 'I should have thought that was hardly an occupation for "the Colonel"! It should have been Rosa's responsibility, if, as I understand it, she is to run the household for him.'

'He used an agency. I have to say that they seem very satisfactory. And dear Giles is so considerate of her.'

'Considerate! Of Rosa?'

'Yes. I am sure he wanted to save her the trouble of having to set about engaging servants the minute she got back. And managing with such a small staff as we had was very difficult.'

'All the same,' said Annabelle, the light of battle in her eye, 'it would have been more tactful if Giles had waited till Rosa's return. It was very high-handed of him.'

Lady Ordway regarded her with a smile. 'You haven't changed, Anna. You were always ready to do battle on Rosa's behalf. And I won't deny that Giles can be high-handed. It comes of having a successful career in the Army. But in this case I'm sure he meant it for the best.'

Annabelle was by no means so sure. The dislike in Giles's eyes had been very obvious. 'You don't think that…?' she began delicately. 'Might Rosa not have felt it showed some lack of trust in her judgement?'

Lady Ordway sighed and said slowly, 'It's difficult to say—I suppose it might. Especially as she is so unsure of herself. Anna, what has Rosa told you? About…about Stephen…and our life here?'

'She said she had given her word to you to say nothing to

anyone about Stephen himself. And she didn't. But all the same, it is clear to me that she has been under stress for a long time. She could hardly avoid revealing the difficulties you were both in during the last twelve months. And that included some of her own problems with Giles Stanton.'

'She kept it all from me, you know. I suppose she thought I was too ill. I thought he was simply being...'

'High-handed.'

'Exactly.'

It was clear that Lady Ordway still had a high regard for her nephew—and, if what Wilson had said was true, he had indeed been very kind to her. So Annabelle said casually, 'It might well have been that. Are you very disappointed not to see Rosa?'

'A little. But I am delighted to see you—especially if it means that Rosa will be properly cured before she comes back. I recommended a longer stay, you know. I even suggested this switch between you myself, though I confess I was not entirely serious!' Lady Ordway smiled. 'But it isn't as if you have never done it before.'

Annabelle grinned, then looked guilty. 'But that was when we were children. And it was only meant to tease. We've never done it in earnest before.'

'No. Are you proposing to sustain your role until Rosa returns?'

'You mean not to tell "the Colonel"? I...I would prefer not to. But it has to depend on you, Lady Ordway. I couldn't do it without your help.'

Annabelle waited in suspense while Lady Ordway considered. She was quite determined to fight for her sister's interests. And, if necessary, she was even prepared to open Lady Ordway's eyes to Giles Stanton's true character. But to her relief there was no need for such drastic measures.

After a pause Lady Ordway said slowly, 'I think we shall keep it to ourselves, Anna. I am fond of Giles, and he has always been very kind to me. But he is a touch autocratic…he certainly doesn't like to be crossed. And he has always been somewhat critical of Rosa, even when she was a child. From what you said, it seems to have got worse, though no one ever talks about it now.'

'Why *should* he be critical of Rosa? I thought they had never met before he came back from France last year.'

'They hadn't. In the old days Giles stayed with us during the school holidays at exactly the same time as Rosa was spending the summer down at Temperley with you and your father. He never saw her then. And after that he was out of the country for ten years, all over Europe with the Army—Spain, Portugal, France, Vienna… He never even saw Rosa and Stephen after they were married.' Lady Ordway turned her head away. 'But he was always fond of Stephen, and Stephen…and Stephen idolised him.'

Annabelle put a sympathetic hand on Lady Ordway's arm. 'Don't talk of it if it upsets you—I'm here to help you forget. But just think! If I'm given a chance I might even manage to persuade Giles to change his opinion of Rosa. You know she would never stand up for herself. Could you…could you regard deceiving Giles as a kind of game? A challenge? Could you find it amusing?'

'Do you know, I think I could!' said Lady Ordway, cheering up a little. 'And then there would be no risk of his sending you back and demanding Rosa's return. Yes! I think I could!'

'Good! Then that is what we shall do. You, my dear Lady Ordway, are about to enjoy yourself.'

'Am I?' Lady Ordway smiled tremulously at Annabelle. 'Then welcome, my dear. You're very good to do this for your sister.'

'Don't credit me with too much virtue, Lady Ordway—'

'You'd better call me "Aunt Laura", or you'll soon be discovered,' said Lady Ordway, entering into the spirit of things. 'And I must remember to call you "Rosa" in public.'

'Very well...Aunt Laura! But I'm looking forward to seeing London while I am here. It's an exciting adventure for me! I'm not just helping Rosa, you know.'

'You will be careful with Giles, won't you, Anna?' said Lady Ordway with a sudden return to her former manner.

'In what way?'

'There are things I don't wish him to find out... You must be very careful.'

Annabelle was puzzled, but she did her best to reassure her hostess of her discretion, and then talked of other things. Quite soon she had her hostess laughing at her description of her ignorance of the rules of Society, and her lack of social graces.

'Surely not, surely not! It cannot be as bad as that. Even in Berkshire they must know more than that!' Then Lady Ordway pulled herself together and said, 'But just to make sure, we shall start a course tomorrow on how to behave, Anna, my dear. We can't have poor Rosa accused of forgetting all I taught her.'

'It won't tire you?' said Annabelle, pleased that Lady Ordway was taking such an interest, but surprised that she thought it so important. They would not, after all, be mixing so very much in society. And it was only for one month!

'Of course not! I shall enjoy it. And if Giles sticks to his intention of entertaining more, you will need to know what to do.'

'Entertaining more?' echoed Annabelle.

'Yes. That's why he has engaged all the new staff. And more are due later this week. Now that he is permanently in London he feels obliged to invite his friends here.'

'Permanently in London?' Annabelle stared. 'Permanently in London? You mean, from now? But Rosa said...Giles is surely going to France for the next month? That was why she had to come back today—to be company for you!'

'He has changed his plans. You, my dear, are going to see a great deal both of him, and of London society.' She looked at the appalled expression on Annabelle's face. 'Isn't that what you wanted?'

Chapter Two

'Not...' Annabelle swallowed. 'Not quite. It's true that I wanted to see London. But I'm not sure I would have embarked on this adventure quite so gaily if I had known I should have to perform in front of Giles for a whole month! I thought we should be alone for most of the time.'

'Oh, I'm sure you'll manage, Anna! Come, my dear! This is not like you!'

'But...but I don't understand! If Giles is to be here all the time, why does he need Rosa?'

'He wants her to act as his hostess. I am not yet well enough.' She looked at Annabelle's stormy face. 'Don't be angry with him, Anna. He may be taking the opportunity to repay his friends' hospitality, but he is really staying in London for our sakes.'

'How very kind of him!' said Annabelle, without conviction. 'How is that?'

Lady Ordway remained patient. 'Giles has arranged to stay in London chiefly because he wishes to get on with sorting out our affairs. Ordway affairs, I should say. It was urgently necessary. Stephen...Stephen left them in some disorder. And between that and the tasks remaining from his duties with

Wellington, I don't believe he has stopped working since he arrived here. Rosa and I owe him a lot.'

Annabelle hardly heard her. The news that Giles Stanton was to remain in London in the foreseeable future was most unwelcome. She and Rosabelle had plotted their exchange on the basis that Giles was to be away, that he and Annabelle would hardly meet. 'He's really going to be here all the time? Here at the house, as well?'

'He has rooms in Mount Street, but he hardly ever uses them.' Lady Ordway looked surprised at the expression on Annabelle's face. 'After all, Anna, the house and most of the things in it are now his. He could have insisted that I remove elsewhere, and it is extremely kind of him to allow us to continue living here at all!'

'Kind of him! It would hardly have added to his credit in London,' said Annabelle sharply, 'if he had refused to give you both a home. Indeed, I don't see how he could have done it! It's not as if he had a wife or family of his own to house.'

She was in shock. Pretending to be Rosabelle, living quietly in London with Lady Ordway for most of the time, while Giles Stanton was safely away in Paris was one thing. But it was quite another to act as the man's hostess, to entertain the *ton* in spite of her lack of experience, to behave suitably at all times—all under the coldly critical gaze of those eagle eyes… Could she manage it?

'Aunt Laura, I'm not at all sure I can do this, after all!'

'Anna, you must! If Rosa has been as ill as you say, how would she manage? Oh, Anna, please do it, my dear—for your sister's sake!' She looked pleadingly at Annabelle. 'I know it is a lot to ask, but please say you will carry on.'

'Dearest Aunt Laura, I think I shall have to! I can't imagine that Rosa would cope, either. But it's far from what I imagined my stay in London would be. And I have few social graces.'

'I am quite certain you will manage very well,' said Lady

Ordway. 'And there are so many ways in which I could help you. Remember, Rosa was very young when she married Stephen, and after the first year they never entertained a great deal. No one will expect you to manage without help.'

'But I'm not even half as…as graceful as Rosa, Aunt Laura! She seems to know by instinct how one behaves. I didn't even mix with my neighbours in Berkshire more than I had to, and it has been hinted more than once that my manners leave a lot to be desired. I've always gone my own way. I suppose I never had anyone to argue with me—'

'That father of yours has a lot to answer for!' Lady Ordway spoke with unusual severity. 'I represented to him several times the desirability of a Season in London for you, but he always put his own comfort before anyone else's convenience. But don't despair. You're a bright, intelligent girl, every bit as charming as my Rosa. With a bit of training from me, and a few lessons in deportment and dancing and so on, you'll do. We'll tell Giles your social skills need a little polishing up after being unused for so long.'

'But surely Rosa went to all sorts of balls and parties! I imagined her having a wonderful time in London.' Lady Ordway had been talking with animation, her manner alert and eager. But now she sank back, a closed expression on her face. Annabelle hurried on, 'Not this last year, of course. But before that…' Her voice trailed away as Lady Ordway shook her head.

'It…it wasn't possible,' she said. 'Rosa and I did not go a great deal into society. Visits to a few friends, the occasional evening at Almack's. We saw very little of balls and parties.'

Annabelle was mystified. Why was the subject so painful? Anxious not to let her hostess fall back into apathy again, she said, 'I'm sure you could teach me a lot, all the same. I don't even know how to dance the quadrille, let alone the waltz!'

'Now that is something I can do! I haven't danced for years, but I remember all the steps. Perhaps we could engage a dancing master! I'll ask Wilson—she knows everything. Annabelle, we shall enjoy ourselves—you'll see!'

If Annabelle had been in a better frame of mind she would have rejoiced at the improvement in Lady Ordway's spirits. It was quite clear to her that her hostess had only needed some stimulus—such as her arrival in London—to emerge from the state of apathy and invalidism she had indulged in for so long. So she encouraged Lady Ordway in the plans she made for her education, and tried to keep any further doubts to herself.

They talked till quite late, but when Annabelle finally went to bed she found herself unable to sleep. She spent half the night wondering how she could possibly take her sister's place for the next month. When her eyes did eventually close her dreams were haunted by visions of herself committing one social error after another, before being unmasked as a fraud before the shocked eyes of half of London, including the Prince Regent himself.

She woke unrefreshed. The room was completely dark and the house seemed to be in silence. Then, as her eyes became adjusted, she saw that there was a narrow chink of light over to her left. Shuttered windows. She got up and gingerly walked over to them. A slight fumbling with curtains and catches and light came flooding into the room. It was bright daylight outside, and by craning her neck she could see sunlight on the trees in Grosvenor Square. She turned and surveyed the room. It was not as large as her bedchamber at home, though the ceiling was higher, but it was very comfortably furnished in the modern style. A closet opened off it, and walking over to it, she found that it was full of dresses, shawls, shoes, pelisses, hats and every sort of accessory. Most of them looked as if they had not been worn for some time, pushed to the back behind a collection of clothes in more sombre colours. Rosabelle had been in mourning for the past year, of course.

She went back into the room. Used as she was to the noises of country life coming in through the windows, this London house seemed unnaturally silent. What time could it be? She peered at a dainty French clock on the mantelpiece. Ten o'clock! Ten! How had she overslept so? What must they be thinking of her! She gazed round. A pretty little washstand stood against the wall and there was still some water in the jug. Annabelle hastily splashed her face and dried it, then dressed herself in a simple dress from the back of the closet— a pale green walking dress with a matching jacket of green velvet. Then she hurried out of the room. She paused outside Lady Ordway's door, but hearing nothing she went on down the stairs and into the dining room. The room was empty, the table and sideboards bare. How strange! A scullery maid was on her knees, washing the marble squares of the entrance hall.

'Oh, ma'am! Pardon, ma'am! I…I…'

'It's all right. Where…where is Colonel Stanton?'

''E went out, ma'am. Ridin'. He allus does at this time o' the mornin'.'

'I see.' Annabelle paused. She would like some air and exercise herself. 'Can you open the door for me?'

'Open the door, ma'am?' The little maid's jaw dropped in astonishment. 'Were you…were you thinking of going out? At this hour?'

'Well, yes, I am. It looks like a beautiful morning.'

It was plain that the girl thought she had gone mad, but she did as she was bid, staring all the while. Annabelle went out into the morning air and walked briskly towards Grosvenor Square. She went round the square twice, watched by various footmen, delivery boys and street vendors, who stopped in their tracks to stare at her. Annabelle supposed it was because she was out without a groom or footman. Even in Berkshire it was more usual for a young lady to be accom-

panied, and when the new footmen appeared she must remember to ask one of them to accompany her.

'Rosabelle!'

A horse and rider came up alongside her, the big bay cur-
vetting and pulling at the reins as he was drawn to a sharp
halt. Giles dismounted.

'What the *devil* are you up to now?'

Annabelle stared. What had she done? Surely the simple
absence of a footman was not responsible for this blistering
tone?

'Good morning, Giles,' she said carefully. 'I'm taking
some air. It's a beautiful morning, don't you think?'

Giles took a step towards her. 'Do you know what time it
is?'

'It must be after half past ten o'clock. I slept late.'

'You slept—' Giles took a look at the grinning crowd
which was beginning to gather round. 'You'd better come
home with me. Here, you!' he called to one of the grooms
among the crowd. 'Take my horse round to the stables.
Sergeant Goss will deal with her.' He tossed him a coin.
Then, taking Annabelle's arm he led her back towards Upper
Brook Street.

'You're walking too quickly, Giles.'

'I want you back where I can talk to you without an au-
dience.'

Annabelle was still casting around in her mind for a clue
to what had caused his annoyance, but she was beginning to
become somewhat indignant herself at this cavalier treatment.

'You're hurting me, Giles. Let go of my arm, if you
please!' He ignored her, and grimly continued his march.
Annabelle put her weight back on her heels and halted. She
was now seriously angry.

'Your military life is showing again, Giles! I am not a
prisoner of war. I will return to my home at a suitable pace,
and if you wish to speak to me there, I shall be pleased to

listen to you—as long as you are civil. I will not be…be frogmarched along the pavement, nor will I be ignored!'

'Your holiday appears to have given you some spirit at least,' he said. 'Whatever it may have done in other respects. Very well. May I request you, ma'am, to accompany me to what is, for the moment, your home. And may I also ask to speak to you over the breakfast table?'

'You may,' said Annabelle with a queenly dip of her head, fastidiously removing her arm from his grasp. To her surprise, this gesture seemed to amuse him, and he gave an involuntary grin. Annabelle was astounded at the difference it made to his face. Humour and intelligence were once more to the fore as his expression relaxed. He was not only very handsome— he was extremely attractive!

But he soon relapsed into his former manner. As they entered the house he said peremptorily, 'In the breakfast room. In ten minutes.' Annabelle looked at him in silence. He sighed. 'Rosabelle, would you do me the pleasure of having breakfast with me? In ten minutes? Please.'

She corrected him. 'Quarter of an hour,' she said, then added formally, 'Thank you, Giles. I should be delighted.'

Giles's eyes followed her as she went up the stairs. There was a puzzled frown on his face.

In fifteen minutes to the dot Annabelle presented herself in the dining room where the table was now laid. The room was empty of servants, and Annabelle guessed that Giles had dismissed them. He was already sitting at the table, a newspaper spread out in front of him, but he looked up when she came in.

'At least you're punctual,' he said.

'Sergeant Goss told me you were a stickler for it. He didn't mention any other virtues—such as courtesy, for example.'

'I have always found empty politenesses difficult. But…'
He rose to his feet, gave a slight bow and said with exagger-

ated care, 'Good morning, Rosabelle. Do you wish me to help
you to some food? A little toast, perhaps? Some honey?'

Annabelle repressed a smile. 'Thank you,' she said de-
murely, 'but I can help myself.' She went to the sideboard
and took a moderately generous portion of bread and butter,
together with some honey. Giles eyed it as she sat down.

'You appear to have a better appetite. You used to pick at
your food.' Annabelle looked at her plate. Rosabelle had
never taken as much as this even at Temperley.

'The country air has done wonders for me in many ways,
Giles,' she said airily.

'I think it has. Even to keeping country hours.' Annabelle
looked up at this remark. 'You must own that before you went
to Temperley you would never have been seen outside your
bedchamber before noon, let alone outside the house! Are you
about to claim you had forgotten town hours? Or were you
trying to demonstrate what a reformed character you are? No
longer vain and idle, but a virtuous early riser? It doesn't
impress me.' He gave a scornful smile. 'A rather cheap trick,
don't you think, Rosabelle? And one which merely exposed
you to the ridicule of servants and tradesmen. Did you enjoy
being gawped at?'

Annabelle had grown pale during this attack, and she had
difficulty in suppressing an angry response. She may have
made a foolish error, one which Giles would naturally not
understand, nor was it one she could explain to him. But his
tone and words were insulting. Rosabelle had never in her
life been either vain or idle. She rose to her feet.

'I find I have no appetite, after all,' she said in a stifled
voice. 'You must excuse me.' She walked to the door.

'I haven't finished.'

'If you wish to speak to me about the arrangements you
are making for the house and its management, I shall talk to
you when you have finished breakfast. Meanwhile I shall see
if Aunt Laura is awake.'

He got up and strode after her. 'You will not upset Aunt Laura, Rosabelle. She is making good recovery at the moment. I will not have any setbacks.'

Annabelle looked at him scornfully. 'I suppose you think I would run to her with complaints? Aunt Laura has never been burdened with tales of our private quarrels, Giles, and never will be from me. But if, as you say, she is recovering and taking more of an interest in the world, then she will soon see for herself how matters are between us—unless you curb your sour, ungracious tongue. Where shall I see you? In the library?'

'In the library.' He went back to the table, his brows drawn once more in a heavy frown.

Annabelle was fuming as she went upstairs. Giles was impossible! How poor Rosabelle must have suffered under this barrage of criticism and harsh words! No wonder she had been in such a state—she had a nature which, above all, needed love and encouragement to flourish. Gentle, vulnerable as she was, she would have no defence against Giles Stanton's attacks. Her charm, intelligence, humour, even her self-esteem would all shrivel in the chilly atmosphere of his disapproval. How fortunate it was that, however much she and her sister resembled one another in appearance, their characters were so very different! Annabelle was neither gentle, nor so easily cast down! She smiled grimly. The prospect of foxing Giles Stanton, of eventually teaching him a lesson, was becoming more attractive by the minute. It wouldn't be easy. He was no fool. If she was to avoid suspicion, she must do more than learn the ways of society in two or three secret lessons—she would have to learn to disguise her own strong will and her readiness to do battle, which was so unlike her sister's desperate need to live in peace. But, she swore, she would do all of it if it killed her!

*   *   *

When Annabelle entered Lady Ordway's bedchamber she found her awake, with Wilson in attendance.

'Good morning, my dear. Did you sleep well?'

'Thank you, Aunt Laura. And you?'

'Well enough. Anna, my dear, I've told Wilson our secret. She will keep it to herself. And we might need her help.'

Wilson was still regarding Annabelle as if she couldn't believe what she saw. She pulled herself together and said, 'I'd be pleased to help in any way I can, ma'am. I'm sure a rest in the country is just what Miss Rosabelle needs. But my goodness, Miss Kelland! You *are* like your sister!'

'In looks, perhaps. Not so much in other ways. But I have an urgent question for you both. What is wrong with my going out this morning?'

Lady Ordway looked surprised. 'Nothing whatsoever! Do you wish Wilson to accompany you—or Lily? The new footmen aren't coming till later—'

'No, you misunderstand me, Aunt Laura! I went out this morning—'

'Already?' Lady Ordway and Wilson exchanged glances. 'Who accompanied you?'

'I went alone.'

'Oh, dear!' Lady Ordway seemed unable to continue, so Annabelle looked at the maid.

'I'm sure you had your reasons, ma'am—'

'You'd better get used to calling her Miss Rosabelle, Wilson!'

'Miss Rosabelle. It's just that I've never known of a lady going out before noon, or even one o'clock. It's not often you see any gentlemen, either, before that hour. I can't imagine Miss Rosabelle, the real Miss Rosabelle, doing such a thing.'

'But by that time half the day is gone!' cried Annabelle. 'What lie-a-beds you all are!'

'The servants are up and about, ma'am. And the tradesmen. But ladies and gentlemen never.'

'So that's why…'

'Did anyone see you, Anna?' asked Lady Ordway apprehensively.

'Servants and tradesmen. And Giles. Now then, Wilson! Colonel Stanton was out and about. What do you say to that?'

'Gentlemen, particularly gentlemen who have been in the Army, ma'am, sometimes exercise their horses in Hyde Park at an early hour.'

'What did he say to you, Anna?'

'He was surprised,' said Annabelle with masterly understatement. 'And he was kind enough to escort me back to the house. I was totally unaware that I was offending in any way, so I was not best pleased.'

'Oh, dear. The sooner we start our classes the better, I think. Wilson, see about my breakfast, will you? I shall get up as soon as I can.'

Annabelle welcomed this sign of enthusiasm in Lady Ordway, but she had to say, 'Er…Giles and I are having a discussion in a few minutes, Aunt Laura.'

'About this morning?'

'Not if I can avoid it. I think he wishes to inform me about his plans. I had better see him, don't you think?'

'Oh, yes! We mustn't keep him waiting. He has so much to do. We can have our lesson this afternoon, Anna dear. I'll try to make some notes. I'm sure I shall forget something vital. Oh, this is just like the old days when Rosabelle was a young girl! Come along, Wilson. My breakfast!'

Annabelle went down to the library better prepared than she had been for anything Giles Stanton might bring up about her morning excursion. To her surprise he did not refer to it again, but was quite businesslike. In fact, the meeting began quite well, with what was almost an apology from him.

'I have engaged several servants while you were in Berkshire. I admit that it would have been more fitting to wait for your return, but things here were getting desperate. The lack of a good housekeeper was very marked, and I could hardly engage a competent housekeeper and then expect her to work entirely without maidservants to support her.'

'Of course not, Giles,' said Annabelle meekly. 'Indeed, it would be quite hard for anyone to manage.'

He gave her a sharp look, then said, 'It is possible that I was overhasty in my judgement of your contribution to the household. It is true that your absence was felt more than once.'

'You mean I was not vain and idle *all* the time?'

He said stiffly, 'No. In fact, I think Aunt Laura and I have reason to be grateful to you for your management of the house in the past year.'

'Why, thank you!' said Annabelle, delighted to have wrung this acknowledgement from him. However, her pleasure was soon destroyed, and the atmosphere took a turn for the worse from then on.

'That is not to say that I have changed my opinion of you entirely, Rosabelle. I still find it difficult to forgive your behaviour towards my cousin.'

'Some day you might tell me exactly what it is you accuse me of, Giles. And at the same time you might show me what evidence you think you have for it.'

He gave her a searingly contemptuous look. 'Don't try your games on me! You must know what you've done—I don't need to tell you. As for evidence—you've already seen it. There was evidence enough for even the most objective reader in Stephen's diary. Or have you conveniently forgotten about that?'

The memory of her sister's bewildered distress as she had talked of the letters and the diary, her desperate denials of any wrongdoing, gave Annabelle the courage to face him calmly. 'I should like to see them, all the same. And the letters you said you received from him.'

'So that you can pick them to pieces?'

'No. Merely so that I can defend myself. Or are we in a wartime court-martial situation here? No argument for the defence allowed?'

There was a pause. Then Giles said, 'I can't let you have Stephen's papers at the moment. I'm working on them. There's still an enormous amount of confusion, and it would take more time than I can spare to separate a few odd sheets from the rest. I am still trying to see if I can rescue any of my aunt's personal fortune from the mess.' He looked at her sharply. 'I'm still sure you could help me if you chose. Or do you persist in your refusal?'

'I tell you, I *can't* help you. I don't know what happened to any of the money.'

Giles got up. 'Stephen, presumably with your help, not only spent all the income—a considerable annual sum—from the trust fund his father set up, he also appears to have persuaded his mother to part with most of her money, too. What did the two of you spend it on?'

Annabelle thought it best to say nothing. She was sure that Rosabelle had no idea, but it was wiser not to enter into any discussion of such a dangerous topic. Giles made a gesture of impatience,

'You see? I am absolutely certain you could help me if you would, Rosabelle, but you persist in remaining silent. Why? I don't believe I am being unreasonable. I've paid off the most pressing of Stephen's debts, I've secured this house and set up a small annuity for my aunt—all out of my uncle's estate—'

'Which Stephen would have inherited if he had lived long enough. Let me remind you of that, since you appear to have forgotten it! Just three more years and it would all have been his, income, capital, this house…everything.'

'But not for long. The Ordway fortune would soon have

gone the way of the rest, if you and Stephen had had your way with it. Between you, you would have got rid of the lot!'

'Perhaps you think it's fortunate that he died when he did?' said Annabelle sharply. She spoke without thinking, enraged by his insistence on Rosabelle's guilt. But the effect of her words on him was electric. He strode over, took her by the arms and shook her, his face contorted with anger.

'You little…! I loved my cousin! Loved him! Which is more than you ever did, you self-seeking opportunist! How *dare* you suggest that I wanted Stephen dead? By God, if it weren't for Aunt Laura, I swear I'd throw you out today, bag and baggage!' He thrust her away from him and walked over to the window, where he stood, clearly fighting to control his feelings. Annabelle was shocked at his violence, but she was ashamed, too. Her words had been ill chosen. She had certainly not meant to imply that Giles rejoiced in Stephen's death.

After a moment's silence, she said, 'I should not have said what I did, Giles. Please forgive me.'

'No, you should not,' he replied sombrely, without turning round. 'I never imagined I would inherit the Ordway fortune, nor did I want or need it. Stephen was so much younger than I was.' He paused, then went on, 'He was still a child at the time of my uncle's death; there had to be trustees then. But the estate should have gone to him when he was twenty-one. I tried to dissuade my uncle from putting those conditions into his will—I fought against it right up to his death, but I couldn't move him. Sir John was adamant. Stephen had either to have a son, or to wait till he was twenty-five. Before that he could live on the income from the trust which had been set up for him, but not touch the principal. I never understood why. And now my cousin is dead, and I am beset with un-answered questions, enigmas, mysteries…and chaos.'

He turned towards her, standing stiffly upright like a man expecting a blow. His face was very pale. 'Rosabelle, I have to know! Will you tell me this at least? I have begun to suspect that…that Stephen committed suicide? Am I right?' He came away from the window again, and stood over her. They were so close that their eyes were only inches apart. Shocked beyond measure, transfixed by that piercing gaze, she couldn't utter a word.

'Tell me, damn you!'

Annabelle was totally unprepared for anything like this. When Stephen Ordway had died, she and her father had been informed that there had been an accident, that he had fallen down some steps and broken his neck. And during her stay at Temperley Rosabelle had said nothing about her husband's death. There had certainly never been the slightest hint that Stephen had killed himself.

She drew back a little—Giles stood waiting, watching her, too close for comfort. She must say something!

'Why should you think that?' she asked carefully.

Chapter Three

'Damn it, why do you always have to prevaricate! You're just like all the rest of your sex!' The pain behind Giles's angry outburst was all too clear. Annabelle tried to answer him as honestly and as patiently as she could.

'I...I don't wish to prevaricate. I...I wasn't there when Stephen fell. I just don't understand why you should think such a thing.'

He turned away abruptly, as if to reject her sympathy, and walked about the room. After a while he said wearily, 'Like everything else, there's a mystery about it. I've...I've been making enquiries—oh, you needn't worry! I've been discreet.' He threw a scornful look in her direction. 'Apart from his doctor, you and Aunt Laura were the only ones allowed near Stephen towards the end, and though I've asked Cottrell he refuses to comment.' He was back in front of her. 'Did my cousin really fall down those steps? Or did he throw himself down? It's quite possible. Quite understandable. The poor fellow was overloaded with trouble—his debts, an unfaithful wife—'

'I...I don't know,' said poor Annabelle. These were deeper waters than she had anticipated when she had so blithely embarked on her impersonation of Rosabelle. Of one thing she was completely certain. It was quite out of the question that Rosabelle had ever betrayed her husband—such disloyalty would have been utterly against her nature. Yet…in another respect she knew Giles to be right. Rosabelle had not loved Stephen as a wife should. She had married him to please her godmother, and had lived to regret it.

'One thing I can assure you of, Giles,' she said steadily. 'Stephen may have had debts, but he did *not* have an unfaithful wife!'

Giles ignored this. 'If Stephen's death was a straightforward accident, why all the mystery?'

'You must ask Aunt Laura that, not me,' she said. 'I can't discuss it with you. I gave my word to Aunt Laura not to discuss Stephen with anyone.'

She shifted uneasily under Giles's brooding regard, but stood her ground.

'You are, of course, aware that I could not possibly approach Aunt Laura on such a matter,' he said finally. 'She loved my cousin too much. But don't place any dependence on my not finding out what happened—eventually. And then, by God, you'll answer for it.'

'Condemned and sentenced without a hearing. Is that it?'

'I've given you your chance, Rosabelle.'

Annabelle was about to argue again, but then the futility of it struck her. His present prejudice was like a brick wall. She reined in her temper and said as calmly as she could, 'Giles, are you sure you want to do this? Aunt Laura is just beginning to live again. Do you really want to revive all the pain, all the distress for her? I honestly don't know whether Stephen killed himself or not. But what good will it do if you establish—somehow—that he did? It won't bring him back. And Aunt Laura will almost certainly suffer another setback.'

'I suppose that would suit you very well!'

Good resolutions faded at the bitterness and contempt in his voice. She said angrily, 'You're impossible! I think it would be better for all of us if I went back to Temperley for good!'

'Oh, no! As I said before you went to Berkshire, you owe something to the Ordway family, Rosabelle Kelland, and you're going to repay that debt at least! God knows why, but Aunt Laura is devoted to you—'

'And I love her, too, Giles! Never forget that!'

'So you'll stay in London and earn your keep. When she is fully restored to health and spirits, then you can talk of escape to Temperley.'

'And where are we going to live till that happy time?'

He looked surprised. 'Here, of course!'

'With a constant threat of eviction over our heads, if I don't obey you? Of being reduced to penury through Stephen's debts? That will hardly be conducive to our peace of mind, will it? You see, I too remember your words before I left for Berkshire!'

'Those debts are paid in full. That was done shortly after you left London.'

Annabelle gazed at him in disbelief.

'Oh, you may look amazed, but did you really believe that I would willingly cause Aunt Laura any further anxiety? Whatever happens, her future is secure. And I suppose that means that yours is, too. Your financial future, that is. And the house is available to you both for as long as you're likely to want it.'

'Even if you marry?'

'I don't envisage marrying for some time—if ever.' His face was closed.

Annabelle suddenly felt exhausted. So many different emotions in such a short space of time—anger, frustration, pity, and now, incredible though it seemed, gratitude! She roused herself to say, 'Giles, little though you may believe me, I am grateful for what you've done for Aunt Laura. And…and me.'

'I could hardly have done less.'

'I know you dislike me. There is little I can do about it, except to hope that with time you will see how unjust you have been. Meanwhile…'

'Meanwhile we shall have to rub along as best we can. Is that what you want to say?'

'Yes. If I am not to return to Temperley then there's nothing else to be done.'

'I suppose not.' He became businesslike again. 'I've been waiting for your return to leave London myself for a few days. It won't be for long, however, and when I return I shall want to start entertaining—I owe a great deal of hospitality. I shall require you to act as my hostess.'

'Do we have servants enough?'

'Not quite. I have asked the agency to send round a couple of footmen. Whitcroft can deal with them. He might think a third is necessary. If so, you must see to it. And the new housekeeper will want to engage more help in the house and kitchen. You'll have to talk to her about it. Apart from that, you'll keep Aunt Laura company.'

'Yes, sir! Straight away, sir!' said Annabelle, with a salute. '*I require you to… You must… You'll have to… You will keep…* Do you ever request anyone politely? Or has Upper Brook Street become an Army barracks?'

'I'm sorry,' he said stiffly. 'I told you, I haven't the patience for empty courtesies. When I travel over rough ground I spend as little time on it as possible. And the ground has recently been very rough indeed. But I should, indeed, be grateful for your help.'

Annabelle could now see that he looked bone-weary himself. 'I suppose that will do,' she said philosophically. 'And I shall give you all the help I can. If only to prove I am not what you think me.'

'That will be difficult,' he said with a return to his former grim manner. 'But we shall call a truce, for the moment.'

* * *

Annabelle escaped with a sense of profound relief, and hastened up to Lady Ordway's room to share the news. With
Giles away they had some time when they could work on her
deficiencies as a social hostess without a need for conceal-
ment.

'But this is very good news!' said Lady Ordway. 'And I
have more. Wilson has found us a dancing instructor, who
will come tomorrow. And she has heard that Mrs Thelwell—
a most respected member of the *ton*, but living in very reduced circumstances—might be willing to coach you in social
behaviour.'

'I should have thought you were more than capable of that
yourself, Aunt Laura!'

'But I get tired, my dear. And we have other work to do.
I intend to see that you have some new and beautiful dresses
to dazzle the *ton*. I used to love buying them for Rosabelle
in the old days. I believe Madame Fanchon is still highly
regarded—'

'But I saw a closet full of dresses this morning in
Rosabelle's room—surely we could make do?'

'That is one of the things you will have to learn, Annabelle!
One does not "make do" when mixing with the *ton*!
Goodness me, girl! Don't you want some pretty new dresses?'

'Yes, but…how will we pay for them?'

'Leave that to me! Giles has restored my income quite con-
siderably, and I shall delight in spending it on clothes. I shall
order some for myself, too. No more objections, if you
please!'

Annabelle had to give in. In truth she could see that the
prospect of preparing for her pseudo-goddaughter's re-entry
into Society was giving Lady Ordway a great deal of pleasure.

From then on Annabelle underwent an intensive course in
learning to be a lady of society. Ridiculous though some of
the rules seemed to her, she meekly worked to learn them,

and since she was an intelligent girl she was soon reasonably conversant with them. She learned to subdue her own stride to a graceful mincing walk, she became versed in the exact depth of a nod, bow or curtsey to give to different levels of acquaintance, she acquired a range of subjects suitable for conversations at table, at routs and balls, for afternoon calls. She was taught the names of those members of society who were approved, and those whom she must avoid.

'Of course, it is much too early, I am sure, for you to be considering remarriage, Mrs Ordway,' said Mrs Thelwell. 'But well prepared is well armed, and it doesn't do any harm to know who would do.' And she proceeded to give Annabelle a surprisingly comprehensive list of eligible bachelors and widowers. To Annabelle's amusement, Philip Winbolt was one of them. But when she mentioned him to Mrs Thelwell, the response was discouraging.

'Ah, yes, Lord Winbolt's grandson. A charming young man, and a most desirable match. But he seldom comes to London, except when he visits his grandfather in Arlington Street. He inherited Shearings, his uncle's estate in Berkshire, and spends most of his time there. He is not a lover of town life. I doubt you will see him enough to become properly acquainted with him.'

Annabelle hid a smile. She was already very well acquainted with Philip Winbolt. The Shearings estate bordered on that of the Kellands', and the Winbolts were their closest neighbours. Philip Winbolt had been a frequent visitor to Temperley since his arrival in Berkshire, and Becky, the Kellands' housekeeper, had been convinced that he came looking for a wife. Annabelle had not been interested. Mr Winbolt was not to her taste—he was far too polite, too much the gentleman. More Rosabelle's style, perhaps… She wondered briefly what Rosabelle would make of him. And what Mr Winbolt would make of Rosabelle. And whether he would notice the difference… He would certainly be far too polite to comment if he did!

Annabelle also took advantage of Giles's absence to inspect the household arrangements, discussing with the new house-keeper how they could be improved. The task was not diffi-cult. She did not doubt her ability to manage the household in Upper Brook Street after her long experience in managing Temperley for her father. There were a few practices and customs that were different, but she quickly mastered these, and was soon confident that the domestic side of her life in London would present no problems.

Her social life was a different matter, but even there she found enjoyment. Mrs Thelwell was a hard taskmistress, but a delight to her pupil. The lady was so dedicated, so serious, so convinced that the only object for any young woman must be to acquire a rich and eligible man—young or, in her eyes, preferably old.

'For you must know, my dear, that older men are so much more reliable in their affections. And never forget, a man of mature years has had time to gather the fruits of his success. Why, look at Lord Osborne—his mansion in Portman Square is a veritable treasure house of elegant furniture, statues, pic-tures and I don't know what else besides. Now, *he* is *devoted* to his young wife. He never lets her out of his sight.'

Something in Annabelle's expression caused Mrs Thelwell to add hastily, 'And there are others…I cannot quite recall at the moment… Oh dear, you will think me a sad scatterbrain.'

'My dear Mrs Thelwell, you have been a mine of infor-mation and instruction! I cannot begin to thank you enough. I am truly not thinking of acquiring a husband for some time yet, but the rest of what you have taught me is invaluable. I now feel so much more fitted to face society.'

'But, Mrs Ordway! You are lovely enough to disarm any

criticism. And I am sure society will be delighted with you, once they know you for yourself.'

This seemed a somewhat cryptic observation to Annabelle. 'Know me for myself? How else should they know me?'

Mrs Thelwell who, for all her apologies and claims to being a scatterbrain, was usually a highly composed creature, looked discomfited. 'Forgive me, I spoke without thinking.'

Annabelle was not satisfied. 'If I am to enter society with confidence again, Mrs Thelwell, I must know what is being said or thought about me.'

Mrs Thelwell hesitated, then said finally, 'It's not about *you*!' She lowered her voice. 'I have no desire to distress you, Mrs Ordway, and I would not dream of saying anything in front of Lady Ordway, but as you have insisted... You did not mix in society a great deal when your husband was alive, so it does not surprise me that you are unaware of what was being said. Mr Ordway, the late Mr Ordway, was not...not...' She was clearly at a loss.

'Quite the thing? Would have been on your list of people to avoid?'

'Er...well, let us say rather that he was not regarded with universal approbation.'

'I see.'

'I hope I have not distressed you. I am sure if he had lived he would have overcome society's prejudices in time. But it was not to be. His accident...' She paused, but when Annabelle did not respond, she went on, 'You need have no fear for yourself, my dear ma'am. I prophesy that you will be a great success.'

Mrs Thelwell was still looking anxious. Annabelle was grateful for the warning she had been given, and had no wish to upset her companion. So she merely smiled. 'If that is indeed the case, then much of it will be due to your efforts. Thank you again, Mrs Thelwell. This past week has been most enjoyable.'

Lady Ordway came in at that moment, followed by Wilson, who was laden with boxes.

'Good evening, Mrs Thelwell. Rosa, my dear, look! The dresses have arrived from Fanchon. She's a dear creature. She must have worked all hours to get these done in the time.'

In the subsequent flurry of activity, unwrapping, exclaiming, trying on, Mrs Thelwell's words were pushed to the back of Annabelle's mind. But that night she lay awake, thinking of Stephen Ordway and her sister's life with him. She was not as surprised as she might have been by Mrs Thelwell's words. Neither she nor Becky had taken to Stephen Ordway on the one occasion he had paid them a visit, not long after he and Rosabelle had married. Golden hair, bright blue eyes, slender, graceful build—he looked handsome enough, and at first they were impressed by his surface charm.

But as time wore on he had become bored in the country, and petulantly impatient with Rosabelle when she had wanted to visit old friends and show him her favourite haunts. He had even begun to make fun of people the twins had known and respected for years, and his scorn for country bumpkins had soon begun to show through. No one had been sorry when the Ordways' visit had come to an end. There had never been another, and Annabelle had never been invited to Upper Brook Street. Rosabelle wrote regularly, but after that sole visit she had seemed to distance herself from her family in Berkshire.

Stephen was now dead, but he still apparently had the power to cause distress to those he had left behind—Lady Ordway, Rosabelle, even Giles Stanton. Giles Stanton. A curious man. Was he a villain? Or was he someone who still thought of Stephen as a boy, an innocent younger cousin who had idolised him, and who now needed to be avenged? Had Giles, too, been taken in by the angelic looks, the apparent charm? From all accounts, he had not seen much of his cousin in later years…

Just as Annabelle was drifting off to sleep, a vision of herself just ten days ago, about to leave Temperley for London, drifted into her mind. She had been laughing, assuring Rosabelle that all would go well with their changeover. She had almost got to the door when Rosabelle, clearly on impulse, had clutched her arm and whispered, *'I gave my word to Aunt Laura that I wouldn't tell anyone about Stephen, but I can't let you go without warning you! He had some strange friends. Don't take any risks.'*

Her sister had been desperately anxious that she should take the words seriously. But what had she meant by 'strange friends'? And why had she thought a warning necessary—so necessary that she had been prepared to talk about her husband in spite of her promise to his mother? The incident was odd, but it had left an impression.

Annabelle sighed and turned over in the bed yet again. What had started out as a lighthearted exercise in deception, merely in order to give her sister more time in the country, was proving to be much, much more complicated. But…but if Rosabelle could be re-established in the eyes of London society, then this visit would have done more good than she could have hoped. So much depended on the next few weeks!

To Annabelle's relief Giles's business kept him out of London for longer than he had planned, and he was away for well over a week. When he did arrive back it was early in the morning and he looked travel-stained and weary. Annabelle was up. She was still unused to town hours, and though she did not go out, she was always awake and active from about eight o'clock onwards. She was in the drawing room when she heard the bustle at the door, and came out to see what it was.

'Giles! You're back!'

'I do believe I am,' he said sourly. 'I had hoped to get to

my room and have a wash and shave before anyone saw me. What are you doing up?'

Annabelle took a breath. 'Was the journey very fatiguing, Giles? It looks as if it was. Shall I send for something to eat for you?'

'I had some coffee when I got off the coach. It was vile.'

'Then you go upstairs and I'll send Sergeant Goss to you, and I'll see Mrs Brooks about some food.' Giles hesitated. 'Go on,' said Annabelle firmly. ''How long do you need? Half an hour?'

'Twenty minutes,' he said with a slight grin. Then he frowned again. 'Why *are* you up?'

'I can't sleep when it is so bright outside. I still haven't managed to shake off country hours. And when there is so much to be done here…'

'Still trying to impress, Rosabelle?' he asked as he started up the stairs.

'What a futile exercise that would be,' Annabelle snapped. Just for a moment she had felt sorry for the man. She was a fool!

He came down after twenty minutes looking brighter, and regarded the substantial breakfast laid out in the dining room. 'Are you not joining me?' he asked in surprise, gazing at the single setting.

'I might. If you can be civil,' she said.

He took a deep breath. 'I'll try. Now sit down and join me.'

They sat down. 'Do you wish to tell me what you've been doing?' Annabelle asked.

'Nothing to any purpose, though I've left a few irons in the fire…' The servant was dismissed with a nod and Giles waited until they were alone. Then he looked at her thoughtfully. 'I'd like to know—'

'Know what?'

'What goes on in that lovely head of yours.'

'If you are about to start being unpleasant again, I shall leave the table and get on with what I was doing before you came.'

'No, don't go!' he said. 'Let me tell you what I was doing. I've been investigating a couple of references in Stephen's diary.' Annabelle stiffened, but though he noted it he made no comment. 'About a man called Da Costa.' He paused. 'You don't know the name?'

'No, I've never heard of him.'

'First I went to a tavern, a wretched hole near Woolhampton on the Bath Road.'

Annabelle dropped her knife. 'But that's not far from Temperley!' she said.

'I hadn't thought of that. Is it a coincidence?' said Giles as he picked up the knife and gave her a clean one.

There was something in his manner which was making her uneasy. 'What else could it be?' she said.

'I don't know. Why aren't you eating?'

'Because I'm listening to you, and waiting for you to get on with it!' said Annabelle, irritated. 'I don't like cat-and-mouse games.'

'Now why should I be playing cat and mouse?'

'I have no idea, but I wish you would stop.'

Giles sat down again. 'Very well, I will! I went to this inn and asked about Da Costa. The landlord knew him. He was most unwilling to talk, but I persuaded him in the end.'

'What did you do?' asked Annabelle coldly. 'Burn the soles of his feet?'

'No, just bribed him.'

'And?'

'The landlord told me that Da Costa was in the habit of meeting someone else there.' Giles was now watching her very closely. 'A gentleman called Selder.'

Annabelle waited. Giles continued to watch her steadily. Eventually she said, 'So? Did he say why they met?'

'Oh, you're good!' said Giles. 'You're very good. Your stay in Berkshire has done wonders for your ability to dissemble. The last time I mentioned Selder's name you jumped a foot.'

'What do you mean? I've never heard the name before—' Annabelle stopped short. 'When…when was that,' she asked.

'You're now claiming you've forgotten? That's going a bit far, don't you think? It was just after I came back to England. When I found Stephen's diaries. But I knew about the affair before that—I've told you before. Stephen had already written to me about it.' He had been bent towards her, but he now sat back and regarded her cynically. 'Why don't you spare me this play-acting, Rosabelle? We both know that Selder was your lover.'

Annabelle jumped up, turning her chair over in the process. 'That's it! I've had enough!' She leaned over the table and glared at him. 'I am telling you for the last time, *Colonel*, that I was *never*— n-e-v-e-r—*never* unfaithful to Stephen. If Stephen says so in these diaries you keep refusing to show me, then he was lying—or mad. I have never had any sort of lover. Do you hear me?'

'It would be difficult not to,' he said unpleasantly. 'You're shouting like a fishwife.'

'Heaven give me patience,' said Annabelle in exasperation. 'What am I supposed to do? Accept everything you throw at me without a word in my own defence? Sit down meekly and say that I'm sorry, I'll never do it again?'

'Since Stephen is dead that would be difficult, don't you agree? But it would probably mean as much as anything else you might say. And why do you keep asking to see the diaries? I showed you the relevant pages before Easter.'

'Did you, indeed? Well, I want to see them again. Now!'

'I really cannot imagine what you hope to gain, Rosabelle. But I'll fetch them. I'll meet you in the library.' He got up, picked up her chair and went out. Annabelle sank back into the chair. She was trembling. She had come within a hair's breadth of betraying herself! Giles must have tackled Rosabelle about Selder before Easter. Oh, why, in Heaven's name, hadn't Rosabelle told her more? But a moment's reflection told her that she was being foolish. Of course she knew why Rosabelle hadn't. Rosabelle had given her word to Lady Ordway that she would say nothing either about her marriage or about the events leading up to Stephen's death. Distressed and ill though she had been, she would not break that promise, either to her sister, or to anyone else—not even to defend herself. Rosabelle was incapable of betraying anyone, least of all her husband, and if any evidence of her absolute integrity was needed, it was this refusal to talk.

Annabelle could not criticise such loyalty. But the result was that she felt she was fighting Giles Stanton with one hand tied behind her back. And with this sort of opponent she needed all her wits and every other assistance she could get. Would the diaries be of any help? They might reveal something that Giles had missed, though it was unlikely—he had obviously studied them carefully. But it was necessary to see them, all the same. She got up and made her way to the library.

Giles was laying out a pathetic collection of papers and torn, dog-eared notebooks.

'How can you claim to understand these...scribbles?' asked Annabelle, after she had studied them for a few minutes. 'Half of them aren't legible, and the rest don't make sense!'

'That's what you said last time.'

'Thank goodness for that!' thought Annabelle, and said aloud, 'It doesn't make it any less true.'

'Let me show you. Here...and here... As you see, he is quite explicit about Selder and yourself.'

Annabelle cast her eyes over them, then turned a pale,

shocked face towards him. 'I…I don't understand some of the words. But I can guess their meaning. I…I…how could anyone mix my name up in this…this filth!'

'You must excuse me. But I didn't force the diaries on you. You demanded to see them.'

'But, Giles! You can't really be taking these…these obscenities seriously! They're evidence only of the disturbed state in which they were written!'

'And whose fault was that?' Annabelle was still shocked. She looked at him briefly, then set her face and was silent. She had said she would not defend herself again. Giles made an ironic gesture of acknowledgment and went over to the window. There was a pause, during which Annabelle bundled the diaries together, put them back in their box, and closed the lid firmly on them. If Rosabelle's husband, and later Giles, had subjected her to this sort of accusation, it was even less surprising that she had eventually collapsed. Annabelle was feeling sick herself. But she must pull herself together, and continue the fight to clear Rosabelle's name!

'I…I find it very difficult to understand, Giles, why you should be so adamant, so rigidly determined to believe the worst,' she began, speaking to his unyielding back. 'I don't believe that you really listen to anything I say to defend myself. Why is that?'

Giles turned round. His face was in shadow. 'I never met you when you were a girl,' he said, almost conversationally. 'Whenever I stayed with the Ordways you were down at Temperley, spending the summer with your father and sister. Aunt Laura was always saying what a perfect daughter you were, how loving, how gentle—how glad she was that she had agreed to foster you. Even then, Stephen distrusted you.'

'B…but how? Why?'

'He thought you had wormed your way into his mother's affections at his expense.'

'That is rubbish!'

'Is it? Stephen believed it to be so. And the terms of his father's will didn't help. He was...humiliated by the thought that he wouldn't be allowed to inherit before he was twenty-five. At twelve or thirteen that must have seemed a lifetime away. His father's rejection of him must have made him all the more possessive of his mother. So I suppose the more she spoiled you, the more isolated he felt.'

'But Aunt Laura adored Stephen!'

'I know she did, and I told him so. But he wouldn't listen to me. He was convinced you were trying to come between them. And I have to say that from his accounts of the arts you employed, the tricks you got up to, it could well have been true.'

Annabelle thought for a moment, wondering how to deal with this. For her, it was simply more evidence of Stephen's duplicity. But Giles would not think so. She said slowly, 'You never questioned what he was telling you? You never suspected that you might be being manipulated?'

'A child of that age? That's absurd! I had known him from babyhood! He was a delightful little chap—open, frank, honest. He was never very strong, but he was full of pluck. Not an ounce of guile in him! Don't try to defend yourself by casting doubts on Stephen, Rosabelle. From beginning to end you were the cause of the deepest unhappiness in my cousin.'

'That he was unhappy I have no doubt. But, believe me, it was not because of anything I did. Aunt Laura loved all her family—that's the way she is. But Stephen was her only son and she worshipped him. She gave him everything!'

'Even a wife he didn't want?'

Chapter Four

Annabelle was shocked again and showed it. 'What are you saying now? That I trapped Stephen into marriage?'

'Stephen was certain that Aunt Laura more or less forced him to marry you because it was the only way she could make your future secure. You had no fortune of your own, and the Ordway money was too well tied up. If you can bear to read more of Stephen's writings, you can read his letters to me. It's all there.'

Annabelle felt a rising tide of anger and frustration. It was so plausible! Had she not known her sister as well as she did, she might even have believed this rubbish herself! But she controlled her feelings. Giles's accusations were unwelcome, but they were at last giving her something tangible to work on. At last she knew the reason why his dislike of Rosabelle went so deep. But flat denials would not be enough. Giles remembered only the delicate, charming little boy he had known in the past, and had believed his cousin's tales.

'These…ravings—' she pointed to the box of diaries '—if Stephen was so indifferent to me, why was he so distraught when he writes about the affair with Selder?'

Giles paused. Blinded by his deeply ingrained prejudice against his cousin's wife, this was obviously something he had not considered. 'Perhaps he loved you more than he realised. Or perhaps he saw that the chances of having the son he needed were in danger.'

Annabelle put her head in her hands. It was aching. For a few minutes neither of them spoke.

Then Giles said, 'I warn you, Rosabelle, I mean to find out the truth. About Stephen, why and how he died, and where his money went. And about Selder.'

'And I am not afraid of that. As long as what you find out *is* the truth, and not a set of prejudices and lies.'

'At least you have more spirit that I credited you with.'

'Thank you. I suppose you mean it as a compliment. I was ill before Easter, Giles, and your bullying made it much worse. But I believe I can stand up to you now, and I will.' She pointed to the diaries. 'You can put these away again. I do not regard them as evidence of anything at all, and the house is tainted by their presence. Though I have done nothing to deserve it, I still feel…ashamed that my name is associated with such filth. They would best be burnt.'

His eyes showed a reluctant admiration. 'If I were not already so convinced of your guilt, I could almost believe you sincere.'

Annabelle said with more than a touch of irony, 'I don't know whether to thank you for that or not. But…believing me guilty, do you wish me to continue to run this house?'

'Oh, I do! I want you where I can see you. And I will not deny that you are needed here. As long as you do not upset Aunt Laura, you will stay.'

Annabelle bit back a retort. Time and patience, she told herself. Time and patience!

Giles went on, 'And now, if you'll excuse me, I shall seek her out. She might even be up already.'

Annabelle looked at the time. It was only eleven o'clock. She would have sworn it was well past noon. These revelations and battles with Giles certainly made the time pass, though as a cure for boredom they were somewhat extreme!

Following Giles's return to London, preparations went swiftly ahead for a reception, to be followed by several evening parties. Though he made no further reference to their conversation in the library, Annabelle was aware that Giles was keeping a careful watch on her. Let him! It had taken a few days to overcome the feelings of disgust aroused by the diaries, but she had managed it. Now, pleased with the success of her domestic arrangements, confident of her ability to move in the best circles without making mistakes, and aware that she had one of the prettiest collections of dresses in London, Annabelle's mind was more easy. She had nothing to hide, nothing to be ashamed of…except when she remembered that she had everything to hide! She was, in fact, not at all the woman Giles Stanton thought her to be. Not Rosabelle Ordway, but Annabelle Kelland, doing her best in difficult circumstances. When she permitted herself to think of it, the thought of his rage and contempt if that piece of outrageous chicanery ever came to light kept her awake at night, and gave her nightmares when she slept.

But during the day she managed to concentrate on her role as Rosabelle, Stephen Ordway's widow, newly out of mourning and about to re-enter society.

On the night of the reception she took more care over her appearance than ever in her life before. Annabelle Kelland had dressed carelessly, negligently almost. But Rosabelle Ordway, real or counterfeit, dressed as the genuine article— a member of London's highest society, about to entertain some of the foremost names in social, diplomatic and military circles.

No one could have faulted Lady Ordway's choice of gown for her. In deference to her recent emergence from mourning the dress was white. But it was far from being the sort of artless creation worn by girls in their teens making their debut in Society. The stiff folds of *peau de soie* gleamed in the candlelight, and the touches of crystal and gold silk in the trimmings echoed the sparkle of her eyes and the rich, dark gold of her hair. It was a highly sophisticated creation by one of London's most skilled dressmakers. Excitement had brought a delicate colour to Annabelle's cheeks and deepened the blue of her eyes. And Lady Ordway had produced a gold, pearl and crystal filigree necklace which completed an exquisite picture.

'My dear girl,' cried Lady Ordway when she saw her. 'You look even more lovely than I had imagined!'

'Pray tell me more, Aunt Laura! I need all the confidence I can muster! And may I say how splendid you look yourself?'

After much coaxing by Annabelle, and a special request from Giles, Lady Ordway had agreed to attend the reception. 'Giles asked in such a particularly pleasant manner that I should come, dearest Anna. I do think you are having an effect on him.'

Annabelle merely smiled, but she had no illusions. Giles had not changed his attitude to her.

This was made clear when she finally entered the white-and-gold drawing room. It was a room which she particularly liked. When she had first arrived it had been full of knick-knacks and gewgaws on all sorts of small tables and stands, and displayed in cases round the walls. The room was ornate in itself—the fireplace alone was an intricately carved masterpiece of rioting cherubs and garlands—and was better left uncluttered. She had recently seen to it that most of the cases and stands, together with their contents, had all been removed and put away in an attic. Now the beauty of the room's proportions, the decorated ceiling and silk wall-coverings, the candles in the delicate crystal chandeliers and gilded girandoles, were reflected clearly and without distraction over and over again in the huge mirrors on either side. The effect was as stunning as she had hoped.

Giles was standing by the empty fireplace, which was now filled with flowers. He was looking moodily at the carved surround, tracing the curls of one of the cherubs with his finger.

'Ah! There you are, Giles!' said Lady Ordway. 'Do turn round! We are both here.'

He turned, and the colour in Annabelle's cheeks grew slightly deeper as he took in her appearance. For a moment his eyes widened, and there was something in his gaze…admiration, certainly, but there was more than that. Warmth, feeling… She had no time to analyse either it, or her own response. It disappeared immediately, to be replaced with his usual, cold regard. Then he switched his attention to Lady Ordway, and smiled down at her.

'This is a great occasion, Aunt Laura.'

'Oh, yes! I don't know who isn't coming, dearest Giles. It has been nothing but acceptances. I had dared to hope for the *ton*—but the house has never before seen such a distinguished collection of ambassadors and attachés. And the service people…'

'That is not what I meant. It's a great day now that you have come down to join us again. I hope it's the forerunner of many such occasions. And I thank you for making the effort.'

'It was no trouble at all! Wilson helped, of course. But Rosabelle here has been such a darling girl—helping me to choose my dress, and the jewels to go with it. But don't you think that gold necklace looks well against her dress, Giles? And doesn't she look a dream?'

'Lady Ordway has been good enough to lend her necklace to me for the evening,' said Annabelle stiffly, as Giles's eyes rested on it.

'My mother had one like it,' he replied. 'I was wondering what had happened to it.'

'So she did! Your dear grandpapa gave her one when she married your papa, and I admired it so much that he had another made for me when I married his son. I had quite forgot! What did happen to it, I wonder? Oh!'

Lady Ordway looked distressed as Giles said harshly, 'I expect it went along with the rest to her… successor, ma'am. Though I cannot imagine it is to my beloved stepmother's taste.' Lady Ordway put her hand on his arm, and Giles forced a smile. 'But such things are best forgotten. I have no wish to spoil your evening. Come, I see Whitcroft is trying to catch your eye.'

'Dearest Giles!' Lady Ordway gave him an affectionate smile and moved away to speak to the butler. She was out of earshot. Giles turned his attention to Annabelle.

'Tell me,' he said. 'What have you done with Stephen's snuff boxes and the rest of his things?'

'They're in the attic,' Annabelle said calmly. 'I thought they were better out of the way.'

His mouth twisted in an unpleasant smile. 'Of course,' he said. 'Of course you would, Rosabelle. They were Stephen's treasures—he spent years collecting them.'

'Giles, please!' said Annabelle. In spite of herself her voice wavered. Her nerves were already so tightly stretched that she could not bear it if he started to attack her now, however discreetly. 'Can we not have a truce—for tonight, at least? It will do you no good if your acting hostess disappears before the evening has even begun.'

He looked at her fingers, twisting and turning on the filigree posy holder she carried, and said stiffly, 'I'm sorry. I'll try to avoid controversy. For tonight, at least.'

'I'll have the things brought back tomorrow, if that is your wish.'

'No. As a matter of fact, I like the room without them.'

* * *

For the rest of the evening Giles's behaviour was impeccable. The huge room soon filled with a chattering, laughing throng, and he moved among them with ease. Annabelle was astonished at his polished charm. Was this the man she had accused of not knowing what to do in civilised society? How mistaken she had been!

She herself was soon surrounded by numbers of people, all wishing to make the acquaintance of the lovely Mrs Ordway. Lady Ordway stayed firmly at her side, keeping her on the right lines when the conversation became difficult or obscure, but, ironically enough, it was Giles himself who actually rescued her from an awkward situation.

She had been caught by an obviously important guest, a distinguished-looking gentleman, covered in orders and decorations. Aunt Laura was too far away to be appealed to, and the conversation was getting a little strained, as Annabelle talked her way through a delicate web of references to people and events about which she knew nothing. It would have helped, she thought bitterly, if she had the remotest idea who the gentleman was! He obviously expected her to know him and was beginning to look somewhat puzzled at young Mrs Ordway's evident distraction. To Annabelle's enormous relief, Giles joined them just in time.

'I had thought you were in Vienna still, Duke.'

'No, m'boy. I came back. M'work is done there. I hear Wellington's finished in France, as well.'

'Yes, Europe seems to be prepared to manage without us, thank God!' Giles turned politely to Annabelle, who was still trying to look as if she knew who her companion was. 'I expect you know that His Grace was in Vienna when I was there, Rosabelle.'

'Just been tellin' her. Best adjutant Wellington ever had.'

'You flatter me, Duke. But…may I take my cousin away from you? There's a group of the old campaigners over there who are demanding to be introduced.'

'I thought I recognised them! "Old campaigners" indeed. Not one of 'em is over forty! Well, my dear, I suppose I'll have to let you go. But you'd better take care with those "old campaigners", 'pon my word, you had! Their campaigns haven't always been on the field of action!' He gave a deep chuckle, then moved away and Rosabelle could breathe again. For once she did not object to Giles's peremptory tone.

'This way, Rosabelle.' He took her arm, and as they made their way through the crowded room he said, 'I must congratulate you on the success of the arrangements. You must be pleased with your efforts.'

'I shall be—but not before it is all successfully over, Giles.' Taken by surprise, she smiled at him. His hold on her arm tightened momentarily, and his face softened. But then, once again, the moment vanished. The barrier came down and his handsome face lost all its expression. At least, thought Annabelle, suffering an unaccountably sharp disappointment, he could hardly look at her with his usual dislike in the middle of a room full of guests!

Giles's friends were fellow officers, none of whom had met Rosabelle before. They laughed, admired, flirted a little, and she, free of the dread of failing to recognise someone she 'knew', was able to relax and respond. They all warmly congratulated Giles on his lovely cousin, and begged him to bring her to the balls and routs which were taking place nearly every day in London in the Season.

'We shall see,' said Giles. 'I suppose we can hardly avoid one or two of them.'

'What a frown, Giles, old fellow!' said a dashing Major, with just such whiskers as Annabelle had expected to see on Giles. 'Don't be such a dog in the manger. And why is it that we have never met this enchanting lady before?'

Looking at Giles's expression, which was growing more forbidding by the minute, Annabelle said swiftly, 'Major Dabney, you must know that Giles has been away for much of the past year. And I…have been living a very retired life since…since my husband died. I have only just started to mix in Society once more.'

This gave them all a moment's pause. But then Major Dabney said, 'I hope you will permit Society to see a little more of you, Mrs Ordway. If Giles finds himself unable to escort you, I should be delighted to offer my services.'

'And I!'

'And I!' The chorus was almost universal.

'Thank you. You are all very kind. And if I should need anyone I shall be sure to remember you. Now you must excuse me. I see my godmother beckoning to me.' With a charming smile to all of them she escaped while Giles was still able to be civil to them. He really was a dog in the manger, she thought rebelliously.

The reception was a triumph. Everyone said so. People came and went throughout the evening, but the rooms were always crowded, and there was the sort of animated hum in the air which betokens success. Lady Ordway took it very well, and though she was still in bed when Annabelle saw her the next morning, she seemed none the worse for the experience.

'My dear! You must be so pleased. I knew you could do it. Look!'

Lady Ordway's bed was covered in cards and letters. 'People have been so kind. They seem genuinely pleased to see me up and about.' Her eyes filled with tears. 'I was afraid…'

'Dearest Aunt Laura,' said Annabelle quickly. 'You must put the past behind you! You must know that people have very short memories—even in the country, yesterday's sensation is quickly replaced by the next. And how much truer must that be in London! I am certain that you would be very kindly received wherever you went.'

'This is your doing. I would never have roused myself without your encouragement, Anna. Thank you, my dear.'

'Nonsense! And it isn't Rosabelle you should thank, but Giles. He was the instigator.' She gave Lady Ordway a warning glance. Giles was on his way upstairs. He came in with a face of thunder, his arms full of flowers.

'I took these from Whitcroft as I came up. There's one for you, Aunt Laura. The rest are for Rosabelle.'

'Why do you always call her Rosabelle, Giles? Why not Rosa, as I do?'

'I've never considered the matter,' he said. 'What shall I do with the flowers? Rosabelle appears to have a brand new batch of admirers.'

'Yes, she has!' said Lady Ordway, happily. 'And the dear girl deserves every bit of admiration. She looked absolutely beautiful, don't you agree, Giles?'

'Exquisite,' he said tonelessly. 'And we are all impressed by her ability to charm. I would not have suspected it before last night.'

'Giles!'

'I think Giles means that he is grateful to me for exerting myself on his behalf,' said Annabelle, smiling sweetly in his direction. 'After all, they were all his guests, most of them friends of his. I am sure he wanted me to make them feel welcome.'

'Indeed! And Dabney, Pettifer and Wainwright obviously felt *very* welcome.' He looked at the cards on the flowers. 'Their requests for further acquaintance are most pressing. But I am surprised not to see the Duke of Armagh's card among them. He is a well-known connoisseur of beauty.'

'Why, thank you, Giles!' The sweetness of Annabelle's smile did not diminish. So that was the distinguished gentleman's name! She went on, 'The Duke was very kind, but out of my league, I believe. However, I find your other friends *very* amiable. Surprisingly so. Or is it a case of the attraction

of opposites? I'll take the flowers, Giles. They should be put
in water. They are too beautiful in themselves to suffer for
their donors' lack of tact in sending them.'

'Lack of tact? Whatever do you mean?' asked Lady
Ordway.

'I'll leave Giles to explain, Aunt Laura. Perhaps he'd have
preferred it if the bouquets had been sent to him!' was
Annabelle's parting shot as she went out of the room to find
the housekeeper.

When Annabelle returned Lady Ordway was alone. Her
face was troubled.

'I should have thought Giles would be pleased at last
night's success,' she said. 'But something seems to have put
him in a bad mood. It was the business of the necklace, I
suppose. I had quite forgotten that my sister-in-law had been
given one just like it. It must have been passed on to Giles's
stepmother, and he hates to be reminded of her. Though why
he should take his ill humour out on you, I cannot imagine.'

'Can't you? He thinks I'm Rosabelle.'

'You mean, this…coolness towards her is as strong as
ever? He is still prejudiced against her? I had hoped that
would fade with time.'

'I'm sure it will soon,' said Annabelle with determination.
It occurred to her that this was an opportunity to talk to Aunt
Laura about Stephen, Giles and Rosabelle. 'Is Giles intending
to come back?' she asked. 'Or have we time to talk a little?'

'He's gone out for a ride. I think he intends to call in at
Tattersall's. He was talking of buying another mare.'

'Good. Aunt Laura, can't you tell me *anything* which will
help me to understand Giles? I know you are fond of him,
and he is good to you. *Why* has he this prejudice against
Rosa? Is it…is it something to do with Stephen? I know so
little about Rosa's husband.'

Lady Ordway plucked at the sheets nervously. She suddenly looked much older. 'I don't want to talk about Stephen, Anna. Please don't ask me to!'

Annabelle was disappointed but tried not to show it. 'I don't want you to do anything that distresses you, Aunt Laura.' She put her hand on Lady Ordway's arm. 'We won't talk about Stephen. But can't you give me a hint of what it is that causes Giles to be so…so unfair to Rosa? He seems to be reasonable enough with everyone else.'

Lady Ordway sighed. 'I love Giles, and I love Rosa. It's such a pity he can't forget the past. Rosa is such a kind, good girl, she deserves better. But Giles was prejudiced against her from the beginning. He never met her in the old days, of course, but he seemed to think that Rosa did her best to come between me and my son. He even tried to warn me about it!'

'He said as much the other day…I told him that it was nonsense.'

'Of course it was nonsense! But then he was predisposed to be suspicious—'

'Of Rosa? But why?'

Lady Ordway sighed again. 'Not just Rosa. Of any personable young woman, Anna.'

'Oh, come! He's a grown man with a successful career already behind him. You don't manage to become a Colonel in the Guards at his age without considerable force of character. Are you trying to tell me that Giles Stanton is *frightened* of women? I would find that very difficult to believe. He certainly doesn't give that impression.'

'He's not frightened of them. I said he was inclined to be suspicious of them. And it's perhaps not so surprising. He learned not to trust one woman when he was still very young.'

Annabelle hesitated. 'This is to do with the necklace, isn't it? And Giles's stepmother, perhaps?'

Lady Ordway hesitated. 'I suppose that now Giles is back in London, the scandalmongers are bound to talk again…'

She paused here for so long that Annabelle had to prompt
her.

'What happened, Aunt Laura?'

'Giles was deeply attached to his parents, particularly his
mother, my husband's sister, Margaret. He was devastated
when she died. It was very sudden, and he was only ten or
eleven at the time.'

'That's sad. He was old enough to realise what he had lost.
Rosa and I hardly remember our mama—we were still so
young.'

'Yes, my dear. And that is sad, too. Your mama was the
most enchanting creature I ever knew. You are both very like
her, though Rosabelle is quieter. But at least your papa genuinely mourned your mother.'

'He still does. Though I could wish… Never mind. What
are you saying? That Lord Stanton did not mourn his wife's
death?'

'Before my sister-in-law had been dead three months,
Giles's father remarried. A young woman half his age, who,
it appears, was his mistress. She was a real beauty—as beautiful as you and Rosa—and she could wind Lord Stanton
round her little finger. He was quite besotted. But…she had
little else to commend her, as Lord Stanton soon discovered.
Her house parties became notorious, and his father was eventually forced to send Giles away. That's why the boy spent
his summers with us. Since then, Venetia Stanton's name has
become a byword for every kind of extravagant and shame-
less behaviour. She eventually left her husband, but not before
she had ruined him. He now lives in retirement on his estate,
and sees no one.'

'Not even Giles?'

'Giles goes to Avenell quite often, but Lord Stanton is in
a sad way. He hardly speaks to his son. He resents him.'

'Resents him? Why?'

'Because when Giles discovered that his father was unable

to keep up the mortgage payments on his lands, he stepped in and bought them up.'

'How could he do that? Or is it since he inherited the Ordway fortune?'

'Oh, no! At least, not if you mean the money my husband left. The Ordways were all fabulously rich, and Giles's mother was an heiress in her own right. When she died Giles inherited the best part of her fortune, though I believe he has spent a good deal of it on his rescue of the Stanton lands.'

'I see. It's a dreadful story. But it happened twenty years ago. Since his mother died Giles has seen the world and mixed with all sorts of people, good and bad. Why has he not been able to put it behind him? It's absurd that he should blame all women for the sins of one!'

'I don't suppose he does. And if he ever met someone who was strong enough to overcome his prejudice he would make a wonderful husband. He is rich, handsome, and he can be very kind.' Lady Ordway gave Annabelle a mischievous look. 'Perhaps you're the one? You appear to have the spirit for it.'

'I think that is most unlikely, if not impossible! Even if I wished to be, I start with the serious disadvantage of deceiving him. If the masquerade ever came to light, can you imagine what he would say? It would confirm all his worst opinions of women in general, and Rosabelle and me in particular! No, I don't think there is any chance of a match between Giles Stanton and me! And think of the quarrels we should have! I am no doormat, you know!'

'That much I had noticed, my dear,' murmured Lady Ordway.

Annabelle was kept too busy in the days that followed the reception to ponder very often on what Lady Ordway had said. A state of armed neutrality seemed to exist between Giles and herself, and they both worked in relative harmony

to maintain the standard of entertainment set on that first
night. She was completely unaware of his state of confusion
about her.

Giles Stanton numbered many distinguished people among
his friends and acquaintances—diplomats, military personnel,
naval officers—people he had known in Spain and Portugal,
in Vienna, Brussels and Paris. After the Duke of Wellington's
return to England and the end of the Allied Occupation of
France many of them had taken up residence in London, and
it was now Giles's intention to return the generous hospitality
he had enjoyed for years as a bachelor at loose in the great
cities of Europe. The house in Upper Brook Street was emi-
nently suited to such occasions, and as soon as the family's
year of mourning after Stephen Ordway's death had ended he
had wasted no time in setting things in motion.

But in deciding to entertain such eminent and sophisticated
guests he had taken something of a gamble. Though his aunt
was now slowly improving, she was not yet ready to take
over the reins of the household. And Rosabelle Ordway had
been an unknown quantity. He had not been at all impressed
by what he had seen of her before Easter—thin, pale, nervy,
apparently ill at ease in company, and far too easily reduced
to tears. He might have forgiven her for all of this, if he had
believed for one moment that she missed Stephen. But it was
clear she did not.

She may have attempted to convince Giles that she had
remained faithful to her husband—and what a vain exercise
that had been with the evidence of Stephen's letters so vividly
in his mind!—but she had never pretended that she had truly
loved his cousin, or that she was sorry he was dead. Her one
saving grace in Giles's view was her indisputable devotion to
Aunt Laura.

He had been puzzled by her. This…colourless nonentity
was a far cry from the seductress portrayed in the letters. He

had even sometimes thought she must be playing a part, though for what purpose he could not determine. He was not a man to be softened by milksop manners and pathetic looks, and it had not been her tears which had moved him into letting her visit her family at Easter. It would have been too unreasonable not to allow her to go.

But he had not thought twice about insisting on her return at the given time, in spite of the change in his plans. He wanted her in London for purely selfish reasons. More than one lady had indicated her willingness to act as a proxy hostess until Lady Ordway was well again, and that was something Giles wished to avoid at all costs. Give a woman a hold over you and you could be stuck with her for life! At least he would be safe with his cousin's widow—he knew her for what she was.

But two weeks after the reception he sat in the library, ignoring the papers spread out in front of him, and coming to the conclusion that he was now more perplexed than ever by Rosabelle Ordway. A month or two ago he would have sworn she was an idle, broken butterfly, incapable of coping with a large household and a demanding social life. He had allowed for it. With a competent housekeeper, a good cook—and Rosabelle as a nominal hostess, kept well in the background—he would manage well enough. Though he could hardly hope to compete with the high standards of entertainment set by his friends, he had hoped for a modest degree of success.

However, it had recently been borne in on him that Rosabelle was, in fact, extremely capable at running the house, and that her skills and energy in organising entertainment of almost any kind were considerable. She had a trick of individuality, making something special of the smallest event, of casting a mantle of novelty over the most mundane occasion. He now discovered that evening invitations to the house in Upper Brook Street were among the most sought after in London. And as for Rosabelle staying in the background...he had difficulty in keeping up with her!

With all this success, Giles wondered why he was not happier. His friends were envious of his cook, impressed with the standard of comfort and elegance in the house, and they all raved about his cousin's lovely widow. It was astonishing, he told himself bitterly, quite astounding, what a pair of dark blue eyes and an enchanting smile could achieve. Such a woman had no need of intelligence or wit. She had only to sit there and look at a man, and before he knew it he was under her spell...

Chapter Five

Giles pushed his chair back impatiently and got up. He knew he was not being completely just. Rosabelle was quite often quiet, almost subdued, especially when she was with people of the *ton*. Was she wary of what members of London society were saying of her? But she was neither stupid nor passive. She could be lively, she was frequently witty, and could hold her own in the most demanding conversations, particularly with his old friends—those who had lived abroad for most of their careers. Even on topics she could know little about, she was able to listen and respond intelligently. And though her battles with him were bitter, she nearly always gave as good as she got. But lively or quiet, witty or subdued, the result was always the same—they all sought her out. Was this what Stephen had not been able to face? Rosabelle's popularity with the gentlemen?

Giles threw himself back into his chair, frowning heavily. She *must* have been playing a part when they had first met, six months ago. One month's holiday in Berkshire could not have brought about such a change. And she was certainly lying when she swore she had not had an affair with Selder! She knew the name very well, even though she had attempted to deny it. He had not forgotten her dismay and horror when he had first mentioned Selder's name to her—before she had been to Berkshire and recouped her forces.

But a few days ago, when he had sprung it on her after his return from Bristol, he would have sworn she had never heard it before! What a consummate piece of acting that had been! Did she really think, however, that he was stupid enough to be taken in by an air of innocent enquiry, dark blue eyes wide, delicate chin lifted in that way she had when waiting for a response… It was a very pretty chin, even when it was lifted even higher in challenge, a refusal to back down…

Damn it! She was a liar and a cheat, however popular she might be with those who didn't know her. He was really looking forward to the day when he had finally solved the mystery surrounding Stephen's life and Stephen's death. No evasions, no denials would avail her then. She would have to admit her guilt once and for all. And then…? Giles pushed the problem of what he would do with her then to the back of his mind.

He was grateful when Whitcroft came in and interrupted his thoughts.

'A Major Dabney to see you, sir. And Goss brought this from the Receiving Office.' He handed Giles a letter.

'Show Major Dabney in, Whitcroft. You'd better fetch some wine.'

The letter was from Charlie Fortescue, and looked as if it might be interesting. It was to be hoped so. After his session with the innkeeper at Woolhampton he had visited Charlie in Bristol, and had spent five fruitless days there making enquiries about Da Costa, and searching the docks and taverns. But he had failed to find any trace of the man. Perhaps this letter would have something—Charlie had promised to enquire further… He was casting a rapid glance at it when Whitcroft showed Major Dabney in.

'Good morning, Dabs! Come and sit down, why don't you? Whitcroft is just about to fetch something from the cellar.'

'Er…well, if it's all the same to you I'd as soon have some ale. Jolly thirsty! Been ridin' in the Park.'

'I'll join you.' Giles nodded to Whitcroft, who disappeared. 'This is a bit early in the morning for you, isn't it?'

'Well, I wanted to talk to you, old chap. Thing is, I was tellin' Mrs Ordway t'other evenin' how pleasant it is in the Park early in the morning—'

'How would you know? You're never up before eleven!'

'I never mentioned *dawn*, dear fellow. Eleven o'clock or noon was what I meant.'

'Go on.'

'And she happened to say how she envied me.'

'Did she, indeed!'

'I was a touch flabbergasted, I can tell you. I've never met a lady yet who wanted to know anything about the outside world before about one o'clock. But apparently Mrs Ordway's an exception. She finds it hard to lie abed when it's so light, she says. Thing is, would you object if I was to invite her to take a turn round the Park one morning? Thought I'd better ask.'

Giles's first impulse was to refuse, but he restrained himself. He really had no reason to. Dabney was a perfectly eligible member of society, he was reasonably rich, and he knew how to behave. Rosabelle would be safe with him. It was unconventional, perhaps, for a lady to be out riding so early in the morning, but Rosabelle was no debutante. She was, or had been, a married woman, and there was nothing questionable in her riding round the park with an escort. Perhaps the question ought to be whether Dabney, whom he liked, would be safe with his cousin's widow! Eventually he said, 'Go ahead and ask her.'

'Thanks, Gil. Didn't think you'd mind.'

Whitcroft came in with two tankards, which the gentlemen quaffed in companionable silence. Then Dabney said with a gesture at the letter, 'I hope I didn't interrupt your work. The

Beau still keeping you busy? You seem to do nothing else nowadays. I thought you'd sold out!'

'This? Oh, this isn't work. It's the reply to an enquiry I made in Bristol. About a chap called Da Costa. I'm trying to find out a bit more about Stephen's activities before he died, but I don't think this can have much to do with them.'

'Ordway's activities, eh? Er...got very far, Gil?'

'Not yet, but it's early days. Why? Do you know anything about them?' Giles asked in surprise.

'No, no! Nothing at all. Never knew your cousin.'

'I didn't think you would have. He was much younger than either of us.'

'Heard of him, though.' Major Dabney stopped.

'And?'

'You been about the town much, Gil? Since you came back from France?'

'Not yet, but I'm planning to. What is all this about, Dabs? It's not like you to be cryptic.'

Major Dabney looked uncomfortable. 'Thing is...'

'Well?'

'I don't want to interfere, Gil, but...it might be better to leave well alone. No sense in stirring things up.'

Giles sat up and looked coldly at his friend. 'Explain!'

'It isn't all that easy! I just thought you might be wiser not to delve too deeply into your late cousin's activities.'

There was a pause, during which Major Dabney avoided Giles's gaze. 'What do you mean by that?' asked Giles softly.

'It's no use using that tone, Gil! It might scare the junior staff, but it don't frighten me! I've known you too long.'

'So?'

'This is damned awkward! I've no wish to offend you, old chap, but the long and short of it is, that, from what I've heard, your cousin ain't too well thought of in London! Some of his activities won't stand close investigation. He mixed with a rum crowd.'

Giles eyed his friend thoughtfully. Then he said, 'Have you by any chance been talking to Stephen's widow?'

'Mrs Ordway?' Major Dabney looked at Giles in astonishment. 'Good God, what do you take me for? I wouldn't mention it to *her*, 'pon my word, I wouldn't! Not at all the sort of thing to do! Bound to distress her.'

'Well, where did you hear it?'

'As a matter of fact I wouldn't know where I heard it first. It…it's fairly common knowledge. But I shouldn't worry. Unless you go poking around in it, it'll die down. Eventually.'

'Is Stephen the only victim of the gossip? What about the rest of the family?'

'Who would that be? You? Lady Ordway? Don't be a fool, Gil!'

'What about…Mrs Ordway?'

Major Dabney stared at Giles. 'What the devil's got into you, Gil? Of course not! Most people seem to think she's well rid of him!' He looked at Giles's set face, and said in a softer tone, 'Sorry if you don't like it, old chap. I know you were quite fond of him and all that, but that's what they say. And everyone I've spoken to is jolly pleased to see Mrs Ordway in society again.'

'I'm sure,' said Giles. 'She livens it up no end.'

Major Dabney looked slightly puzzled at his tone, but ended by saying, 'She certainly does. Lovely woman. A star. So, it's all right if I ask her, then?'

'Ask her what?'

'To ride in the Park!'

'Of course. I'm not her guardian.'

'Er…is she up?'

'I'm sure she is. I'll ask Whitcroft to find her for you.' He pulled the bell rope by the fireplace, then came back. The two men waited in a slightly uneasy silence for Whitcroft to appear.

Just before he came the Major said awkwardly, 'I hope you

didn't mind my mentioning what's bein' said about your cousin, Gil.'

'Not at all. You weren't very specific, though. Does that mean that rumour is vague?'

'Er…no. But I've said all I'm going to say. Just wanted to warn you. Didn't want you to get into difficulties.'

'You're quite right, Dabs. Thanks.'

Whitcroft came in to say that Mrs Ordway was in the drawing room and Major Dabney went out. Giles picked up the letter again, and tried to concentrate on it.

Dear Gil,

There is absolutely no need to thank us, we were very pleased to see you…

The sound of laughter came through the door. Dabney had left the damned thing open in his eagerness to present his invitation to Rosabelle. He had plenty of address—Rosabelle would probably accept it… Giles went to the door and shut it. It was nothing to him what she did. He picked up the letter again.

I've had an encounter with another of the Excise Officers. He was out of Bristol when you were here…

Rosabelle knew that he went out every morning. They had met on that first day after her return. If she was so anxious to go riding why hadn't she mentioned it to him? Something could have been arranged… Giles looked down at the paper in his hand and sat down at his desk. Charlie Fortescue's writing was like a spider trail across the paper! It made it very difficult to concentrate…

…but has now returned. I talked to him at some length…

Perhaps she wasn't all that taken with riding! Perhaps it was just an excuse to have some time with Dabney. It must add to a woman's consequence to have a handsome chap like Dabney escorting her everywhere. An officer, too.

A most interesting chat…

Pettifer, too, had been here the other day to see if she would go to the theatre. And Wainwright had been quite cast down when she had had to refuse his offer of a drive out to Kensington. All those sensible men, good officers, falling over themselves to please her! What fools men were! Giles gave a snort of contempt and returned to his letter.

and I think you'll be surprised at what I have learnt about your friend…

Not all of her beaux were officers, of course. Monteith had called yesterday to arrange to take her to Kew… Supercilious type. The son of an Earl. Aunt Laura had been in a flutter… And there was another whose name he couldn't recall… That damned woman had them all twisted round her little finger…! Giles got up impatiently and took the letter over to the window. The light would be better here, and he could perhaps read it without distraction.

Da Costa has been known to my contact for some years. He has been involved with a good few things in his time, but it is suspected that, for the past few years, he has been working on pirate ships…

Giles's attention was at last securely caught. Piracy! He sat down on the window seat and read more carefully…

There's a thriving trade for these villains in and
around Bristol. They fit up here, and then, with information supplied by spies in the shipping trade, they prey
upon merchant ships, concentrating on the more profit-
able cargoes, chiefly in the Mediterranean. One such, *Le
Faucon*, operated by a Frenchman called Legrand, was
sunk off Algiers last autumn, but there are always others.
My friend believes Da Costa brings information to the
ships. He would be very interested in anything you can
tell him.

Sara and I hope that your plans to entertain London
are going well. We may take you up on that invitation
to visit you, but not yet…etc, etc…

The letter continued for a page more, but there was nothing
relevant to his enquiries… More sounds of laughter penetrated from the hall. Dabney brayed like a horse! He must be
leaving. Good! But what had Rosabelle said to him? Giles
got up and went out into the hall.

Dabney had hold of Rosabelle's hand and they were smiling. But when Rosabelle saw Giles her smile faded and she
drew back.

'Dabs, I forgot to ask you—'

'Good morning, Giles,' said Rosabelle clearly.

'Good morning. I hear you are still unable to get used to
town hours. Why didn't you say?'

Rosabelle gave him a speaking look, then said, 'Major
Dabney has found a solution. I gather you don't object?'

'Of course not. Why should I object?'

'Why, indeed?' She turned to Dabney. 'The day after tomorrow, then? I'll consult Goss about a horse.'

'I could bring one along,' said Major Dabney eagerly. 'I
have the prettiest little mare. You cannot imagine—'

'Don't put yourself out, Dabs. Absolutely no need for it,'

said Giles, overriding the Major's protests. 'The stables are full of horses badly needing some exercise. I'll see to it.'

'Right! I'll take my leave, then. Wait! What was it you wanted to ask me, Gil?'

Giles looked blank, then said, 'Oh, yes. Is Nicholson back yet, do you know?'

'He's not due for another three weeks. I thought I told you that the other day?'

'So you did! I'd forgotten. Right.'

The Major shook his head and said, 'I told you all that work wouldn't do you any good, Gil. Get some fresh air yourself. The day after tomorrow, Mrs Ordway. Eleven o'clock! Gil!' He saluted them both and strode off.

Giles walked back towards the library deep in thought. At the door he stopped and looked back. Rosabelle was about to go upstairs again.

'Rosabelle!' He walked back. 'I'd like to make sure the mare I have in mind for you will do. Have you ridden much in London?'

'Er…not a great deal. But I've ridden a lot down at Temperley.'

'Open fields and country lanes. Not the same thing at all. Can you be ready to go out in half an hour?'

'Where?'

'Riding in the Park, of course!' He repressed a smile at her obvious desire to ride battling with that independent spirit of hers, and decided to make it easier for her. 'Rosabelle, if you are free for an hour this morning, I should like very much to take you riding. Would you come? Please.'

She looked at him suspiciously. 'Why?'

'It's a pleasant morning. I feel like fresh air. And I should like to make sure that you will be safe with Dabney.' When she still looked sceptical, he added irritably, 'And I think it would look better in the eyes of the world if your first excursion into Hyde Park was with a member of the family!'

Her face cleared. 'Ah, that sounds more like it. Half an hour?'

'Half an hour. I'll go and see Goss.' Giles walked away, satisfied. He had done his duty by the family, he told himself. And it wouldn't do her any harm to see the sort of person she might meet at this hour in Hyde Park.

Annabelle went up the stairs with a light step. The prospect of some exercise and fresh air was very attractive. But did Rosabelle possess a riding habit? And would her sister's boots, supposing there were any, fit her? To her relief, at the back of the closet was a dark green riding dress and some tan boots which fitted perfectly. The dress was just a fraction tight, but was perfectly wearable. Rosabelle must have been quite young when she had last worn it—it had obviously lain in the closet for years.

Lily found a white lace-edged kerchief, which she tied into something like a man's cravat, allowing her to leave the dress open at the neck. Tan leather gloves, and a dark green hat with a small plume completed the outfit. After a quick check in the looking glass Annabelle was satisfied that she would do, though she had a fleeting regret for the new and very stylish habit she had left behind at Temperley. She went downstairs with two minutes to spare. Giles was waiting in the hall.

'I will say this for you. You are more punctual than most women of my acquaintance,' was his greeting.

'Heavens! A compliment! A real one.'

'Real?'

'One of the first things I was told about you was that you believed in punctuality.'

'Who told you that?' he asked as he escorted her outside, where Goss was waiting with the horses.

'Why, Sergeant Goss here.'

'Goss wasn't with me when I arrived at Christmas.'

Annabelle kept her head. 'I meant the first thing Sergeant Goss told me, when I came back from Temperley,' she said fluently, then hurried on, 'Have we at last found a virtue I possess? Punctuality. It's not a very noble one, but I suppose it will do.'

Goss handed her up and they set off along Upper Brook Street towards the Park.

'You're wrong,' Giles said. 'Punctuality is a very important virtue. In wartime it can be vital.'

'I can well believe that to be so. Giles, I should like to hear of your adventures in the Peninsula. Spain has always held my imagination.'

They negotiated the crossing into the Park. 'They weren't adventures, Rosabelle, as in a romance. Men died in them.'

'I'm sorry,' she said quickly. 'You are right to rebuke me. I didn't think before I spoke.'

He looked at her downcast face and said more kindly, 'I lost some good friends out in Spain, but for all that there were adventures which we all enjoyed—times when we laughed, and times when we were simply glad to be alive with a good horse under us, and the plains of Estramadura before us.'

'What is Spain really like?'

'You cannot imagine how different it is from England. The countryside is harsh, unyielding, with no shade or hill to break the monotony. It can be unbelievably hot in summer, and men can die of the cold in winter there. But it has its own, stark beauty—vast skies and endless horizons.' Giles was lost in thought for a moment. Then he looked back at her and said with a smile, 'But there were many times when I longed for a more temperate climate, green grass, lazy rivers, the dales and moors of England…'

'You never came back to England during that time?'

'No.' His face closed up. 'No, I didn't. I chose not to.'

The ghost of Stephen…and someone else?…floated between them. A hazy picture of a beautiful woman wearing a necklace of crystal, gold and pearls, a woman who had taken his mother's place, disgraced it, then cast it carelessly aside. Giles was frowning, and Annabelle, reluctant to let the unusual mood of camaraderie go, cast around in her mind to find something to say.

'Lord Monteith is of the opinion—' she began. Her choice was clearly an unfortunate one. He interrupted her.

'I heard him airing his opinion on the wars in the Peninsula the other night. He must have been all of fifteen and at school when Talavera was fought and men died by the hundred. Spare me the inanities of such a supercilious ass!' Giles's tone was savage. 'Why are we riding at such a funereal pace? The horses need more than this to get the fidgets out of them.' His bay jerked forward at his master's urging and set off at a gallop.

One did not gallop in the Park, it was simply not done. Annabelle knew that very well—it was one of the many rules Mrs Thelwell had carefully instilled. But, after a second's pause, she let her horse have its head and followed Giles's example. It was glorious!

By the time they drew up they were at the far end of the Park. Giles was standing by his horse, adjusting one of the girths, when Annabelle reined in. He went to help her dismount.

'That was wonderful, Giles!' she laughed, as she leapt gracefully down. 'That bay of yours is a magnificent animal, but this mare is superb! She goes like the wind. I should love to try her out on a proper stretch of ground.' She looked up at him ruefully, the laughter lingering in her eyes. 'But not here! Society will disown me if I ever gallop like that again here. I must look a wreck!'

Giles looked at cheeks flushed with excitement and exercise, eyes sparkling with enjoyment, the sheer vitality of the woman before him. His hands were still at her waist... With an effort he drew away.

'I'm afraid your hair is coming down, Rosabelle. Do you wish to fix it?' he said coldly.

The pleasure slowly drained out of her face. 'Of course. Thank you.' She turned away from him and raised her arms to take off her hat, hooking it on to the saddle. She was still panting after the gallop, and it was easy to see the rise and fall of her bosom in the closely fitting riding habit. He had always thought of her as slight, but she was, in fact, a very shapely woman... He gazed in fascination as she bent her head and started to coil her hair. It slipped through her fingers like molten gold...

'Why are you staring so, Giles? I'm sorry if my appearance offends you, but it is entirely your fault. If you had told me we were going for a gallop, I would have made sure my hair was more secure. I suppose you will now call me a hoyden.'

'I...no, I will not call you a hoyden.' Giles was forcing himself to speak calmly. He was shocked at the feelings roused when his hands had been round her waist, and again at the sight of Rosabelle twisting her rope of hair. They were not the sort he had ever felt for a respectable woman before. Not in his life. This sudden desire to take her into his arms, to let that dark golden hair flow over him, to loosen the delicate lace at her throat and kiss the hollow thus revealed...

She had her back to him. He put his hand out to pull her towards him... The big bay horse sidled away and pulled at the rein. By the time he had brought it under control again she had finished tidying herself and was looking cool, neat, remote even. But the lace at her throat was still rising and falling more rapidly than usual, and one small tendril of hair was still curling round her ear... He looked away, angry with himself and her. His horse's movement had saved him from making a disastrous mistake—the damned animal had more sense than its master!

'Shall we go back?' he said abruptly.

'Of course,' she said.

Once again he helped her as she mounted, but this time she was silent. They rode back towards the gate. Giles was working hard to bring his feelings into line, full of scorn for his own weakness. How could he account for that sudden, almost overwhelming desire to make love to Rosabelle Ordway, there on the spot? He had always prided himself before on his cool approach to such matters.

There were women to whom one made love—charming, sophisticated beauties who surrounded Wellington and his officers—to whom love was a game, who knew how to please a man in return, of course, for certain favours, without any thought of long-term commitment. And then there were what one might call respectable women, women with pretensions to virtue.

A sensible man avoided the slightest romantic involvement with any of these, for before you knew it she was talking of wedding bells and trousseaux and you were caught. Caught in a lottery where the chances were heavily weighted against you. Caught as his father had been. As Stephen had been. Women of virtue! He smiled grimly. Rosabelle Ordway, a woman of virtue? What a fool he was! How could he have forgotten, even for one moment, Stephen's anguished letters?

He stole a glance at her. She was looking withdrawn, sad almost. The flush in her cheeks had died down, her breathing was more even. You might say she was the perfect picture of a young society matron about to take a short, sedate ride in the Park! The trappings of respectability were there, certainly. Her behaviour in public was impeccable, and even in his own circles she had so far won approval from all sides—and that included the most rigidly hidebound sticks in the War Office. Charming she might be, original she certainly was, but she never overstepped the mark in public.

But she *must* be playing a part! Stephen had written of his wife in terms which could never be applied to a respectable woman. He had known the wanton in Rosabelle Ordway. And Selder, he must suppose, had known it, too. How long would it take before Dabney, Wainwright, or one of the others…? No! The smooth pace of Giles's horse faltered as he tightened his grasp on the reins. That was too much! That idea was one he could not even begin to tolerate. He found he was struggling once again to bring his feelings into order. What the devil was wrong with him? Why was he unable to believe that Rosabelle Ordway would run true to form? The problem was that he was finding it increasingly difficult to reconcile the woman he was getting to know with the picture drawn by Stephen in those damned letters. He was as big a fool as all the rest!

Goss was waiting for them at the gate to the Park. When they were within sight of him, Giles said curtly, 'I see no reason why you should not go with Major Dabney tomorrow morning. But I don't advise going as far as we did today. Keep to the more frequented paths.'

She looked at him mockingly. 'Major Dabney has a greater sense of propriety than you, Giles. I don't imagine for one moment that we will go above a slow trot, or out of Rotten Row.'

'As well for him, perhaps.' She looked at him, clearly puzzled by his tone, but said nothing. When they reached the house, Giles watched as Goss took charge of Rosabelle's horse and was rewarded with a charming smile. She couldn't resist trying to enchant everyone! Absolutely everyone!

Annabelle went up to her room to change. She felt…strange, unsettled. Why had she been so tinglingly aware of Giles's hands on her waist? Why the sensation of shivers running down her spine when she met his eyes…? It wasn't the first time by any means that a gentleman had helped her thus from a horse, so why, this time, had she felt

so breathless, as if she was on the threshold of something...something unimaginably exciting? His hands had
tightened as he held her. Had he seen the effort it had cost
her not to put her arms round his neck?

She had done her utmost to hide the feelings he had
aroused, but had he been aware of them all the same? Was
that why he had been so curt, so cold? He was quite right, of
course. No decent woman would even think such things. The
trouble was, these new and powerful emotions had taken her
completely by surprise. She had never experienced anything
like them before. Was she a wanton? And later, when she had
turned away to avoid his eyes, had concentrated on tidying
herself as quickly and as neatly as possible, had he thought
she was deliberately flaunting her hair before him?

No one had ever before regarded her with such stony disapproval. She had deserved it. How could she be so shame-
less! She must make quite certain that such a thing never,
never happened again!

Her resolution was not put to the test in the days that followed. Giles seemed to be avoiding her, and once again
Annabelle felt deeply shamed that he thought it necessary.
However, she maintained her air of calm, and when they did
meet managed to treat him politely, but at a distance. She
rode out most days with one or other of her cavaliers, and in
the evenings entertained at Upper Brook Street, or went out
with Lady Ordway. They were frequently escorted by Giles,
but though she seldom lacked partners she was never invited
to dance with him, and their conversations were limited to
banalities. During the day he spent a great deal of his time
in the library, or out and about, presumably with his friends.

For the rest she rejoiced to see Lady Ordway growing happier and more active with every day that passed, and she
herself was still fresh enough to town life to take pleasure in
the endless round of soirées, balls, concerts, and all the rest.

She had become adept at appearing to understand a comment or observation without having the slightest notion of what was meant, and had learned to switch effortlessly to safer topics before any discrepancies became obvious. In fact, this constant challenge to her wits added secret spice to Annabelle's social life. Otherwise, deprived of her verbal battles with Giles, she might eventually have become bored with the frivolities which made up the London Season.

Chapter Six

Annabelle was growing anxious about the length of her stay in the city, and said so to Lady Ordway.

'Good gracious, Anna! Is it so long since you came here? I am surprised. How time has flown!'

'That's one of the most pleasing things you could have said to me, Aunt Laura! It proves that you really are better. Can it be that you are even enjoying yourself?'

'Well, I am! More than I have for years. You and Giles have both been so kind, and my old friends have made me so welcome. But I suppose you are pining for Temperley?'

'No, not exactly... But I can't be Rosa forever. You wouldn't wish me to, I'm sure.'

'No, that's true. I miss Rosa. But I should miss you, too!'

Annabelle started to laugh. 'You can't have both of us. I don't think Papa would like that, and just think how London would regard us. They'd think they were seeing double!'

'Well, they would be, wouldn't they?' Lady Ordway joined in Annabelle's laughter. But after a few minutes they both became sober again.

'I have to say, Anna, that I cannot at the moment see how you and Rosa could possibly change places. Giles would be bound to suspect something if you suddenly insisted on going to Temperley again so soon.'

'I agree. And even if we managed that, I can already foresee some difficulties Rosa's re-entry into society will create. It wasn't easy for me to take her place, but I had one advantage. She had been seen but seldom in public during her year of mourning, and society had rather forgotten exactly what she looked like, how she spoke and behaved. But the *ton* have seen so much of me in recent weeks that it would be much more difficult now to deceive anyone.'

'Especially Giles.'

'Especially Giles. In fact…in fact, I'm beginning to be of the opinion that *that* might be impossible. He's very astute. Sooner or later one of us will be required to confess the plot to him.'

Lady Ordway sighed. 'Oh, dear! I hadn't foreseen all this…'

'Nor had I,' said Annabelle ruefully. 'It's all his fault, of course. If only he had gone to France as he promised, instead of entertaining half of Europe here!'

'But…I thought you were enjoying yourself?'

'I am! I love it in London.'

'Rosa seems to be loving it at Temperley… Perhaps she would like a little longer there? There's a Mr Winbolt…'

'Philip Winbolt? She has met him?'

'Yes. I had a letter today. She can't say much, of course, but I gather she was rather impressed by him. Do you know him, Anna?'

'Yes, I do. Well, well! Rosabelle and Mr Winbolt…'

'Did you like him? Do you think he and Rosabelle might suit?'

'I found him over-solicitous. He seemed to think that every woman of his acquaintance was a delicate creature, needing his protection and help. You can imagine how I felt about that, after years of running Temperley single-handed! But

Rosabelle is different… Do you know, Aunt Laura, I rather think they might be an ideal pair! And if Rosabelle was attracted to him, it would be a very good match for her. Mrs Thelwell considers him extremely eligible. '

'Then he must be. I don't know how she gathers her information, but I've never known her to be wrong!'

'If it did come to anything… How would you…what would your feelings be?'

'I know what you are thinking. My poor Stephen. But…I know now that Rosabelle was too young when she married him. I've known it for a long time. It was just…I persuaded her into it because I thought it might change him. But it was a disastrous mistake.'

'Change him? How?'

'To be…to be…' Lady Ordway's lips trembled and she shook her head. 'No! It's no use, Anna. I can't tell you. But I have bitterly regretted that marriage. Though I loved Rosa so much, I ended up trying to make use of her. I nearly ruined her life. If she could find happiness with someone else— someone who would love her the way she deserves—then I would be the happiest woman in London, I think.'

'Well, then,' said Annabelle briskly, anxious to turn Lady Ordway's mind into a more cheerful direction, 'it can't do any harm to leave matters as they are for a week or two. Meanwhile, we must put our minds to the problem of effecting an exchange when the time is ripe! Perhaps when the season finishes?'

Just a few days later Lady Ordway came in from an afternoon drive in a state of eager excitement. She said triumphantly, 'Anna! I have the answer to our problem! I have just been talking to Mrs Arbuthnot, and she has the highest opinion of the waters at Bath. They have done her no end of good, she says.'

'And?'

'We could go there! Giles had talked of going to his estates in the North at the end of the season, but I am sure I can persuade him to take us to Bath instead. And the Bath Road passes within a few miles of Temperley.'

'But if we stayed at Temperley, Giles would meet Rosabelle there! And as soon as he saw us together he would know instantly what we had done. It wouldn't work, Aunt Laura.'

'Wait! Giles and I would not go to Temperley. I have some very good friends at Reading whom I haven't seen for years. We would stay with them and you—'

'—would pay a visit to Temperley, ostensibly to see my father… I see!'

'And after a day or so Rosa would join Giles and me at Reading, and the three of us would carry on to Bath!' Lady Ordway sat back, looking very pleased with herself. 'Is that not a good plan?'

'An excellent one! It would mean that Rosa's return to London would be postponed as well. Society will have a chance to forget me. But…what reason can we give for your not coming to Temperley with me? The house is big enough for twenty visitors.'

'Your papa is an invalid, Anna! We could not possibly foist ourselves on him. Besides, I should really like to see the Chamberlaynes again.'

'Very good. The next most important question is—can you persuade Giles to take you to Bath?'

'I'm sure I could. He's so very kind. The difficulty will be to find him at home for long enough to bring the question up! He spends so much time out of the house nowadays.'

Annabelle bit her lip. She too had noticed that Giles was seldom at home, and thought she knew the reason for it. Odious, conceited man! Did he not realise how much she regretted that moment of weakness in the Park? How small the danger was that she would repeat it? There was really not the slightest necessity for him to spend so much time with his friends!

But later that night, as she lay in bed, Annabelle asked herself why she was not more pleased at Lady Ordway's ingenious plan. Her task was accomplished. Rosabelle had enjoyed an untrammelled month—more!—in the peace of Temperley, and she had seen more than she could ever have imagined of London and its Society. If the Bath project succeeded, Rosabelle Ordway would return later in the year to London, and Annabelle Kelland would settle down again to her busy but quiet life at Temperley.

It might take Rosabelle a while to accustom herself to the life in society again, but she would manage. And if the affair with Philip Winbolt was serious, he would visit her there. She did not doubt for a minute that if Mr Winbolt truly fell in love with her sister, he would forgive her for her deception. He was as gentle and as understanding as Rosabelle herself. With Mr Winbolt to protect her and to believe in her, what would it matter if Giles remained unconvinced of her innocence?

It was all very satisfactory, so why was there this pain somewhere inside her? What did it matter to her—this conviction that Giles would quite certainly never forgive her for deceiving him? That it would only confirm his jaundiced view of women in general, and of Annabelle Kelland in particular? Annabelle reviewed his character defects in detail. She rehearsed in her mind the insults, the harsh orders, the unreasonableness of his behaviour... But nothing seemed to chase away this feeling of sharp regret that she would soon never see him again.

Giles was not seeing his friends as often as Annabelle believed. He was busy seeking out people who had known Stephen Ordway. He told himself that his aim was to prove Dabney's view of Stephen totally mistaken. And if he should discover more about Rosabelle Ordway in the process, then well and good! But, as time went on, he began to realise that any attempt to prove Dabney wrong was vain. Instead, he grew more and more troubled at the picture of Stephen which was emerging.

His cousin *had* mixed with one of the most unsavoury sets in London Society. His word, his honour, his integrity *had* been compromised time and time again. And while no one knew, or no one would say, what he and his friends had been up to, they all condemned him without hesitation. When Giles suggested that he might have been weak, foolish, easily led, the world agreed with him. But one man, who had been close to Stephen in the old days, added that though he had always been weak and foolish, he had also been a liar and a cheat.

'You're wasting your time on that cousin of yours! He wasn't worth it! Oh, he could charm the skin off a cat, when he was in the mood, but it was all show. Look, Gil, I was at school with the fellow, and I know. What's more, I'm not afraid to tell you—not like some of these others. Believe me, Stephen Ordway was a bad lot from the day he was born. A manipulator and a liar.'

Giles rejected this, of course, immediately. This was not the Stephen he knew. But in the end he had to admit that Dabney's advice had been sound. He had stirred things up which would have been better left alone.

However, he found he could not leave it there. Stephen was dead, beyond the reach of harm or censure, but his widow still lived. What part had Rosabelle Ordway played in all this? In all his researches, there had not been the slightest hint of criticism directed against her. But then, he had never heard any mention of Selder's name, either. It was evident that the pair had kept their activities very discreet. Giles was convinced that there must be someone in London who knew more about Selder, and he set about trying to find whoever it was.

His quest took him into curious byways, and among those

who lived in the twilight of London's underworld. He learned one or two names of men who had been part of Stephen's circle, even came to recognise one or two—a blond giant called Fraser, and a small, stocky man called Burrows. But he never heard a whisper of the name of Selder.

Lady Ordway eventually managed to broach the question of a visit to Bath with her nephew.

'I am much improved in health, dearest Giles, but Dr Cotterell has persuaded me that a short visit to one of the watering places would be beneficial. To Bath, say.'

'Then you must go to one. Indeed, it would suit me very well to take you.'

'It would?'

'I had intended, as you know, to go north, at the end of June—I've even started to make some arrangements. But I had been wondering what to do about the house here. I don't like the idea of leaving you in London without someone to keep an eye on you. Especially in the heat of the summer months. But if you and Rosabelle were to spend a few weeks in Buxton, then I could escort you there. You would be quite safe there while I pay a visit to my father at Avenell, which is only a dozen or so miles away. Then I could later join you, and escort you back again.'

'Buxton!'

'Yes, why not? The facilities there are first class. The waters are considered to be as good as any in England, and the Crescent is very handsome, with two or three excellent hotels and apartments.'

'It's such a long way away!'

'A mere sixty miles further than Bath! Have you ever seen anything of Derbyshire, Aunt Laura? It's very beautiful, I assure you.'

'I visited Avenell once—just after your uncle and I were married. I remember that the journey seemed endless!'

'We could take it in easy stages. Several friends of mine live on the route, and they would be delighted to welcome you. Or there are one or two excellent inns I have come to know, too.'

'Mm…I…I wondered if we might go to Bath, Giles? The beauties of Nature are all very well, and I'm sure your friends are delightful, but I prefer life in a city. Bath is such a *civilised* place, and there would be amusement for Rosa, too. The Assembly Rooms there are a great deal more fashionable that anywhere so far north as Buxton could be. Who has ever heard of Buxton?'

'I thought it was the waters you were anxious to take, Aunt Laura? But…' Giles looked at Annabelle. 'I suppose it is your wish to go to Bath?'

'Yes,' she said bravely, putting up her chin. 'I've always heard that it's a beautiful city, and that the shops and entertainments there are quite outstanding. Buxton could hardly compete.'

'Frivolity and fashion. Is that all you think of?'

'Giles! I would prefer to go to Bath, too. Rosa was merely supporting me.'

'Was she? Well, I suppose I could go north later—in the autumn. I'll think about it, Aunt Laura. I'll have to ask my agent if there's any pressing business at Avenell first.'

'Yes, do, dearest Giles! I am persuaded that everyone at Avenell Hall could do very well without you till the autumn.'

'We could always go without you, Giles,' said Annabelle with a mocking look. 'We should be safe enough with a suitable number of grooms and servants. We could then indulge our love of frivolity and fashion without denying you your chance of worth and achievement at your country seat.'

Giles looked at her blandly. 'I wouldn't hear of it. We shall all three go either to Bath—or to Buxton.'

The two women exchanged a glance. Their beautiful scheme was in danger of going sadly awry!

* * *

A day or two after this debate Giles took them to the theatre. It was intended to be an evening of harmless amusement, one of many such. But this particular visit resulted in a sequence of events which was to have a far-reaching effect on several lives.

As they took their places in the auditorium Giles stiffened. His eyes were fixed on three people sitting in the box opposite theirs, and Annabelle wondered what could possibly interest him in such an ill-assorted group. On the left was a generously proportioned lady in black, looking around with good-humoured self-assurance. Her plump face was thickly powdered, and it was very clear that her sable hair owed more to art than to nature.

On the right was another lady on the shady side of forty, equally heavily made up and with hair as spuriously golden as her friend's was black. She wore a low-cut red dress and a great deal of jewellery—several rings and necklaces, and a long string of milk-white pearls wound extravagantly among the brassy curls. Between these two sat a young man in his late twenties.

Annabelle could hardly believe her eyes. He was almost too handsome to be real—more like a statue out of classical antiquity! Tall, broad-shouldered with classically perfect features and lint white hair—what on earth could he be doing with the two harpies?

Annabelle raised her opera glasses to her eyes…and gave a gasp as she caught a glimpse of one of the necklaces worn by the woman in red…

'Give me those!' Giles said sharply. He held them to his eyes, then gave an exclamation of disgust and turned to Lady Ordway. 'Would you please excuse me, Aunt Laura? The play is one I have seen before, and there is something else I really ought to be doing at this moment. I shall return before it is over and wait for you in the anteroom. Winterton is in

the next box—I'm sure he would accompany you downstairs.'
He was very pale.

Lady Ordway looked at the woman in the box opposite,
and nodded. 'Of course we shall be perfectly all right, Giles,'
she said. 'We shall see you after the play.'

Giles bowed, thrust Annabelle's glasses back into her hand,
and disappeared.

'Poor boy!' said Lady Ordway, shaking her head. 'That
dreadful, dreadful woman!'

Annabelle fingered the necklace round her own neck. 'Who
is she, Aunt Laura? Is it…is it Giles's stepmother? The necklace she's wearing is the same as this, isn't it?'

'Yes,' said Lady Ordway bitterly. 'That's Venetia Stanton.
And she's wearing Margaret Stanton's necklace. But not only
that. The pearls in that…trollop's hair—they too belonged to
Margaret. She inherited them from my mother-in-law, who
had them from her mother.'

'It's a lovely string of pearls.'

'They are worth a king's ransom! So large and so perfectly
matched. But that isn't the point, Anna. Margaret Stanton and
her mother Emily before her were both decent, well-bred gen-
tlewomen. The value of those pearls goes far beyond their
intrinsic worth—they represent pride in family and reputation.
And to see them flaunted in that shockingly vulgar manner…
I do not blame Giles's revulsion!'

'Who are her friends?'

'The woman in black was Nellie Marsden before she married a German aristocrat. A camp follower. Now she's the
Baroness Leibmann.'

'Is that the Baron sitting between them?'

'Good Lord, no! He's eighty if he's a day! No one ever
sees him. I don't know who the Adonis in the box is, I haven't
seen him before.'

At the end of the play Annabelle and Lady Ordway made
their way, escorted by Lord Winterton, down to the anteroom.

But there was such a crush on the stairs that Annabelle was separated from the two older people. She could see the feathers on Lady Ordway's headdress waving on the other side of the staircase, and at the bottom of the stairs she tried to cross over to rejoin them. But the tide of people was too strong, and she merely succeeded in losing her fan, as it was torn from her in the mêlée. A strong arm swept her to one side into a safe corner, and a minute later her fan was returned.

'Ma'am?'

'Why, thank you! You are very kind, sir!' said Annabelle with a slightly nervous smile.

The gentleman smiled back, and though he was not precisely handsome, Annabelle thought how charming he was. She started to smile more widely. But then, quite unaccountably, she found herself trembling, chilled to the bone as if she was suffering a sudden attack of ague. Her skin crawled as he spoke again.

'Why, Rosabelle!' he said. 'What a piece of good fortune! I've been hoping to see you.' He cast a glance up the staircase. 'But this isn't the place. We'll meet again before long.'

Then, before she could say anything, he disappeared into the crowd. Annabelle leaned against the wall. What was the matter with her? The crowd had pushed her, but there had been no real danger. Why this sudden reaction? It couldn't have been the gentleman who had rescued her fan—she had never seen him before in her life. Yet…who was he, and what had he meant? He knew her twin, so much was certain, but she could not somehow imagine Rosabelle making a friend of him. A second shiver ran up her spine. Annabelle passed a hand over her forehead—was she sickening for something? The room was hot, but she felt chilled… She nearly jumped out of her skin when a hand descended on her shoulder. Turning, she found Lady Stanton peering at her throat.

'Look, Fraser!' the lady cried. 'It's the girl with my necklace!' The woman's fingers stretched out like talons to touch it. Annabelle's head swam as a waft of perfume threatened to overpower her, and Venetia Stanton's heavily powdered face was thrust close to hers.

'Who the devil are you, my dear?' demanded Lady Stanton. 'And what are you doing with a copy of my necklace? Don't tell me that my toad of a stepson has a *petite amie* at last! Did *he* have it made for you?'

Annabelle felt sick. 'I beg your pardon,' she said as clearly and as coldly as she could. 'You must excuse me.' She tried to get round the side of the group. The tall, fair man was in her path.

'Let me pass, sir!' cried Annabelle, frantically. She had never before felt so trapped and ill. Suddenly Giles was there at her side, and she turned towards him gratefully, clutching his arm. The man called Fraser instantly stood aside and bowed.

'I'm sorry if I frightened you, ma'am,' he said. 'I had no intention of doing so, believe me.'

His tone was indifferent, with a touch of surprise, and Annabelle felt slightly ashamed at her panic. She nodded stiffly and he turned away.

'Are you ready to join us again?' Giles's tone was curt. Annabelle became conscious that she was still holding his arm more tightly than necessary, and with a murmured excuse she released him. Her knees were weak, as if she had just been through some deadly peril, and she was by no means certain she could walk. Berating herself for her stupidity, she took a step towards Lady Ordway, who was standing over by the door.

But Lady Stanton had not finished with them. 'What, no greeting for your own stepmama, Giles?' she called shrilly. 'How uncivil of you!'

Without even a glance at her Giles replied, 'I do not owe you any civility, ma'am. Excuse me.' Lady Stanton let out her breath in a long hiss at this set-down, but Giles ignored it. With a frown he took Annabelle's arm and skilfully steered her through the crowds. A carriage was waiting for them and he saw both ladies into it, treating Annabelle, who still shivered occasionally, with gentle consideration, patiently parrying Lady Ordway's anxious questions.

This was a side of Giles Annabelle had not seen before, and she was disarmed by it. If only he could be like this all the time, she thought wistfully. She felt safe, cherished. In the darkness of the carriage she smiled wryly to herself. She had scorned Philip Winbolt for the very qualities that Giles was now displaying. Why was it so different?

It was still quite early when they reached Upper Brook Street, but Lady Ordway announced that she was very tired, and was going to bed. The evening had not been without its difficulties.

'And if you take my advice, Rosa, you will do the same. You look quite worn out. Thank you for taking us to the theatre, Giles. The play was delightful, though…' She decided not to finish the sentence, bade them both goodnight cheerfully enough and then went upstairs. Giles raised an eyebrow at Annabelle.

'Are you too tired, too? Or would you have a glass of wine or ratafia with me? It might help you to sleep.'

This was an unexpected gesture. Since the ride in Hyde Park Giles had been careful to keep his distance. What was in his mind? Whatever it was, it would surely be wiser to follow Lady Ordway's example and go straight to bed! She cast wisdom aside and said, 'I…I'd like a glass of wine, Giles. And some *pleasant* conversation!'

He laughed and escorted Annabelle into the drawing room. Whitcroft brought the wine, poured out two glasses, then left the decanter on a table by the sofa. Giles stood in his favourite place in front of the fireplace.

'You're looking better,' he said. 'I thought for a moment

you were going to faint in the theatre. I was afraid I should not reach you in time. Was it the crush? The lack of air?'

'I don't think so. I am not normally affected by such things. No, it was more like a passing attack of fever. It has quite gone now.'

'I saw you drop your fan—that was when I started to make my way to you. Who was the man who returned it, do you know?'

'The dark gentleman?' Annabelle repressed a shiver, and spoke without thinking. 'I've never seen him before.'

Giles regarded her for a moment in silence. 'Strange!' he said, and drank some wine. 'Did…my stepmother say anything to upset you?'

Annabelle looked blankly at him, and he went on stiffly, 'I thought Aunt Laura would have told you who she was. The woman in red in the box opposite. I saw her talking to you just before I reached you.'

'Aunt Laura did tell me—I'm sorry, Giles, I was wool-gathering. No, she didn't frighten me, though I…I didn't like her. She asked about this necklace. She…thought you might have given it to me.'

'I see. Well, whatever the cause, I'm sorry I left you to fend for yourself. I shouldn't have done it. I should have stayed with you in the box.' He turned and put both hands on the mantelpiece, looking blindly down at the garlanded cherubs. 'It's just that…I cannot bear to look at her. Especially when…'

'Yes, I know,' said Annabelle softly. She rose and came over to the fireplace. 'Aunt Laura told me the story, Giles. I'm sorry.' She put her hand on his arm.

He stared at it in silence. Annabelle, suddenly confused and embarrassed, worried lest he should think this an unmaidenly advance, jerked it away.

'No! Don't go! Rosabelle…' He pulled her back and took

her into his arms. She looked into his eyes, and what she saw there made her heart thump. She suddenly felt breathless.

'Don't go!' he said again slowly, and bent his head. His lips touched hers in a featherlight kiss. Annabelle felt more shivers running down her spine, and her knees felt as if they might give way beneath her, but this time the sensations were entirely pleasurable. She moved closer, grasping his shoulders for support. Giles tightened his hold and kissed her again, more firmly. A ripple of feeling ran through her veins, unlike anything she had before experienced.

She found herself responding, tentatively at first, then, as the strange new feelings increased, more eagerly. For a glorious moment she was lost in a swirl of sensation, eyes shut, her body pliant and yielding. But it did not last long. Reason soon returned and she was suddenly nervous. This was uncharted, alien territory for her, and she did not trust it.

'Giles,' she murmured, putting her hand between them and pushing him away. He caught the hand and took it to his lips. Annabelle watched, fascinated, as he turned it and kissed the centre of her palm. She gave a little cry of delight, and he laughed and pulled her back to him. He started to kiss her again, and this time Annabelle was half lifted off her feet as he swept her into a passionately deep embrace, muttering her name, his lips on her eyes, her hair, then back to her lips… For longer than she later cared to remember she responded with a fervour equal to his, but when he started to urge her towards the sofa, her fears returned.

'No, Giles!' she panted, and using all the resolution she could muster she dragged herself away from him. She became aware that her hair was halfway down her back, her dress was crushed and in disorder, and her lips felt bruised and sore. As sanity returned, as her sense of fitness, of outraged propriety gradually overcame the tumult of her emotions, she felt deeply ashamed. She turned away from him and bent her head. 'This is not right! It cannot be right! You…you despise me already, I know, but I am not a wanton, whatever you may think.'

Giles was equally roused. He was breathing rather fast, and his hands were trembling. It was almost as if he had not heard her words. He stepped towards her and, taking her hand back in his, pulled her roughly towards him, trapping her in one arm, while he forced her chin up with his other hand, bending his head over hers…

'No!' cried Annabelle again, and gave him a sharp, hard push. He paused, but instead of letting her go, he held her away from him, staring at her with a dazed expression in his eyes. Then slowly the wonder died, and a curiously cynical smile took its place. He released her, and turned away, back to the fireplace. For a moment or two there was silence in the room.

Then he said evenly, 'Forgive me! I…I forgot myself. God damn it, Rosabelle, what are you? I thought I knew all the tricks women can employ, but you have me mystified.'

She was shocked, and her face showed it.

His voice was harshly impatient as he exclaimed, 'Oh, for God's sake, don't look at me with the eyes of a hurt child! That was no child's behaviour just now.'

'I…' Annabelle swallowed painfully. 'I was not play-acting, Giles. I am aware that I behaved badly, that I should have put a stop to…to our lovemaking long before I did. Indeed, it should never have begun! But…but I don't know what came over me! I had never felt such a strong…such a strong attraction before—never even knew such…such a thing existed. And…and it took me by surprise.'

'Oh come, Rosabelle! Don't try my credulity too far!'

'You may disbelieve me if you wish, Giles. But I assure you, it was a…a new experience.' She stopped and swallowed again. 'Putting an end to it was one of the hardest things I have ever done. But I had to. For my own sake and yours.'

'How extremely noble of you!'

'Please…! If it had gone any further, we would both have regretted it. There are too many barriers between us for love to flourish.'

'Love! My dear girl!' His scornful tone made it clear what he thought of love, and she flinched.

But after a moment she continued steadily, 'You know I am right. Thinking what you do about me, you would surely have despised yourself later for succumbing to the impulse, the weakness of the moment. And…' she faltered, then went on firmly, 'And for me at least, only love, sincere and lasting love, could excuse such behaviour. I am ashamed of myself.' She lifted her chin and regarded him proudly. 'But I employed no tricks. Forgive me, if it seemed to you that I did.'

Chapter Seven

Giles found her honesty curiously convincing, and was disarmed by it. Others in similar circumstances would have burst into dramatic tears, indulged in furious accusations of an attempt to seduce them, gathering up a cloak of outraged virtue around them—conveniently forgetting their own eager responses just a moment before. But Rosabelle Ordway had rejected such histrionics, and he was impressed. No other woman of his acquaintance would have been so frank about her own feelings.

'Perhaps I was wrong to accuse you of tricks. My excuse is that I, too, was…taken by surprise.' He stopped as he realised how true this was. It was not normally part of his nature to be so carried away, so lost to the world around him. He frowned and went on, 'This was not what I intended when I invited you to a glass of wine. I saw that you were distressed at the theatre. I meant only to comfort you, to soothe your lacerated nerves. But then you offered me comfort instead…'

Annabelle could see that he was genuinely disturbed by what had happened and decided to accept what he had said—it was, after all, an apology of sorts. Her own feelings were still in turmoil, and she wanted nothing more than to escape

to her room before she betrayed more than she wished. She
nodded, not meeting his eyes and turned towards the door.

'No, don't go yet!' he said. 'You haven't finished your
wine. And there's something more. Something I must ask
you. Please stay.' The words were abrupt, but this was a plea
rather than a command. She hesitated, then came slowly back
and sat on one of the chairs.

'Thank you.' He brought her glass over, put it beside her,
and then went back to the fireplace. He stood for a moment,
obviously marshalling his thoughts.

'Rosabelle, it is true that I had certain prejudices before we
ever met which have given me a jaundiced view of you—a
view which seemed at the time to be perfectly justified.' He
stopped. Annabelle held her breath—was Rosabelle about to
be vindicated?

Giles went on, 'I told you, I believe, that I intended to find
out more about Stephen's life and death. And I have recently
been searching London for people who knew him.' His face
grew sombre. 'It hasn't been pleasant. It has gradually been
borne in on me that the boy I knew…the boy I thought I
knew…existed only in my imagination. I may have made a
mistake in believing everything he told me without question.
It is possible that the faults in your marriage to Stephen were
not on one side only.' He paused, obviously waiting for her
to respond. But Annabelle was not ready to say anything. If
Giles had been talking to people who had known his cousin,
then he probably knew far more about Stephen and his marriage than she did!

He gave a sigh and went on, 'I can see that it will take
time for you to believe me sincere. And I don't blame you.
If I have been wrong, I must have hurt you badly in the past.
But—at the risk of offending you yet again—can you really
tell me nothing of Selder? He is the stumbling block to every
enquiry I have made. Don't shake your head, Rosabelle!
Believe me, I am not at the moment pursuing the question of

an affair between the two of you. Even if that were the case, I am prepared to accept that, however wrong it may have been, you may have been seeking consolation for the failure of your marriage.'

Annabelle remained silent. Giles had always been so convinced of Rosabelle's guilt that it would be a waste of breath to deny the existence of any affair. But his next words surprised her.

'I have even begun to ask myself whether your involvement with Selder might have been a figment of Stephen's disordered imagination... No, don't say anything—I know you have always denied its existence. But let us put that to one side for the moment... It is only one piece—a very important piece, but one of many—of the puzzle surrounding Stephen's relationship with Selder. To solve the whole I need to know more about Selder himself. So far he is a figure in the shadows, a cipher. Can't you tell me *anything* about him?'

For the first time since coming to London, Annabelle wished passionately that she had never embarked on this stupid, senseless, dangerous masquerade. Rosabelle just might have been able to respond to Giles's appeal, but she herself was totally in the dark about the man... And now what was she to do? The choice before her was stark. She could confess to Giles, on the spot, that she was Annabelle Kelland, and therefore knew absolutely nothing about Stephen, Selder, or anyone else. Or, as Rosabelle, she could apparently persist in her refusal to talk of Selder.

Giles would be disappointed, angry even. But that would be nothing compared with his anger and disillusion if she, Annabelle Kelland, told him that she had been deceiving him systematically, constantly, for the past six or seven weeks! Especially only moments after he had said he might be beginning to trust her! She simply could not face it.

'I...I cannot,' she said in a low voice. 'I know nothing of

Selder. I have no idea where he can be found, or anything else about him.'

The air was filled with his sharp disappointment, but he took it better than she had thought. 'I half expected that,' he said. 'Your acquaintance with Selder must have ended some time ago. And Selder is a very elusive creature. But, if you ever find that you know something after all and feel able to confide in me, I should be very obliged to you, Rosabelle.'

'I assure you, Giles, that I will,' said Annabelle with all sincerity. 'And now I should like to say goodnight and go to bed.' He escorted her to the foot of the stairs, where he stood for a heartstopping moment, looking down at her.

'I wish I could make up my mind about you,' he said. 'Perhaps, with time, we may yet come to a better understanding?'

'I'd like that,' she said. But she spoke sadly, and he wondered why.

Annabelle was not sure how to face Giles the next day, but in the event he made it easy for her. There was no consciousness of the evening before in his manner, as he enquired if she had slept well, whether she felt more herself.

Lady Ordway answered for her. 'She certainly seems it. I was quite worried about her last night. Tell me, Rosa, will you be fit enough for the Marchants' ball? You have only to say the word and I shall send a note of apology to Countess Carteret.'

'I am quite recovered, Aunt Laura. Thank you both for your concern, but it really isn't necessary any longer. I don't know what came over me last night.' She felt colour rising in her cheeks, and, avoiding Giles's eye, she added, 'At any stage. But I am quite well again this morning.'

'That's good! Giles, have you heard from your agent yet?'

'No, Aunt Laura, but I shall in the next few days. Hathersage would have replied immediately if there had been anything urgent, so it seems highly likely that we shall be able to go to Bath. You could begin to make plans on that basis.'

'I shall tell Barker to write straight away to enquire about houses. Somewhere near the Assembly Rooms, I think...' She hurried off to write a note to their man of business. Giles and Annabelle were left alone.

'I...I must see the housekeeper...' Annabelle's voice trailed away under Giles's continued steady regard. 'Please don't look at me in that way, Giles!'

He shook his head as if to clear it. 'I don't know what the matter is with me,' he said irritably. 'I was certain that cold light of morning would bring me to see reason. But even now you are still exercising your damned enchantments, Rosabelle.'

'I have no enchantments!' she cried. 'You must abandon this nonsense, Giles! Last night was an...an aberration which we should both forget.'

'I know, I know! And I am sure it will pass. Very well.' He took a breath and became businesslike. 'If Hathersage's report is favourable, and I think it will be, we can leave London at the beginning of July. Aunt Laura tells me that you would like to visit Temperley on the way?' Annabelle nodded. The thought of Temperley and what it meant depressed her.

He went on, 'Shall I escort you there?'

Annabelle's heart gave a jump, but she managed to say casually, 'Er...you could, I suppose. But perhaps it would be better for you to stay with Aunt Laura. She hasn't seen these friends for so many years, she might need your support. I can ask my sister to send a carriage to Reading to collect me and bring me back. It isn't far.'

'I suppose you're right.' He started walking to the door. 'Have you any commissions for me in the town?'

'No, but...Giles!'

'Yes?'

'Are you… Do you plan to be at the Marchants' ball?'

'I think so, yes. But I shan't ask you to dance with me.'

'Why not?' demanded Annabelle in absurdly sharp disappointment.

Giles raised an eyebrow. 'I might find it impossible to "abandon this nonsense" if I found you in my arms again—during a waltz. I can't put my reason under such a strain. Not twice in one week.'

'We…could dance something else?'

'Very well. We might dance the boulanger together. Will that do?'

'If I am free for it,' Annabelle said primly.

His sudden grin flashed out. 'You will be, Rosa! You will!'

The Marchants' ball was held in Berkeley Square. It was one of the last functions of the season proper, and as such was well attended. Indeed, it would probably reach the ultimate accolade of being declared a sad crush by those who attended. The rooms were crowded almost beyond their capacity, but even so, the lovely Mrs Ordway still created a stir when she entered the ballroom. The experiences of the night of the theatre visit, far from giving Annabelle hollow eyes and pale cheeks, had added a bloom to her complexion, and deepened the sparkle in her lovely eyes. She was wearing another of Fanchon's creations, a pale blue-green silk overlaid with silver embroideries on net.

Lady Ordway had sighed when she had first seen it, and talked of water nymphs and the like, and at the ball her sentiments were fervently echoed by more than one admirer. Giles looked increasingly bored at the comparisons with mermaids, water sprites and naiads which permeated the conversation, and said roundly that he preferred on the whole to dance with a woman, not a fish. But he took good care to sign her card for the boulanger before it was quite filled up, and then added his name for a set of country dances as well.

'Aren't you going to ask her for one of the waltzes?' asked Lady Ordway, looking on with pleasure at this improvement in relations between her nephew and so-called daughter-in-law.

'No, Aunt Laura! Not in public. She will have to be satisfied with the boulanger and the country dances.' As Annabelle gasped in indignation at this high-handed approach, Lady Ordway laughed.

'But why, Giles?'

'Safer,' he said enigmatically. 'Besides, Rosa has every other dance booked. I'm lucky to have two.'

Annabelle's first partner came to claim her, and she was swept away on to the floor. From then on, apart from the boulanger Giles had booked, he saw little of her before supper, for she danced without a break. They were a lively party during the supper interval, and Giles had every opportunity to observe just how well Rosabelle Ordway could behave. He could not fault her behaviour, and once again he was cast into a most unaccustomed state of indecision. What sort of woman was this? And, more important, why did she have such a confoundedly disturbing effect on him?

After the interval several of the younger ladies disappeared to tidy themselves up. Dancing was resumed and Giles stood with the Duke of Armagh, watching the gaily dressed crowd swirling by in a waltz, while he waited for Rosabelle to reappear. He caught sight of her on the other side of the room and was just about to excuse himself and make his way across, when he saw that she was engaged in conversation with a stranger. Something about the man caught his attention. He had seen him before... But where?

'Who is that over there, do you know, Duke?' he asked his companion.

'What? Talking to Mrs Ordway? By Jove, that's Falkirk! He's back, then.'

'Falkirk?'

'Yes. He's a distant connection of the Banaghers. That's a strange affair, Stanton. He couldn't have imagined for a minute that he would ever inherit the title, but it looks very much as if he will. There's something wrong with that family— dead or dying, the lot of them, and not one of them with an heir. One or two went in the wars, of course—they're an Army family. But the rest…no surviving children. It sometimes happens. So, when old Arthur Falkirk goes, which could, I gather, be at any moment, young Julian, against all the odds, will be the fifth baron. It's to be hoped he's a bit more fertile than the rest of his family! He looks as if he might be.'

'I don't believe I've met him at all.'

'I'm surprised—he was an Army man, too. Mind you, he's always been a touch come and go, Stanton. Very elusive kind of a fellow. But perfectly sound. Plays at all the best clubs when he's in town. Actually, he usually gives this sort of do a miss, he's not much of a party beau. But perhaps, in view of the change in his circumstances, he's planning to join the marriage stakes. Eh? It's good to see him in society again— we haven't seen him for the past year or so.' He regarded the two across the room, then added, 'He's a lucky dog! Mrs Ordway seems quite taken with him.'

Falkirk shifted his stance a little, and came more clearly into view. Giles remembered where he had seen him before— at the theatre, just before Rosabelle had been taken ill. He ought to go over…

A few minutes before this exchange took place, Annabelle had just re-entered the ballroom when she heard the voice behind her.

'Rosabelle!'

She swung round, puzzled. Where had it come from?

'I hoped you'd be here.' The gentleman who had rescued her fan at the theatre came up to her and bowed over her hand. The doors leading to the garden behind him were wide open, and Annabelle suddenly felt cold. Pulling herself together she smiled. There was absolutely no need to feel so very nervous. She had not the faintest idea who he might be, but it was a situation she had dealt with many times in the past. She gave the stranger a brilliant smile.

'How…how nice to see you! I can't remember when we last met before I saw you at the theatre. It must be…er…let me see…' He was laughing.

'Excellent! I would never have imagined you could do it! And with such verve. You are looking surprisingly well. I can hardly believe the improvement in looks and spirit!'

She must be overheated—this cool draught of air was causing her to shiver. Or had the attack of fever returned? She had an absurdly strong impulse to seek Giles out, to feel his protective presence once more.

'Rosabelle! You're shivering!'

There was no sympathy in his voice, no concern. He did not even seem surprised. In fact, had it not been absurd she would have said he was pleased! She did not like this man.

'I…I think I am not well, sir,' she said dismissively. 'You must excuse me.'

'Of course. But before you go I'm afraid I must ask you for a meeting elsewhere in the next few days—somewhere where we can talk more privately, perhaps?'

'I don't think so, Mr…' Her voice died away. She was feeling so ill that she could no longer dissemble. 'Forgive me, sir. I'm afraid I've forgotten your name.'

'What a pity!' he said. Why was there so much mockery in his voice? Or was she just imagining it? Was it a symptom of the fever, which seemed to be growing worse? He regarded her for a moment, then said, 'It's Falkirk, my dear. You have my permission…indeed, my injunction…to forget any other. My name is Julian Falkirk.'

What on earth did this strange, menacing man mean by that? Had he really said those words—or was her illness playing tricks with her imagination? But she was very happy to have an excuse not to see him again. She said brightly, 'Well, Mr Falkirk, I'm afraid it is quite impossible for us to meet again. We are very shortly leaving London for Bath, and I'm afraid…'

'It's a matter of some papers—papers you must have, which belong to me.'

'Papers?' They were standing in comparative isolation, ignored by the dancers, but now she saw Giles's tall figure threading his way towards them. Annabelle was smiling brilliantly in relief as she turned to Mr Falkirk. 'I'm sorry, Mr Falkirk! I haven't any papers. You must ask Colonel Stanton about them.' She nodded her head briefly and went to leave him.

Julian Falkirk caught her arm as she moved away. 'That won't do! You don't escape me so easily, Rosabelle. We must speak again.'

Annabelle removed her arm from his grasp. 'I've told you, sir—I cannot! I have no time before we go.'

'Then I shall have to see you in Bath! Perhaps you will have remembered about Stephen's papers by then. I do hope so.' He bowed gallantly. 'I shall look forward to Bath.'

Annabelle paid no attention. She didn't even hear what he said. Giles was now only a step away, and she turned to him gratefully, not bothering to hide her delight that he had found her. She had no idea how pale and nervous she looked.

Giles took both her hands in his. 'You're ill again! You should not have come out tonight. Come, I'll take you home.'

'I…I think it has passed, Giles.' She looked back, but the sinister Mr Falkirk had disappeared. 'Yes, I feel much better, really I do!'

'At least come and sit down for a few minutes. We could sit in the conservatory where it is cooler.'

'Thank you.'

They wove their way through the dancers to the small winter garden which had been built on to the end of the ballroom. Here they found a table and two chairs, in public view, but obviously meant for those seeking some quiet refreshment.

'Wait here!' he said. 'I'll find a waiter. Wine?'

'No, I'd like some lemonade, please. I…I feel thirsty.'

'Are you sure you wouldn't prefer to go home? I could easily find Aunt Laura.'

'I shall soon be perfectly restored, I promise you. I don't know what came over me, but it has passed.'

Giles found a waiter who brought a glass of lemonade for Annabelle, and some wine.

'Now, tell me. Who was the man you were talking to?'

Annabelle jumped. She wished he had not reminded her of Falkirk. 'I…it was Mr Falkirk,' she said uneasily. 'I don't know him very well. I…I don't like him.'

'Wasn't it the same man who returned your fan at the theatre?'

'Yes. Yes, it was.'

'It looks as if it is Falkirk who puts you into a quake. What did he want?'

'I can't remember…'

'Didn't I hear something about papers?'

'Yes! He asked if…if I had some papers of Stephen's… I said I hadn't anything at all, and…and told him to apply to you…' Annabelle had the strangest feeling of reluctance to discuss Mr Falkirk. However absurd it seemed it was as if the power of his personality had put a spell on her and she felt that she was courting danger by even mentioning his name. All she could think of was that she wanted to forget him as quickly as possible. 'Giles, can't we talk of something else?' she said desperately.

Music sounded in the ballroom. 'Mrs Ordway,' said Giles getting promptly to his feet. 'Would you give me the infinite pleasure of dancing with me?'

'Why, thank you, Colonel Stanton! I should be delighted.' Annabelle got up and shook out her skirts. She took Giles's proffered arm and gave him a mischievous look. 'How delightfully formal you are. And to think I once accused you of not knowing how to behave!'

'Oh, I know all the rules of good behaviour, Rosa. But you have an astonishing talent, which I have never before encountered in any other female, for tempting me to abandon them!' He looked down at her with a wicked glint in his eye, and it took all the self-discipline Annabelle possessed to ignore it and take the floor with him.

They danced in perfect harmony, their steps fitting as if they had practised for years, and Annabelle had never felt such a sense of rightness, of happiness and, curiously enough, security—though this was not something she had ever prized before. It was not that Giles held her particularly close. He was careful to keep the correct distance from her, never allowing, even in the turns, the space between them to diminish. But as he guided her confidently through the crowded ballroom, his hand at her waist was sure, and his other hand held hers in a firm grip. And, whenever their eyes met, which was often, the expression in his was, for once, warm, with a touch of humour and...something else, not so easily defined. But definitely exciting.

The waltz ended and they rejoined Lady Ordway. For the rest of the evening Giles did not leave her side except when other partners claimed her for their dances. His attentiveness clearly caused disappointment in some feminine hearts, and Annabelle was able to feel proud at being sought out, looked after, by a man she was growing increasingly to respect and admire...though these words seemed almost too cool, too ra-

tional for the unfamiliar emotions she was beginning to experience.

She lay awake that night, going over the evening in her
mind, re-living the waltz with Giles and his subsequent behaviour. She spent some time examining this strange, new
feeling of shared warmth, oddly mixed with something less
reassuring—something exhilarating, but frightening too, as if
she were about to take a step into territory hitherto unknown
to her. Whatever it was, she knew she trusted Giles, relied on
him in a manner she had never before allowed herself with
anyone else. He had been so kind to her after her conversation
with Falkirk…

Her happy musings came to a sudden halt. Why did she
react with such strong dislike to that man? His very name
sent shivers up her spine. She drew the bedcovers more
closely round her. Giles could hardly have been serious when
he suggested that talking to Falkirk had caused her mysterious
attacks of fever! And yet…it was a curious coincidence…

Annabelle was suddenly wide awake. What if it was not
she, but *Rosabelle* who suffered this strong reaction to
Falkirk? What if it was Rosabelle's horror of him which was
being transferred by some strange sympathy to her identical
twin? Was that possible? They had occasionally felt each
other's injuries, though not often, and only when the pain had
been severe. And she had been worried about her sister long
before Rosabelle had arrived, looking like death, at
Temperley. That must be it! Rosabelle, for some reason or
other, was terrified of Falkirk!

Annabelle tossed and turned for a long time. In a week or
two she and Rosabelle would be changing back. Was she
prepared to abandon her sister to the unsolved mysteries, to
throw her back to deal with Falkirk alone? And more than
that, could she bear to leave her growing friendship with Giles
to wither away, without making the slightest attempt to per-

suade him that her intentions in taking Rosabelle's place had been honest, even if her actions were not? These and other disturbing reflections kept her awake till morning.

Captain Pettifer had suggested some time before that Annabelle might like to visit Vauxhall Gardens, and since she had heard a great deal about them she was eager to accept the invitation. But Lady Ordway had at first demurred.

'For you know, my dear, though Vauxhall is a charming place, a delightful experience with all those lights, and the entertainment, and I don't know what else besides—a lady has to be *careful* when she goes there. One never knows who else will be there.'

'What do you mean?'

'Well, it's not like Almack's or an entertainment at a private house. All the world will be admitted, as long as they pay the fee for entrance.'

'I'm sure Captain Pettifer will look after me, Aunt Laura.'

'But I'm not sure, either, that it's quite the thing for you to be going there alone with a young man you hardly know!'

'Rosa will be safe enough with Richard Pettifer,' Giles said tolerantly. 'But if it would make you feel happier, Aunt Laura, we could add ourselves to the party.'

'I certainly think it would be more fitting if Rosa had a chaperon. But would Captain Pettifer be pleased, Giles? And what about Rosa?'

'Well, what about Rosa?' asked Giles, turning to Annabelle.

'I have no objection, if you can arrange it, Giles,' said Annabelle innocently. 'I wouldn't wish to rouse criticism. And Captain Pettifer is your friend, surely?'

As a result of this conversation, Lady Ordway, Annabelle, Giles and Captain Pettifer found themselves being sculled across the Thames to Vauxhall the next evening towards the sounds of music emanating from Vauxhall Gardens. They were all in good spirits as they landed and were escorted to a comfortable booth near the centre, where they would be able to see the entertainments, and later, the fireworks. Altogether the evening augured well.

Soon after their arrival, music struck up in the Pavilion and Richard Pettifer was prompt to ask Annabelle to do him the honour of dancing with him. They spent an energetic half-hour, after which they returned to the booth. But Giles had apparently taken Lady Ordway for a stroll round the grounds, for it was empty. Annabelle sank down on to one of the chairs, and gratefully accepted the glass of lemonade her partner had managed to procure for her.

After a few minutes Annabelle's attention was caught by a figure in a brightly striped dress making a slightly unsteady way towards them. She was accompanied by a tall young man with white-blond hair... The latter stopped to talk to someone, but Lady Stanton carried on, and, with some dismay, Annabelle saw that she was making straight for the front of their booth.

'Why, if it isn't Giles's *petite amie*! You're not wearing your necklace tonight, dear. Why not? Oops!' The lady was quite definitely the worse for wine. Captain Pettifer stood up, looking embarrassed.

'I don't think, ma'am...'

'No, no, no! You're going to say I shouldn't be here, aren't you? But you're wrong, soldier! You sh'd treat me with respect! My name, dear fellow, is Venetia Stanton, and I am Giles's stepmama!'

'Quite! Captain Richard Pettifer, ma'am. And this lady is the widow of Colonel Stanton's late cousin, Mrs Stephen Ordway. I still don't think—'

'Well, well, well! So this is the famous Rosabelle! Oh, what a lot of trouble you caused us all, my girl!' said Lady Stanton, waving an uncertain finger. With a sense of nightmare Annabelle saw Giles and Lady Ordway approaching. At the same time the blond man came up and took Lady Stanton's arm.

'Leave me alone!' said the lady, wrenching her arm away. 'It's all right, Fraser! This is Rosabelle Ordway—did you know? I never met her, of course, in the old days. But it's all right to talk to her. She's friends with Selder again. I saw them together at the theatre just a night or two ago.'

'Venetia—'

Opposition merely made Lady Stanton more argumentative. She said more loudly, 'It's all right, I tell you! You were there, too! You must have seen them, Fraser! Don't you remember?' She smiled foolishly into Fraser's furious face, and said cajolingly, 'Don't frown like that, Fraser! They're friends again, I tell you! She was talking to Selder and they were smiling.'

Giles stopped in his tracks, his face suddenly pale.

'You must excuse me, Lady Stanton, but you are quite mistaken. I don't know anyone of that name,' said Annabelle desperately.

'What nonsense! Of course you do—' It was not quite clear to the rest of them what Fraser did then, but Lady Stanton turned round with a little cry of protest. 'Fraser!' Then her voice died, and she suddenly looked old and frightened. 'Oh God, I forgot! She's right—we've been told to forget him…I forgot, I tell you! I won't do it again, Fraser! I just forgot! I won't mention him again. I swear I won't. He doesn't exist any more.'

'It's time you went home, Venetia,' was all Fraser said. But his eyes were cold, inhuman. 'Come!'

'Wait!' Giles was standing in their way. He regarded his stepmother with ill-disguised dislike. 'When was it you saw her?' he asked grimly. 'The night before last? Talking to Selder at the theatre?'

Lady Stanton started to nod. 'That's right—'

'That's enough, Venetia!' Fraser's voice was like a whip. Giles turned on him.

'I asked a question, sir! And I'd like an answer.'

Fraser looked dangerous for a moment and Richard Pettifer stepped forward to range himself by Giles. Then, with a graceful gesture of surrender, Fraser looked at Lady Stanton and said, 'Very well. If the lady really wishes to talk to you, I won't stop her. Venetia?'

'I…I don't think I will,' she mumbled, with another scared look at Fraser. 'I'm tired. I want to go home. No, really, Giles. I…I've forgotten all about it.'

Giles took a step forward, but Richard Pettifer put a hand on his arm. 'I don't think you'll get anywhere, Gil. And you don't want to make a fuss here. The ladies…'

Giles looked as if he was about to argue, but then, with a glance at Annabelle, he said, 'I suppose you're right, And there are other ways.' He turned to Fraser. 'But I shan't let the matter drop. It's too important to me.'

'By all means do your best, sir!' said Fraser. He gave Annabelle a look from those light, inhuman eyes. 'I don't think you'll find Mrs Ordway very forthcoming, either.'

He took Lady Stanton's arm with apparent solicitude, but Annabelle saw the lady wince again. The two walked off towards the exit.

Chapter Eight

'Who is this man that dreadful woman was talking about, Giles?' asked Lady Ordway. 'And why do you wish to find him? Is it…is it something to do with Stephen?' Her voice wavered, and she put a trembling hand on Giles's arm. 'Don't meddle with it, Giles! Leave well alone, I beg you!'

Giles took her hand and said reassuringly, 'It's only to do with some of Stephen's money, Aunt Laura. Nothing serious. We'll talk about it when we are at home. It's nothing to worry you.'

'No, but—' Lady Ordway was not reassured. She had sensed the drama which lay behind that small exchange. Her lips trembled and she grew very pale. Annabelle came out of her trance, took her arm and helped her into a chair, murmuring words of comfort.

'I'm sorry to intrude,' said Captain Pettifer. 'But I think the ladies have had a bit of a shock, Gil. Might they prefer to cut the evening short?'

'Indeed, I think my aunt would be better at home, sir,' said Annabelle gratefully.

'Giles can take me back, my dear,' said Lady Ordway. 'Pray don't spoil your own and Captain Pettifer's pleasure.'

'I think,' said Giles with great force, 'in fact, I am sure, that Rosabelle should accompany you, Aunt Laura. Richard will understand.'

'Of course, of course. I'll see to procuring a boat for us. Excuse me.' Captain Pettifer hurried away.

'Giles, I—'

'Later, Rosabelle,' said Giles. His voice was neutral, but his eyes when he turned to look at her were stony. 'Aunt Laura must be seen to first.'

The journey back to Upper Brook Street was accomplished in near silence. When they were back at the house, Captain Pettifer wasted no time in taking his leave, but not before assuring Annabelle that he hoped to make up for the night's disappointment by taking her to the theatre as soon as it could be arranged. Annabelle smiled non-committally, wished him goodnight and turned to see Lady Ordway up to her room. She delivered her into the capable hands of Wilson, who instantly prescribed bed and a sedative.

'But I must see Giles!' Lady Ordway said fretfully. 'He must stop these enquiries into Stephen's affairs at once!'

'You can talk to him tomorrow, Aunt Laura. I am sure he will listen to you. But tonight you should really settle down and rest. It will do no one any good if you are ill again.'

'Tomorrow then, 'said Lady Ordway. 'I shall see him tomorrow.'

'Good. I'll tell him.' She went to the door.

'Anna!'

'Yes, Aunt Laura?'

'Anna, come back here for a moment!' When Annabelle reached her bedside, Lady Ordway clutched her hand. 'I can see Giles is angry with you. But please don't tell him tonight that you and Rosa have changed places! Try to wait until we go to Bath. It isn't very long now.'

'But, Aunt Laura—'

Clutching her hand even more tightly, Lady Ordway said

desperately, 'Please say you won't tell him. He will be in such a fury with all of us, and I don't think I could stand it, Anna. He would send you packing, I am sure. He might even refuse to have Rosa back! And I could not bear it if I had neither of you.'

Anna bent over and kissed her. 'He couldn't do that, Aunt Laura. We both love you—he couldn't keep us away!'

'But a scandal will ruin Rosa's prospects with Mr Winbolt, and I have such high hopes for them both! And if Rosa does return now, Giles will be impossible with her, and she will be ill again, and…and…' Painful tears rolled down her cheeks. 'Things have been going so well. I couldn't bear it if we went back to all the misery of last year, Anna, I really couldn't! Promise me you won't tell!'

Annabelle hesitated. Giles was certainly going to quiz her about this man Selder. How could she keep silent?

Lady Ordway was growing agitated again. She looked ten years older than she had at the beginning of the evening. Her fingers sought to hold on to the sleeve of Annabelle's jacket. 'Promise me, Anna!' Wilson moved forward anxiously and shook her head.

Annabelle could not help but respond to the desperation, the fear, the anguish in that voice. With a deep sigh she said slowly, 'I promise. Now will you try to rest?'

Lady Ordway sank back and closed her eyes. 'Thank you, my dear. Thank you.'

Annabelle went downstairs with a heavy heart. She had been mad to give her word! But what else could she have done? And there was some justice in what Lady Ordway had said. Giles *would* be furious. He *would* react badly to being told that he had been made a fool of for so long. Rosabelle, Lady Ordway and herself—all three of them would suffer the full force of his anger. Whereas, if she kept silent, he would be angry only with her. She stopped where she was on the stairs. And how very angry he would be! He must now be convinced that she had known Falkirk's real name from the beginning. For that must be it. Falkirk and Selder were one and the same man. Lady Stanton had only seen her once before—and that had been at the theatre, when Mr Falkirk had returned her fan. From a distance, their conversation must have looked friendly.

She might just have persuaded Giles that the meeting in the theatre was a casual encounter, that she truly had not known who Falkirk was. But the meeting with the man at the Marchants' ball, witnessed by Giles himself, was far more damning. There she had done her best to pretend she knew who he was, to acknowledge him as an acquaintance, if not a friend. It was really exquisitely ironic! Apart from feeling a prickling horror of the man, she had not known what he meant by anything he had said. But Giles, who had observed it, and had questioned her about it afterwards, would never believe her. He would regard her as a liar and a cheat, and her promise to Lady Ordway would stop her from defending herself with the truth. Her budding friendship with Giles was over. Annabelle was shocked at the sharp pang of regret which this caused her. She stopped again, took a deep breath, then braced herself and walked down the rest of the stairs.

Giles was waiting for her in the hall. 'How is Aunt Laura?' he asked.

'I left her in Wilson's hands. I think she will be all right. She's anxious to see you as soon as possible tomorrow.'

'I shall make a point of seeing her as soon as she is awake. Though I know what she wants—she hopes I will stop uncovering her son's disreputable past. But it's too late for that. I only wish she had told me herself... However, I can at least promise to conceal as much as I can from the rest of the world.' He took a breath, then said formally, 'I'd like to see you for a moment in the library, Rosabelle. It won't take long.' He led the way along the hall, stood to let her pass

before him into the library, then came in and shut the door.
To Annabelle it sounded like the door of a prison cell closing...

Giles walked past her and stood at the other end of the
huge writing table. They faced each other along its length.
Annabelle looked down and saw that Stephen's diaries and
notebooks were scattered between them.

'There they are,' Giles began. 'A record of a young man's
degradation. I had begun to believe that they might be no
more than that—drug-induced fantasies, a release of spite and
spleen against a world which had not given Stephen Ordway
what he wanted. But in one respect they are true after all.'

'Giles, please—'

'No, Rosabelle! Spare me any further lies. I really do not
want to hear any more about your relationship with Selder—
or with anyone else! What I heard tonight was pretty well
conclusive, and I don't think I could stomach any more. You
and Stephen were well suited.'

Annabelle said in a low voice, 'Are you then abandoning
your search for the truth?'

'Why should truth interest you? But since you ask, no, I
am not. I shall continue my efforts to find out what happened
when Stephen died. I owe something to the Ordway name.
And, if necessary, I shall then bury the facts decently, for the
same reason. But you...I want as little to do with you as
possible!' He paused for a moment. When he continued his
tone was almost conversational.

'You know, Rosabelle, you will never know how close you
came to achieving your aim.'

'My aim?'

'I must suppose you intended to share in the Ordway fortune, if not through Stephen, then through me.'

'You!'

'I had begun to have some regard for you,' he went on,

ignoring her exclamation. 'Not just a feeling of lust for that lovely flesh, which you were so expert in arousing. I found myself enjoying your company, respecting your wit, your intelligence…even the display of compassion you put on for my benefit. How galling it must be for you, Rosabelle, that my revered stepmother let the cat out of the bag just a little too soon.'

'Believe me—'

'Believe *you*? What a ridiculous concept! I'd as soon believe…that whore who calls herself my stepmother.'

For the first time his iron control slipped, and Annabelle saw how very angry Giles was. His voice was harsh and ugly, and after one searing look at her, he turned away as if he could not bear the sight. 'I was filled with shame tonight at the thought of what a stupid, gullible fool I had been,' he said with bitter contempt. 'God knows, the evidence was clear enough, but a smile or two, a few melting looks from a pair of blue eyes, a touch of sympathy, and there I was, just like the rest, ready to ignore it all, rushing headlong into the snare. Till tonight I had honestly thought better of myself. Till I heard that you had been, after all, one of them.'

'That is not so!' cried Annabelle passionately, roused at last by this accusation. 'Lady Stanton was mistaken!'

'You mean that Falkirk and Selder are not one and the same person?'

'No! Yes! At least…'

'Well?' he asked ironically, as her voice died.

'I was not smiling at Selder at the theatre. We are not friends.' Giles turned away with a contemptuous laugh, and even to Annabelle this sounded hopelessly feeble. She felt defeated, unable to defend herself as she wished, hobbled by her wretched promise to Lady Ordway. 'What…what do you propose to do?' she asked miserably.

'I don't know.'

'Are you…are you going to send me away?'

'Believe me, there is nothing I would like more! But I don't want to upset Aunt Laura more than I have to, and she depends on you. However hard I work to save Stephen's name, I won't be able to conceal everything, and she is bound to be distressed. You will stay with her.'

His peremptory tone roused Annabelle to rebellion. 'And what is to prevent me from walking out of this house and returning to Temperley? Taking Aunt Laura with me if necessary.'

'As a hostage? If you do that, Rosabelle, then I will surely ruin you.' He said this quietly, but with such menace that she felt chilled. 'And the same is true if I learn that you have communicated with Falkirk again. I won't have a spy in our midst.'

'I am no spy, Giles,' said Annabelle proudly, trying not to show how affected she was by his manner. 'I wouldn't communicate with Mr Falkirk, even if I could.'

'Wouldn't you?' Giles gave her a cynical smile. 'Whatever you say now is a matter of indifference to me, I'm afraid. But I meant what I said. Try to get in touch with Falkirk again and the world will learn how sadly it has been deceived in the lovely Mrs Ordway. So if you have any regard for your family in Berkshire you will pay heed.' Giles went to the door and opened it. 'Goodnight.'

As Annabelle passed him she hesitated and looked up. It seemed impossible to her that this could be happening after the feeling which had been aroused between them. Surely somewhere deep inside he must *know* she was honest, whatever the evidence? 'Giles…' she whispered.

He stared down at her cynically. Then, without warning, he put his arms round her, pulled her to him and kissed her. The kiss was rough, bruising, without respect or consideration. She struggled to free herself but he held her easily, forcing her to submit…

When he finally released her Annabelle stood back. She

had lost the battle to maintain her composure. Slow, painful tears were trickling down her cheeks. 'Why, Giles?' she asked. 'Why?'

'For old times' sake, my dear! To get rid of the memory of other kisses of yours. When I was in danger of becoming yet another of your poor deluded victims. But don't worry. They won't be repeated.'

'God forbid they should, Giles!' she said bitterly. 'You should be ashamed of them.'

As Annabelle went back upstairs to her room she impatiently wiped the tears off her cheeks. This was no time for weeping and wailing. Tears were a weakness she had always despised. She must pull herself together and plan what was to be done. The situation was potentially catastrophic. In a week or so, she would go to Temperley, and Rosabelle would join Lady Ordway and Giles on the trip to Bath. Giles was certain to notice the substitution very soon—he was too astute not to—and would then realise that he had been duped by the sisters.

But far from improving the situation, it would probably make it much worse. Giles would be even less inclined to give either of the sisters credit for honesty or good intentions when he realised how they had deceived him. In his eyes they would be identically lovely in looks, and identically shameful in their behaviour.

Annabelle felt perilously close to tears again at the thought that she had lost Giles's good opinion again. She walked in a daze to her room and allowed herself to be undressed and prepared for bed without really noticing what was happening. For some minutes after the maid had gone Annabelle stood quite still in the centre of the room. It wasn't, she told herself carefully, it wasn't that she was in *love* with Giles Stanton. That was out of the question, an absurd idea. How could this possibly be love? She *disliked* him! He was rude, arrogant, high-handed, authoritarian, impatient... He had judged and condemned Rosabelle and herself without a hearing, and had treated them both abominably.

She had worked hard to run his house and entertain his guests, all without a word of praise or gratitude, only censure. And then he had kissed her against her will... She tried to hold on to the disgust and revulsion she had felt towards him after those kisses, but her thoughts slid away to the memory of others on the night of the theatre visit. She had felt neither disgust nor revulsion then—she had enjoyed them. She must acknowledge the fact, if only to herself...

But she *wasn't* in love with him. She wasn't! So what did that make her? The wanton Giles thought her? It might be true. Before coming to London, she had been a complete innocent in such matters. The various hopeful young men who had called at Temperley in the past had never aroused more than a mild feeling of friendship, which quickly turned to impatience if they became too attentive. She had certainly never felt the slightest desire to behave with them as she had done with Giles. Lost in his kisses, feeling that a door to new, previously unsuspected delights was opening...

But perhaps that was just the effect that any experienced man could have on an ignorant girl...? Annabelle smiled wryly. Until Giles had kissed her she had begun to believe that she was not someone who *could* feel very deeply. She had begun to reconcile herself to the idea of leading an uneventful life at Temperley for the rest of her days, incapable of either rapture or despair! How wrong she had been!

She moved slowly over to the bed and sat down. She had experienced such a turmoil of emotion in the past week, such an intensity of feeling, that she was in danger of losing her famous ability for cool, rational judgement! She must pull herself together before it was too late. It was total folly for Annabelle Kelland even to think of falling in love with Colonel Giles Stanton, autocrat and her implacable critic.

Annabelle lifted her head proudly. Fists clenched, she made herself a promise. She would retain her own self-respect, whatever Giles thought of her. And there would be no further thought of love.

Giles did not go to bed at all that night. He sat up, staring at Stephen's diaries, an ever-diminishing bottle of brandy at his elbow. He was concentrating fiercely on Stephen, Falkirk, the inn at Woolhampton, the question of piracy, Stephen's debts...anything, in fact, but the thought of Rosabelle Ordway. He must tackle Selder, or Falkirk, as he must now be called. That was absolutely vital. Then perhaps he could clear up this whole affair and start life afresh. He had always wanted to see the Americas. Perhaps he could take off for a year or two? Travelling alone was much better than...

He poured some more brandy and drank it down. Of course travelling alone was better! There were always women to provide companionship, if one needed it. They didn't have to have hair of molten gold and dark blue eyes, and a defiant, delicate chin... Hell and damnation! Giles put his glass down with such force that it broke. He stared at it, then got up, went to the window and opened the shutters.

Daylight poured into the room, dazzlingly bright daylight, and he groaned and held his head. After a minute he lifted it again and started for the door. Action was what was needed. A bath, a shave, a ride in the Park first to clear his head, then he would set about finding Falkirk. Calling for Goss, he strode out of the library and took the stairs two at a time to his bedchamber.

He spent most of the day in a search for his stepmother, finally ascertaining that she had left the protection of her latest lover and was living in Cavendish Square with her friend, the Baroness Leibmann. By the time he had discovered this Giles was jaded and in need of distraction. Thoughts of Rosabelle

Ordway intruded into everything he did, and it was driving him mad! Tracking Falkirk down among the London clubs seemed a much more attractive prospect for the evening than talking to a woman he had avoided all his life.

At the very least, it would give him an excuse to spend some time in convivial, masculine company. So he collected a few of his friends and together they visited a number of the gaming clubs around St James's. At each one Giles played high and won considerable sums. It gave him no pleasure, no relief from his obsession with Rosabelle Ordway, and when Captain Wainwright congratulated him on his winnings, he was hard put to it to reply civilly.

'By Jupiter, Gil,' said his old friend, 'the cards are running your way tonight! I hope you're not in love, old chap!'

'Why the devil should you worry about that?' said Giles, somewhat disagreeably.

'Well, you know what they say—lucky at cards, unlucky in love, eh, what?' Captain Wainwright roared with laughter at his own witticism, though he failed to notice that Giles did not join in.

But at last Giles's patience was rewarded. Halfway through a game at Watier's he observed that Falkirk had appeared across the table from him. He studied his opponent with interest. Black hair, strong features, with a flashingly white smile—the man was not exactly handsome, but there was something engaging about him. He was obviously popular—several prominent members of the club greeted him cordially as they passed. He played well, but in spite of a stylishly nonchalant air, he placed his bets cautiously, always with a good eye for the odds, and with the sense to know where to stop. An interesting man—the polished charm obviously hid a clever, self-disciplined, and probably dangerous animal.

When play stopped for a while Giles made his way over to him.

'Mr Falkirk?'

Falkirk turned. Giles watched him closely. Falkirk must recognise him, must know him for Stephen's cousin, but there was nothing in the man's demeanour to indicate this.

'Yes, I'm Falkirk. But…I'm afraid you have the advantage of me, sir. Do I know you?'

'I'm Giles Stanton. I believe you knew my cousin.'

'And who might that be, Stanton?'

'Stephen Ordway. May I talk to you? There's an empty table over in the corner. We shan't be overheard there. I'll get the waiter to bring a bottle of wine.'

There was a wary look in Falkirk's eyes, but he smiled amiably enough. 'Of course. You intrigue me, sir.'

They went across to a distant corner of the room. The waiter brought a bottle of burgundy, poured some, and withdrew.

Falkirk took a sip of the wine. 'Excellent! But I'm afraid I don't know a Stephen…Ordway, did you say?'

'Now that is not worthy of you, Falkirk! I saw you.'

There was a sudden stillness in the air, and the chatter and laughter faded further into the background. Then Mr Falkirk smiled again. 'Saw me?' he asked with an air of surprise. 'You might well have. I talk to a lot of people I don't really know. Yourself, for instance. Tell me, sir, why the inquisition?'

'To be exact, I saw you talking to Mrs Ordway at the Marchants' ball the other night. I believe you mentioned some papers to her?'

'Ah, yes! The lovely Rosabelle.' He smiled again and looked discreet. 'I'm not sure I ought to discuss my conversation with her. It was…a private matter. Between the two of us. May I ask what your position is?'

'I try to guard the interests of our family. And to prevent any gossip.'

'Gossip? But surely a widow is free to talk to whom she chooses without causing comment?'

There was a short silence. Then Giles said blandly, 'If you haven't heard of my cousin, Falkirk, then how do you know he is dead?'

He was pleased to see he had made a hit. But Falkirk recovered so quickly that anyone watching him less keenly would have missed the momentary chagrin. 'I remembered him as soon as you mentioned Mrs Ordway. You must forgive my lapse, Stanton. When one is enraptured by the wife, one tends to forget the existence of the husband, don't you agree? I'm afraid I never knew him well.'

'And these papers? I believe Mrs Ordway referred you to me?'

'I see. Rosabelle has been confiding in you, has she? I am surprised.'

'No,' said Giles evenly. 'Not as much as I would like. But I'm learning. I seem to learn more every day, from various sources. Including my cousin's diaries.'

'Diaries?' Falkirk's tone was sharp. 'Stephen Ordway kept a diary?'

'Yes. I haven't deciphered them all, but they're a sad record, I'm afraid. Towards the end of his life my cousin was quite distressed, particularly by his wife's interest in a certain Mr Selder. And there are some matters in them concerning this Selder which puzzle me. I'd like to talk to him. Do you know him?'

Falkirk was prepared for this. He had regained his former relaxed manner. 'Selder? No, I don't think I do.'

'He seems to be a difficult man to trace. I would think he didn't exist except that…'

'Except what?'

'I'm sorry, I'm boring you about my family affairs, when I should be offering you help with the papers you wanted. Mrs Ordway seemed to think that they might be among my cousin's effects, though I have to say I haven't yet come across anything of that sort. Were they so very private?'

'We'll forget the papers,' Falkirk said curtly. 'I was wondering if I could help you about Selder. Can you describe him?'

'Not yet.'

'Surely Mrs Ordway…?'

'She seems to be very reluctant to talk about the fellow at all.' Giles watched as Falkirk imperceptibly relaxed. 'But I'm hoping to have a description soon,' he added affably. 'From someone who saw him quite recently at the theatre. I could pass it on to you, if you are serious about helping me.'

Something ugly showed for a moment in Falkirk's eyes. He suddenly stood up. 'Please do.'

'Thank you,' said Giles, also getting to his feet. 'Er… there's one more thing. I have no desire to offend you, Falkirk, but Mrs Ordway has asked me to convey a message. She desires me to tell you that she no longer wishes to continue with your acquaintance. She would prefer not to talk to you again.'

'Really?' This was said with a distinctly ironic tone in the voice. 'You have indeed been taking charge, Stanton! Still, if that is what the lady says…'

'I'm afraid she does, sir. So, if you think there are papers of yours among my cousin's effects, I suggest you deal with me. Believe me, I can be very discreet. Can you tell me what they are?'

Falkirk appeared to be considering this for a moment. Then he said with an indifference which Giles was certain was assumed, 'They are not at all important. If you come across anything you think is mine you might pass it over to me. I am lodged in Clarges Street. I, too, can be discreet—you might tell Mrs Ordway that, and tell her also that I will, of course, respect her wishes. But—' he looked up at Giles and smiled '—allow me to give you a word of warning. I am not usually so complaisant. It would be most impolitic of you, or anyone else, to try to interfere otherwise in my affairs. I don't like having my plans upset—I'm sure you understand, Stanton.'

'May I ask what your plans are?'

'Why, to enjoy life, of course!' The smile flashed even wider. 'I'm a very simple fellow, Stanton. All I want is to be free to enjoy life in my own way. And, when my cousin dies, to take my proper place in society. There can't be much wrong with that, surely?' He bowed and walked away. Giles watched him go. Mr Falkirk was taking his time, nodding to someone here, exchanging words with another there. But there was a sense of urgency about him, and the effortless grace of his previous movements was no longer there. Though he was doing his best to disguise it, Mr Falkirk was seriously shaken. So much the better!

But Giles was shortly to learn just how seriously his words had shaken Mr Falkirk, and to be shocked, horrified even, at the result. He knew Falkirk for a villain. But he still had not quite realised how ruthless and dangerous a villain the man was…

The next day Giles presented himself at the Baroness Leibmann's house in Cavendish Square. He was confident the Baroness would receive him, for they were old acquaintances. He had known her in Holland, when she had still been Nellie Marsden, living under the protection of a minor Dutch aristocrat. It had been one of the jokes of the army when she had left him, just when he was on the point of turning her out, to marry the practically senile Baron Leibmann. Nellie always landed on her feet.

But when he arrived he found the house in confusion. Servants were running here and there, carrying clothing, silverware and other valuables, and two of them were struggling up the stairs with a huge chest.

'I'm afraid the Baroness is not receiving visitors, sir,' said the butler. 'She is very distressed.'

'Distressed? I'm sorry to hear that,' said Giles, looking with some curiosity at the bustle. 'Perhaps you would take up my card? In fact, it is Lady Stanton I have actually come to see.'

Consternation showed in the butler's face. 'That is quite impossible.'

'Impossible? Why should you say that? Come, man. Take my card to one of the ladies, Lady Stanton for preference.'

'Her ladyship…passed away yesterday, sir. Last night, in fact.'

'What?'

'Her ladyship is dead. Baroness Leibmann is not at home to visitors.'

'Good God! Look, here is my card. She must see me.'

The butler was about to refuse, but then glanced at Giles's card. His eyes widened in surprise, and he looked more human. 'Colonel Stanton!'

'Lady Stanton was my stepmother. It is imperative that I see the Baroness.'

'If you will wait in the hall, sir, I'll take your card up.'

'I have a better idea,' said Giles impatiently. 'I'll take it up myself.' He brushed past the butler, and found the right room by the simple expedient of following the raucous sound of Baroness Leibmann's voice. In the panic of the moment Nellie Marsden of Stepney was in the ascendant.

'What are you doin' 'ere?' she demanded, when Giles went into the room. She was surrounded by dresses, fans, shoes, thrown all over the chairs and sofas. Open boxes and bags lay everywhere. On her lap was a large jewel case into which she was cramming jewels of every kind. Among them was a long string of pearls which Giles had last seen wound in Venetia Stanton's hair.

'I came to speak to Venetia.'

'Well, you can't! She's dead.'

'So I understand. It was surely unexpected? She looked

in…perfect health when I saw her at Vauxhall the night before last.'

Nellie Marsden's busy hands were stilled for a moment. She looked up at Giles and made a visible effort for control. 'You saw her? Did you speak to her?'

'I couldn't. She was with a gentleman called Fraser, and he wouldn't permit it. What is all this, Nellie?' He gestured at the chaos around them.

'I'm leaving London. I'm needed in Germany. It's urgent.' She started putting the jewels in the box again. Giles walked over and removed the pearls.

'These were my mother's. I'll take care of them. Nellie—' He took her face in his hands and held it still. 'Tell me what's happening,' he said urgently. 'How did Venetia come to die?'

'Oh, get out! I've no time to talk to you!' she said, shaking him off. 'I've things to do.' Giles regarded her grimly. Nellie Marsden, one of the toughest and most experienced campaigners of them all, was in a panic.

'Heart attack?'

'Who? Venetia? No.'

'Has Baron Leibmann had a heart attack?'

'Oh, 'im! No, nothing like that. He just wants to see me.'

'So, why are you so frightened? Nellie, *how did Venetia die*? I shan't go until I know.'

Chapter Nine

Nellie didn't answer immediately. Instead she asked, almost reluctantly, 'When you saw Venetia at Vauxhall...what was it she said?'

'That she was pleased to see that Mrs Ordway and Selder—'

He stopped. The jewel box had slipped from Nellie's lap and fallen to the floor with a crash. The woman's cheeks were ashen.

'So that's it!' she whispered. Then she got down on her knees and started scrabbling the jewels together, piling them carelessly into the box again. 'I've got to go, I've got to get out of London now,' she muttered.

Giles got down beside her and put his hands on hers. 'You're not going anywhere till you tell me what I want to know,' he said harshly. Now they were so close he could smell her fear, see the terror in her eyes.

She whispered rapidly, 'Venetia was found by the watch last night. By the Chesterfield gate in Hyde Park. She...' Nellie swallowed. 'She'd been beaten over the head. They say it must have been done by a gang of vagabonds. Her jewels had all been taken.'

'Vagabonds? Are they...are they sure?'

'Of course!' Her voice was shrill.

'Then why are you in such a panic? Tell me, Nellie!'

'Why shouldn't I be in a panic? My friend has been clubbed to death!'

'By vagabonds in the Park? I don't believe it!' He held her eyes. 'Nor do you. Did…did Selder have anything to do with this?'

'Don't!' she screamed, clearly terrified. 'Selder doesn't exist any more, I tell you! He told us, all of us. We're to forget 'e ever existed. Otherwise… Oh God, I'm so frightened!'

Giles got up and walked about the room in an effort to keep a cool head in the face of this appalling news. He turned back to the Baroness. She had collapsed in a heap on the floor and lay there moaning.

'Nellie, this won't do! Calm down!' Giles went over, helped her up and settled her on the sofa. 'What's in this glass? Brandy? Have some.'

Nellie gulped the brandy down. It didn't do much good. Her teeth were chattering and she was trembling. 'It was always the same when she'd 'ad too much wine—she couldn't hold her tongue,' she muttered. 'But 'e warned 'er. She should've kept her mouth shut!'

'You mean,' said Giles incredulously, 'Venetia was killed just because she mentioned Selder's name?'

'That's about the sum of it, yes. Fraser must've told him about it. Or someone.' Nellie seemed to come to her senses. She looked sharply up at him. 'And that's all you'll learn from me. I've no ambition to have my battered corpse found by the Watch. I'm gettin' out.'

Giles controlled himself with an effort. This was not the moment for guilt or self-recrimination, he had to learn what he could from the woman before him in the time left. It was obvious that further questioning would be useless without a powerful incentive. Would money serve? He thought not. Nellie more than likely had enough salted away, and her husband was rich. Help in saving her neck? That would be more to the point. He thought for a moment, then said, 'You're quite right. You must get away, of course. Heaven knows what Selder will do next. I can see to it, Nellie. I'll arrange for you to leave secretly for Germany tonight, if that is your wish. Selder and the others won't catch you, I promise you.'

Nellie was rightly suspicious of such a generous offer. 'What's the catch?'

'Tell me more about Selder and his band. My cousin was mixed up in it somehow and I must know what the connection was. And how and why he died.'

Nellie considered carefully. 'Tonight, you said?'

'There's a courier going to Antwerp tonight. You probably know him—Captain Foster. I can arrange for you to travel with him.'

Nellie poured herself another glass of brandy. 'Young Foster, aye? I knew 'im years ago when 'e was just a lad...' She made up her mind. 'I can't tell you much. Selder was always very close.'

'Tell me what you do know.'

'I'll tell you one thing for free!' she said with intense seriousness. 'There's nothing, not one thing, that Selder wouldn't do. I don't set myself up as a pattern of morality, but Selder...that one has no morals at all. He's a ruthless fiend. And if he don't get his way by usin' charm, then he'll use blackmail, threats, and...worse. He went out of sight when Stephen Ordway died, but he's in London again now, and very anxious we should know that he's turned 'is back on the old ways.'

'Where does he say he's been all this time?'

'Abroad, with the Army—just like yourself, Colonel. In London just for the odd leave. But if that's true, then he spent his leaves on business as well as pleasure! Selder made a fortune out of the likes of Stephen Ordway. He had a villa out in Kensington... We 'ad some rare old parties there in

the old days. Wild, they were. But there were some we
weren't invited to—and I wouldn't 've gone if I *had* been
invited, neither. I'm not exactly what you'd call respectable,
but I do draw a line at some things.'

'For example?'

'I don't want to talk about it… Look, men and
women…that's one thing. A bit of fun, a lark, plenty of
drink—and more. And if the punter wants to show his appre-
ciation, that's all right by me! But…grown women weren't
welcome on those special nights.'

Giles felt sick. Were there no depths to which his cousin
had not sunk? Nellie went on, 'Selder wants to forget all that
now. He's made 'is money, he's got another name, and he's
all set to be a respectable member of the aristocracy. It's
natural he should want to cut his connections with the likes
of us, but I just don't like 'is way of doin' it, that's all. And
you needn't ask me what 'is other name is, for I won't tell
you, not if you promised me the Crown Jewels.'

Giles did not waste time trying to persuade her. He already
knew Selder's other name. 'We'll call him Selder,' he said.
'Tell me this…how did my cousin die? Do you know?'

'They used a bit of persuasion on him. Too much. They
didn't mean him to die, that I do know. But 'e was always a
bit of a lily, and they must 'ave 'it 'im too 'ard.'

'You mean…they beat him to death?' said Giles incredulously.

'I told you, you don't know what Selder's like! Specially
when he's mad. Look, Stephen Ordway and Selder used to
be very thick, till they fell out over Rosabelle. It was all right
again for a while, but then there was a row which was a lot
worse. A real break. Ordway found something out about
Selder—something that could ruin him. And after Johnny
Kingsley died 'e threatened to use it. Imagine! Threatenin'
Selder! He must have been out of his mind. Anyway, that's
when they tried to teach 'im a lesson, and 'e kicked the

bucket. And the rest of us will go the same way if we aren't careful.'

'So Stephen didn't fall down the cellar steps, after all?' Giles asked.

Nellie shook her head. 'That was a story put about by those two poor women—his mother and his wife. They're your sort, Colonel. They put the family name and all that above everything else, too. They knew what Stephen Ordway was, and they didn't want no enquiries made.'

'And his wife was anxious to save her own reputation, no doubt.'

'Oh, no! She wasn't like that! Well, I can't say that for sure. I never knew her—but from what the others said... I do know that Selder was really mad for her for a while, though.'

Giles put this aside for later consideration. Time was moving on. 'Who were ''they''? The ones who wanted to teach Stephen a lesson. Apart from Selder.'

'I don't know. I wasn't there, was I? But I bet Fraser and Burrows were mixed up in it. They're Selder's shadows—they do 'is dirty work.'

'Who was Kingsley? Was he murdered, too?'

'Like as not. I never asked. He was a nice young gentleman—I could never understand how he got mixed up with that lot. He wasn't rich, he had to work for a livin'—at Lloyds. But I reckon the second bust-up between Stephen Ordway and Selder was something to do with him.'

'How?'

'That I really cannot tell you, 'cos I don't know. Selder, Stephen Ordway, and the others—they were the...what we called the inner circle. Venetia and I never knew what went on inside that. Men's affairs. No females allowed.' She got up and said very determinedly, 'And that's enough. I've told you all I can. Now I expect you to keep your word, Colonel. I can be ready at six this evening.'

Giles eyed her and decided that he had got all he could out

of Baroness Leibmann. It was clear that, even if she knew any more, she was not going to talk about it. He promised that a carriage would be sent on the dot of six, and she would be given a pass which would see that she got to Germany without delay. He took his leave and went to the door. Then he stopped. It was no use—there was one more thing he had to know.

'Stephen and Selder fell out over Rosabelle Ordway, you said. Was it because they were having an affair?'

Nellie gave him a look that was hard to interpret. Then she said baldly, 'Yes.'

Giles was not surprised, but all the same, his heart sank like a stone. He turned to open the door.

Then Nellie went on, 'But it wasn't a quarrel over an unfaithful *wife*, Colonel.'

'What do you mean?'

'Work it out. You're not stupid.'

Giles frowned. 'You mean Stephen was in love with *Falkirk*—'

Nellie Marsden's terror returned in full force. 'Oh Gawd! 'ow do you know that? I never told you that!'

'Isn't that what you were implying?'

'No! I mean his name! I never told you 'is other name.'

'Oh, I knew that before I came here.'

'You did? Well, you'd better forget it!' said Nellie intensely. 'People who know that link tend to get sick and die, Colonel Stanton. Like Venetia. Very sick, and very dead! Why do you think I'm gettin' out?'

Giles tried to get more from her, but it was useless. Nellie was finished. She could not get rid of him quickly enough. Assuring her again that everything would be in order by six o'clock that evening, he departed.

Giles's first action when he left the house was to despatch Goss to Upper Brook Street with orders that he was not to let Mrs Ordway out of his sight until further notice. Then he went to the War Office and made arrangements for Nellie's journey. After this he paid a call on the coroner. What he learned there sickened him. Venetia Stanton had been brutally attacked and murdered, but there were no witnesses and no clues. Robbery was assumed to be the motive, and 'Murder by persons unknown' would be the verdict.

Giles did not debate for long whether to tell the coroner what he knew. What could he say? He was quite certain that Falkirk had swiftly eliminated someone he regarded as a threat to his safety, but he had no evidence of that. Conjecture and hearsay were not enough and he had given his word to Nellie that she would not be involved. He consoled himself with the thought that, if things went as he hoped, Falkirk would not long escape reckoning.

He left the coroner's office and walked through the streets of London oblivious to the crowds around him, thinking over the events of the last twenty-four hours, a prey to the bitter pangs of conscience which now attacked him. How badly he had underestimated Falkirk's capacity for speedy, ruthless action! He had, after all, been warned. To think that he had actually congratulated himself on disturbing Falkirk's complacence! Venetia may have been a poor specimen of womanhood, but she had not deserved to die that way... He walked on for some time, his face grim. Venetia's death had served one useful purpose. He wouldn't underestimate Falkirk again.

He arrived back at Upper Brook Street to find the ladies immersed in plans. The fourgon carrying some of the servants to the house in Bath, together with a load of dresses and household linens, was due to leave the next day and they were busy deciding what personal possessions they would send in advance with it. Giles left them to it. There might well be changes in store, changes which would not meet with their approval, but he needed time before he announced them.

* * *

That night he walked about his room with a heavy heart. It was now perfectly clear that the delightful boy he had known as Stephen Ordway had never existed. A liar and a cheat all his life, they had said. And Nellie had hinted at something worse—real viciousness. Had Stephen lied and cheated about his wife? But Giles suppressed that unbidden hope before it developed. No—Venetia and Nellie had both said that Falkirk had had an affair with Rosabelle Ordway, and they had no reason to lie. The man himself hadn't troubled to deny it.

But he was now haunted by the thought that Rosabelle Ordway was an obvious target for Falkirk's ruthless policy of extermination. It was an inevitable conclusion. She was one of the few people outside Falkirk's 'inner circle' who knew that Selder and the respectable Mr Falkirk were the same person. Indeed, it was surprising that Falkirk had not already made an attempt to silence her. He was not a man to hesitate—once Venetia had been perceived as a possible danger she had been swiftly eliminated. The same could happen to Rosabelle…

Or…was she being spared for some particular reason? Was Falkirk still in love with her, perhaps? Unlikely. From all accounts he was not a man to risk all for love, yet he had risked a great deal in approaching her in such a public place as the Marchants' ball. So what other reason could there be for that? Self-interest was what motivated Falkirk, first, second and last. What could he want of Rosabelle?

Giles concentrated hard in an effort to recall Falkirk's words… *'I shall have to see you in Bath!'* he had heard him say. *'Perhaps you will have remembered about Stephen's papers by then. I do hope so.'* When he asked Rosabelle what Falkirk had wanted, she had said with apparent bewilderment, *'I can't remember… Yes! He asked if…I had some papers of Stephen's… I said I hadn't anything at all, and…and told him to apply to you… Giles, can't we talk of something else?'*

How much of what Rosabelle said was truth, and how much prevarication and lies? Did she in fact know what Falkirk had wanted of her? Was she playing some devious game of her own? She was a fool if she was...a vision of Venetia's body suddenly filled him with horror. Rosabelle must not end like that, dear God, not Rosabelle, too! But how the hell could he protect her when he was working so much in the dark! He had absolutely no idea what was in her mind.

One thing was patent—Rosabelle Ordway was in danger. Until he knew the true extent of her involvement with Falkirk, until he could persuade her to abandon any ideas she might have about him, she must be taken somewhere out of Falkirk's reach. He dared not risk anything else—not when he had so little to work with, and two women to protect. He needed time...

Giles made several decisions that night, and in the morning they were carried out with the efficiency and despatch he had acquired during his years of command. Goss was given a list of men he was to find within twenty-four hours. They were all ex-soldiers, and now, like Goss, out of the army, and possibly looking for a bit of adventure. They all had two things in common. They were reliable, and they could be trusted to keep their mouths shut. Some would be asked to stay in London to keep Falkirk and his associates under observation.

'Falkirk is a dangerous man, Goss. He has already killed once to protect himself, and will kill again without a second thought. Make sure there are enough funds for a couple of them to travel if they have to. Falkirk may go to Bath.'

'That's where we're going, isn't it, Colonel?'

Giles shook his head. 'No. It's where Falkirk believes we're going. But the ladies and I are making for Buxton, Goss.'

'If you'll excuse me one moment, Colonel, I'll just step outside and delay the waggon. It's just about to set off.'

'On no account! I want that fourgon to set off as planned and with as much fuss and noise as possible. Let it go!'

'Er...the ladies' luggage, sir? They won't be best pleased if they are in Buxton, and some of the servants, a lot of their clothes and all of the household items are in Bath.'

Giles nodded ruefully. 'I know. But that's a small price to pay. I want to put Falkirk off the scent. With any luck he'll assume we shall follow, and leave London himself. The servants and the goods will be looked after in Bath.'

Goss privately thought that it was the ladies who would need looking after, but he said nothing.

'Now to business again,' said Giles. 'One of the men is to set off immediately with these—a letter for Captain Daventry in Leicester, another for Avenell and a list of inns where rooms are to be engaged. Send Gregson. But not a word to anyone else—no one at all!—about any of this.'

'Right, sir! Anything else?'

'Yes. I want you to continue to keep a special eye on Mrs Ordway, even when we are travelling. That's important, Goss. Three of your men will travel with us, too—one as footman, and two as grooms. And there's one more thing. There'll be letters to be posted from here—but not for a day or two *after* we have left London. There's one to a Mrs Chamberlayne at Reading, and one for the agent in Bath. And there'll be another to Temperley.' Giles smiled grimly at the thought of the probable contents of Rosabelle Ordway's letter to her sister. She was going to be furious! But...she would be safe.

It was this thought which was the driving force behind all Giles's plans. It was perfectly true that he felt he ought to inform Lord Stanton in person that his estranged wife was dead. It was undoubtedly true that Buxton was a more convenient base than Bath for directing various schemes he had in mind for the Stanton estates. But the overriding motive, the reason for all his elaborate precautions, was this fear for Rosabelle Ordway's safety. Whether she knew what Falkirk wanted from her or not, whether she was stupidly dishonest or perilously innocent, as long as she was within Falkirk's reach, she was in danger.

Meanwhile, the ladies were leafing through guide books to Bath, reading accounts of activities in the Pump Room, and planning excursions to local places of interest. A house had been found on Sydney Street, and the Chamberlaynes had been written to—they had sent a most civil response, inviting Lady Ordway to stay not two nights, but three. Rooms had been reserved at comfortable inns on the rest of the way, and, reluctant though she was, Annabelle had written to Rosabelle to let her know that the time for the sisters to change back had at last arrived.

Then, out of the blue, Giles suddenly announced that he had changed his mind. They were to go to Buxton, after all.

'But you can't do that!' cried Annabelle desperately. 'I've written to my sister, Aunt Laura has arranged to stay with the Chamberlaynes, we've rented the house—'

'I am aware of what you have done,' said Giles, in the tone he now normally used towards her—cool, impersonal, distant. 'But the arrangements for Bath are not irreversible.'

'But I *must* go to Bath!'

'I've no doubt Bath would suit you better, Rosabelle. Buxton is a poor second to Bath, I grant you, in every respect except the qualities of its waters. It would certainly provide you with fewer opportunities to parade yourself before the eyes of an admiring and frivolous society. But since my primary concern is not to administer to your vanity, but to see that Aunt Laura has the treatment she needs, I have decided to take you both to Buxton. All the arrangements are made. We set off early tomorrow morning.'

'Tomorrow morn— But…but this is absurd! What can I possibly tell my sister? She is expecting me at Temperley at the weekend!'

'You will naturally write her a letter. I will see that it gets to her. Tell her that, since I have urgent business in Derbyshire, I have changed our plans. Come, it is not so long since you last went to Temperley. You are surely not claiming that she will miss you?'

Annabelle was speechless. It was Lady Ordway's turn. She had not been quite herself ever since the night at Vauxhall, but she did her best.

'A change in plan is quite out of the question, Giles! You forget, the fourgon with all our luggage has already left for Bath! And Lily has gone with it! What will Rosabelle do without a maid?'

'That's right!' cried Annabelle. 'We won't have a thing to wear! You must see how ridiculous you're being, Giles!'

'I'm sorry about the maidservant, but all the rest has been taken care of. Trust me, Aunt Laura,' Giles said, ignoring Annabelle. 'I have very good reason for my decision. We shall take the journey in very easy stages, and I've arranged for us to spend the weekend with friends of mine near Charnwood Forest—that should break the journey for you. You'll like Selina Daventry very much, I know you will.'

Lady Ordway was by no means so sure, but she lacked the energy to argue further and Annabelle was left to fight her own battle. But all her arguments were in vain.

'He's impossible, quite impossible!' Annabelle said, stormily pacing up and down in Lady Ordway's room. 'He offers us no explanation, no excuse—he simply refuses to discuss anything at all! We are to go to Buxton. And that's the end of the matter!'

'He has always been a touch high-handed,' said Lady Ordway weakly.

'So you have said before. But this is positively Gothic! I could scream with fury! What are we to do?'

'I don't know, Anna dear. But he did say that his business was urgent.'

'And you believe him? I think it's because he can't bear to see us enjoy ourselves. He thought I was looking forward to my stay in Bath.'

'No, no! You are not doing Giles justice! He would not be so petty.'

A snort from Annabelle showed what she thought of this.

'Really, Anna, I do think he has important business with his father. He isn't even going direct to Buxton. He plans to spend some time at Avenell beforehand.'

'Then why cannot he go to see his father, and allow us to make our own way to Bath? Can't you ask him?'

'I couldn't do that!' Lady Ordway was really shocked. 'Giles has assured me that his reasons for taking us to Buxton are sound. We must trust his judgement.'

Without Lady Ordway's support Annabelle was powerless. In the end she was forced to bow to the inevitable, and, with no very charitable feeling towards Giles, sat down to write another letter to her sister. This was going to be even more difficult than the last one.

But as she sat at her writing table and considered the situation she grew calmer. Perhaps this delay was not so disastrous after all? It would provide time in which Rosabelle's relationship with Mr Winbolt could develop, and the more she thought about those two, the more convinced she was that they would suit each other perfectly. Any delay was surely to the good there! And her own case? Ah, there she was less sanguine. But at least she had been given a few more weeks to try. She started writing more confidently, and, in the end, the letter was in the same light-hearted vein as all her others. There was even less point at the moment in worrying Rosabelle with her own problems.

Dearest Sister
   This will be as great a shock to you as it is to me.

Colonel Stanton—for I cannot bring myself to call him anything else, unless it is The Monster—has decided in his wisdom that we should be better off going to Buxton! He is quite adamant.

Apparently, he intends to visit his father in the vicinity, though he has not informed me of the fact. I had to learn even that much from Aunt Laura! I suspect that this is not his only reason, however, though I cannot imagine what any other could be. He can surely hardly be serious when he hints that my character may have something to do with his decision! I wonder whether Aunt Laura and I made the mistake of appearing too pleased with the notion of going to Bath? For such a killjoy as Colonel Stanton, the temptation to change his plans must have been quite irresistible. But let us forget the less pleasant aspects of life in Upper Brook Street!

The sad truth is that by the time you receive this letter we shall be on our way north to Buxton, and it will be impossible for me to see you for seven or eight weeks! Words cannot express how sorry I am. I assure you, my darling sister, I would have hired a chaise and come alone if it had been possible, but the change of plan was sprung on us with hardly a day's notice, and I have been kept exceedingly busy. Colonel Stanton is all consideration! I expect he wanted to spare us the pain of learning too soon that we were not to enjoy the excessive dissipations of life in Bath! I understand that Buxton will provide me with 'fewer opportunities to parade' myself. I quote.

Since I shall not be seeing you in person for some time, I send you my love, and best assurances that I am happier than I may seem! Life with The Monster in the house is at least never dull. And you may have an easy mind about Aunt Laura. She continues to improve, and, however little I deserve it, she seems to be very happy with

Your loving Twin.

As she folded the letter Annabelle even smiled. If Giles read it—as he probably would—it would do him no harm to see what she thought of him!

They left London in Giles's comfortable new travelling coach at seven o'clock the morning after. It was an impressive cavalcade. Lady Ordway and Annabelle sat inside, Wilson and the new footman sat behind, and luggage was piled on the roof. One groom sat beside the coachman, and another rode postilion. Giles, accompanied by the faithful Goss, rode alongside. It was so early that the streets were deserted, and within the hour they had reached the Edgware Turnpike gate and had turned right to join the Holyhead Road at St Alban's.

Giles was as good as his word. They took the road north in very easy stages, and since the carriage was well sprung and could be opened up when it was warm, they were reasonably comfortable. They spent the second night at Woburn, and in the morning they visited the great house there. The housekeeper was very pleased to show them round, and they were all impressed with the interior furnishings and designs. But afterwards Lady Ordway refused to accompany them on a tour of the grounds, pleading that she had walked enough.

'Though I should like you to have some fresh air and exercise, my dear,' she said with a smile at Annabelle. 'Let me take the carriage back to the inn. I could have a rest there, while you and Giles walk back through the trees.'

Annabelle was not sure she wanted a tête-à-tête with Giles, and doubted he would wish for one with her. But to her surprise Giles received the suggestion kindly.

'It isn't far,' he said, seeing her hesitate. 'Not more than half-an-hour's walk.'

Annabelle eyed him suspiciously. She could not imagine that he desired her company for any pleasant reason. Giles had something to say to her in private. But in the end, curiosity prevailed.

'Then I should like to do it,' said Annabelle. 'Thank you.'

Chapter Ten

At first they walked in silence, taking pleasure in the fresh air, the sunshine glinting down through the massive canopy of trees overhead, and the peace of the countryside. Giles seemed to be in no hurry to begin.

Annabelle, too, was reluctant to disturb the apparent harmony, but after a while she said, 'Giles, may I ask you a question?'

'Certainly. Though I do not guarantee to answer it.'

Undeterred, she went on, 'I have no desire to spoil a very pleasant excursion, but what is in your mind, exactly?'

'In what respect?'

'I am not stupid—'

'It is some time since I last thought you were, Rosabelle.'

'I am not stupid,' she repeated, 'and I should like to know why you are taking so many precautions.'

'Precautions?'

'Or is it merely that you do not trust me out of your sight?'

'That would not be unreasonable, surely?'

'That's what I thought at first,' said Annabelle, maintaining her tranquil tone, 'when I couldn't go anywhere during the last days in town without falling over Goss. I became quite annoyed with the poor man, but when I asked him about it, he came up with a hopelessly inadequate excuse.'

'Now Goss didn't tell me that.'

'I expect he didn't wish to worry you, Giles,' Annabelle said affably. 'We all know how devoted he is. And it can't be pleasant to be asked to spy on the lady of the house.'

'He was not spying on you.'

'Well, I've come to see that. And though it seems mad, I now think you had commissioned him to protect me! Can that be so?'

He looked down at her with a hint of admiration in his eyes. 'You're certainly not stupid, Rosabelle. On the contrary.'

'I can't accept too much credit. It didn't occur to me immediately. But after that you were so…I won't say *unusually* tyrannical, but so extremely tyrannical! Not just with me—I have come to expect it from you as far as I am concerned— but with Aunt Laura, too. At first I was so incensed by your overnight decision to reverse all our arrangements and take us to Buxton that I couldn't think rationally. But then…this sudden change was *so* discourteous to the Chamberlaynes, *so* upsetting to the agent in Bath, that you must have had a very pressing reason for it. And then, when I thought again about Goss's behaviour, I came to the very odd conclusion that you were doing it for my sake.'

Giles's tone was repressive as he replied, 'I'm afraid you're flattering yourself. There were other considerations.'

'I am relieved to hear it! Knowing your opinion of me, I was completely puzzled as to why you were prepared to go to such lengths to look after me. I wondered if you had gone mad. Er…would you mind telling me why you think I need protection?'

Giles walked on in silence for some time. Then he said, 'This conversation must remain between ourselves, Rosabelle.

I do not want Aunt Laura to be disturbed by it. Do I have your word on that?'

Annabelle gave him a twisted smile. 'If you think it worth having.'

'When Aunt Laura is concerned I do not doubt your good intentions. And what I am about to tell you might upset and frighten her.'

'Then you have my assurance that I won't say anything.'

'Good!' He seemed not to know how to continue. Annabelle waited. This line of communication which had opened up after days of silence was so slender, so fragile, that she dared not risk breaking it.

At last he said abruptly, 'Your friend Falkirk is a very dangerous man, Rosabelle. Did you know that?'

Annabelle recalled the irrational feelings of terror the man had aroused in her on the two occasions they had met. That they had been communicated by some strange empathy from her twin, she had no doubt. She said gravely, 'He is not my friend, Giles. He never was. And I have always thought him dangerous.'

He stared at her so intensely that she grew uncomfortable. 'That is true,' she said at last. 'Though I know that you do not believe me.'

'I wish I could!'

'Giles, this journey to Buxton will prove very tedious if we cannot come to some sort of a truce. I know your position, you think you know mine. Only time and circumstances can change either. But if we are to spend twice or three times as long on the road as we need—'

'Why do you say that?'

'It's obvious we shall, if you carry on avoiding the post houses, and insist on using your own horses all the way. For some reason you wish us to travel to Buxton without being followed or traced. And I suspect the new grooms are there to look after more than the horses...' She gave him a straight look, then said, 'It's Falkirk, isn't it? He is the reason for all these measures.'

'My stepmother is dead, Rosabelle.'

Annabelle stopped and stared at him in shock. 'Lady Stanton? But…how?'

'She was murdered. I think Falkirk was responsible.'

'Murdered? But, no! That cannot be! Falkirk can't…'

'I am as certain as I can be that he got rid of her because she knew too much! And you…you are in the same danger. For God's sake, Rosabelle, don't try to defend him! Even you might find that difficult.'

Annabelle was distraught. 'I was not trying to defend him in the least! Oh, why won't you trust me?' She turned her face away.

Giles watched her in brooding silence. At last she managed to speak again.

'I…I am grateful to you for telling me about your stepmother. It must be painful for you to speak of her. I am sorry. Tell me what causes you to think I am in danger.'

'Because you know the link between Falkirk and Selder.'

'So do you!'

'Falkirk doesn't know that. Not for sure. Besides, I am well able to look after myself.'

'But why does it matter?'

'Oh, come! We have both agreed you're not stupid. Falkirk is a respectable member of the *ton*, accepted everywhere and ambitious for more. When his cousin dies, Falkirk will be Lord Banagher. Any association with the name of Selder would ruin him, if it came to light. Selder was the leader of a gang of villains of the lowest possible sort, up to every conceivable vice. Murder was the least of their crimes. And Stephen was one of them. Don't try to tell me you didn't know!'

She looked at him blankly, and Giles thought for a moment she was going to faint. He took her arm, but she removed it.

'I…I need to sit for a moment. Excuse me.' She was deathly white. Slowly she went over to a seat nearby and sat down. For a moment she had forgotten he was there. 'I didn't know,' she whispered. 'I really…didn't…know. Why didn't she tell me?' Then she buried her face in her hands.

The impulse to take her into his arms, cradle her, comfort her, until the look of horror disappeared from her face, and some vestige of colour came back to her cheeks, was almost overwhelming… But Giles remained where he was, his face devoid of expression. He was far from convinced that Rosabelle Ordway was as innocent as she claimed, and until he was, he would not give in to these irrational and dangerous feelings. However, it was perfectly possible she had not known the full extent of Selder's villainy. Nellie Marsden had said as much.

After a minute or two he said gently, 'I'm sorry if I shocked you, Rosabelle. I see now that Stephen must have kept most of his activities concealed from both of you. I doubt that Aunt Laura could have told you anything more than you already knew.'

Annabelle looked up at him, wondering for a moment what he was talking about. Then she realised with relief that he had misinterpreted her unguarded exclamation. He had taken 'Why didn't she tell me?' to refer to Aunt Laura. She resisted a strong impulse to tell him the truth there and then. It would be stupid to say or do anything irrevocable while she was still so shaken. She got up, and strove to speak naturally.

'Forgive me. I'm better now. It was a shock. Shall we…shall we carry on?'

'Take my arm.'

'No. Thank you. I am well able to walk without assistance.'

It was Giles's turn to be tentative. 'Rosabelle, an opportunity to talk in confidence like this may not occur often. May we talk it over a little more?'

'Yes, yes. Of course!' said Annabelle, bracing herself.

'The papers Falkirk mentioned at the Marchants' ball…he seems to regard them as important. Do you really know nothing about them?'

Annabelle didn't know what to say. She knew nothing herself, of course, but Rosa might! 'I…I can't remember, Giles,' she said in the end.

But her hesitation had been noted, and Giles's manner grew cooler. 'A pity,' he said. 'It might have helped me.'

'Giles, why *are* we going to Buxton? Would it not have been better to try to expose Falkirk for what he is, instead of running away?'

'I'll stop him somehow or other, never fear. Indeed, I have set things in motion in London… But I have other considerations—you and Aunt Laura, for one. Your life, and perhaps that of Aunt Laura, would be too great a price to pay for the satisfaction of tackling Falkirk face to face at the moment.'

'You really think our lives are at risk?'

'Falkirk is ruthless. And frightened. That's a dangerous combination.'

She nodded and fell silent.

Giles went on, 'Also, I want to destroy Falkirk, if I can, without exposing the true extent of Stephen's villainy. Not only for Aunt Laura's sake—my mother was an Ordway, too, don't forget, and I must do what I can to protect their name. And…I am also going north to see my father.'

'You wish to tell him yourself about your stepmother?'

'That, yes. And…it's time I made my peace with him. After all, Venetia was the chief source of dissension between us.'

'Was she? Aunt Laura said that he resented your acquisition of the family lands, after he had…sold them.'

'So she has talked to you, has she? It's certainly true that you cannot trust a woman to keep her mouth shut!'

'Giles! Aunt Laura told me some of the story in an effort to excuse your conduct.'

'My conduct?'

'Yes—she attributed your general ill-humour and over-bearing ways, not to mention your distrust of women, to the unfortunate experiences in your family.'

'Whereas we know that my distrust of women has recently been more than justified. Is that not so, Rosabelle?'

Annabelle sighed in exasperation. 'How long do you think we shall spend on this visit to Buxton?' she demanded.

'Seven or eight weeks, all told. Why?'

'I'd like to make a suggestion. You say my life is in danger. That isn't a pleasant thought, and the journey is bound to be somewhat nerve-racking, whatever precautions you take. But life is going to be even more unpleasant for us all, if we snap at each other all the way to Buxton and back! Can we not come to some sort of accommodation, just for two months? A kind of truce—however insincere? I would endeavour not to do anything to provoke you, and you in your turn would have to try to avoid being quite so critical of me. Let us, just for a short time, be kind to one another, Giles. Or, if being kind is impossible, then at least we could try to be civil! What do you say?'

He looked doubtful.

'I'm not asking you actually to like me, or…anything else,' said Annabelle, faint colour rising in her cheeks. 'I know you don't. This is not an effort to persuade you to change your mind about me. It is merely an attempt to make the journey easier for all of us.'

'I suppose you're right,' he said at last. He turned to her, and she would have sworn there was a look of genuine regret in his eyes. 'I cannot say that I trust you, Rosabelle, much as I would like to. The evidence against you is still too over-whelming. But—' He held out his hand. 'Yes, I will agree to your truce.'

They shook hands, and then resumed their walk.

The weather remained kind, and the travellers continued to
enjoy their leisurely journey through the English Midlands,
particularly as there was not the slightest sign of any interest
in their progress. Giles was as good as his word, and he and
Annabelle had many lively, but perfectly friendly, conversations with each other. The inns where they stayed were modest, but comfortable, and in the evenings they went for walks,
or talked, or played cards. The shadows of deception and
danger, lack of trust, and all the rest were firmly kept in the
background.

Eventually they turned through the walls of a pleasant
country estate, where they were to spend a couple of nights.

'I must say, I had never expected the journey to pass so
pleasantly,' said Lady Ordway, as they drove up the drive to
the Daventry home. 'Though I have yet to see natural beauties
to rival the architecture of Bath, Giles.'

'You shall, Aunt Laura, you shall. Only have patience.
These Midland counties are not impressive, I agree, but
Derbyshire will astonish you with its beauty.'

Lady Ordway was not moved. 'I visited Avenell when you
were a baby, Giles. I know what Derbyshire is like.'

'Then you have to agree with me. It is of all places the
most beautiful I have ever seen.'

'You are not being partial, by any chance, are you, Giles?'
laughed Annabelle.

'How could you suggest it? But look—we are expected.'

What seemed to be a vast crowd of people was waiting on
the steps of the Daventry home. They were greeted enthusi-
astically by all of them. After a few minutes of confusion,
Annabelle finally managed to sort out Captain Daventry, his
wife Selina, his mother Mrs Daventry senior, and five children. Captain Daventry bore Giles and the children away to

the stables, and the four ladies mounted the steps to the front door.

'We are so pleased to have you here, Mrs Ordway,' said Selina Daventry. 'We see Giles three or four times a year, but this is the first time he has brought someone with him. I gather you are on the way to Avenell?'

'We're actually making for Buxton—Lady Ordway is to take the waters there, but I think we are to visit Avenell on the way.'

'Really?' said Mrs Daventry. 'I'm very glad indeed to hear that.'

They went into the big saloon and sat down. The two ladies of the house were obviously very interested in their guests, and it became clear that Giles was a great favourite with them. He was young James Edward's godfather.

'I cannot tell you how kind he is to the child—to all the children, in fact,' Mrs Daventry said.

The senior Mrs Daventry broke in. 'Mirry and Lucy are twins, Mrs Ordway,' she said. 'Colonel Stanton has told us that you have a twin sister, too?'

'Yes,' said Annabelle. 'Though we haven't lived together since we were six years old.'

'How very sad! Why was that?'

'My mother died, and—'

'I badly needed a daughter, Mrs Daventry,' Lady Ordway intervened. 'So I begged Mr Kelland to let me bring Rosabelle up in London, and he agreed, on condition that I let her spend the summer months each year with her sister in Berkshire.'

'I think my father was quite glad to be relieved of one of us. And it has worked out very well.'

Perhaps sensing that the subject was a difficult one for her guests, though not, of course, even remotely guessing why, Mrs Daventry had the good manners not to ask any more questions. Instead she suggested that she should take them to their rooms. 'Take as long as you need to refresh yourselves after the journey,' she said gaily. 'Captain Daventry and Colonel Stanton will be some time yet, if I know them! James has recently acquired a couple of very handsome hunters.'

'Have they known each other long?' asked Annabelle.

'Ever since they both joined the army. But James sold out after Waterloo. His father wished him to take over the management of the estate, and I have to say that I was very happy that he did! Of course, Giles went on to further glories. We are very proud of him.'

While Lady Ordway sat in the saloon with Mrs Daventry's mother-in-law, the rest of the family took Giles and Annabelle on a short tour of the estate. Annabelle found herself walking with Captain Daventry, and the two boys, and she was so absorbed in what they were telling her that she was surprised to find they had outstripped the rest of the party. With a laugh, they stopped and sat down on a fallen tree trunk to wait. The two little girls came running up, each clutching a bunch of flowers, which grew in profusion in the hedgerows.

'Mrs Ordway, these are for you, we picked them our own selves! Aren't they pretty?'

'I think they're very pretty. Mmm…and they have such a nice smell, too! Thank you. It's a long time since I had such a delightful bouquet. I shall ask your mama if I may put them in my bedroom. Do you think we could find a few fern leaves to put with them? For greenery.'

The two little girls towed her away, assuring her that they knew just where to find such ferns. The rest of the party followed them more slowly, until the boys suddenly took to galloping down the hill. Giles and the Daventrys were left alone.

'What a delightful girl! Oh, forgive me! I should have said young woman. But when you told us of your cousin's wife I had imagined someone more sophisticated, Giles.'

Giles's eyes followed Annabelle as she went back down the path with the twins. They had each taken a hand, and the three of them were laughing and chattering as if they had known each other forever. When would he begin to fathom the contradictions in Rosabelle Ordway's character?

'She…she has a happy knack of fitting in wherever she goes, Selina.'

'That is certainly true!' Captain Daventry said. 'She was very interested in what we are planning to do with the farms here.' He looked guilty as his wife gave an exasperated groan.

'James! You promised me you wouldn't!' She turned to Giles. 'He will keep boring our poor guests with his wretched ideas, Giles. He gets carried away when he talks of his plans—he simply cannot see that changes in farming methods can't possibly be an interesting topic of conversation for town-bred visitors. I'll have to explain to Mrs Ordway as soon as I have an opportunity.'

'Well, I don't think you need worry, Selina! She was far from being bored! Indeed, she made one or two very pertinent observations.'

'That only increases my admiration for her manners, James! How could she possibly be interested?' She laughed and shook her head at her husband. Then she turned to Giles. 'Tell me, Giles, are Major Dabney and Captain Wainwright well? And has Richard Pettifer's aunt finally declared him her heir yet?'

The talk turned to other matters.

But later that evening the subject came up again.

'So you're making for Avenell?' Captain Daventry said. 'Do you plan to stay there long?'

A shadow came over Giles's face. 'No—three or four days at the most. I…I have to see my father. And then I need to take a little time to see how the estate is faring.'

'Are we to stay with Lord Stanton, Giles?'

'I…I'm not quite sure, Aunt Laura. I've reserved some rooms at an excellent inn nearby. You would be very comfortable there. My father may not be well enough to receive visitors.' Giles's tone was restricted. The Daventrys, fully conversant with the situation between their friend and his father, hastened to change the subject.

'Mrs Ordway, I hear that my dreadful husband has been teasing you with his views on farming,' cried Selina Daventry. 'You must forgive him. Since he left the Army he has taken with enthusiasm to being what he calls a modern landowner. He is really quite a rational creature, but on this subject he is sadly blind. He forgets that ladies of the *ton* are neither interested nor informed on such matters.'

'I've told you, Selina. You are quite out. Mrs Ordway displayed an astonishing grasp of our problems.'

'Oh?' said Giles, turning to Annabelle. 'Is this a new talent, Rosabelle? Where on earth have you learned about farming? Who has been teaching you?'

'I…I… You forget, Giles. In my youth I spent every summer down at Temperley.'

'Children's games?'

'No, indeed! Annabelle ran the estate from a very early age, and, like Captain Daventry here, was eager to convey her knowledge to anyone who would listen.' She turned to her host. 'My father is an invalid and was happy to delegate the running of Temperley to my sister. She takes a keen interest in the land. I'm sure she would enjoy talking to you, Captain Daventry. You would have a lot in common.'

'A gel! Running an estate!' cried the older Mrs Daventry. 'How odd!'

'I suppose it is, ma'am. But I think Annabelle is happy to do it.'

'She must be an able teacher,' said Captain Daventry with a smile. 'But then you are twins, are you not? So perhaps there is an extra line of sympathy between you.' His wife interrupted him.

'Are you very alike? I was rather disappointed when I found that our two are not.'

Annabelle hesitated. This was a dangerous moment. But Lady Ordway came to her rescue. 'There are similarities of appearance perhaps, but they are not at all alike otherwise. They have led such very different lives. I pride myself that Rosabelle is the prettier, but you might call me over-partial, I suppose. Annabelle has always led such an outdoor life— she was sadly brown when I was last at Temperley. Tell me, Mrs Daventry, is this delicious dessert made with your own fruits?'

The moment passed and Annabelle breathed again. The rest of the visit passed without incident, and when the time came for them to leave she did so with regret. She had developed a fondness for the Daventry family, but doubted very much that she would ever see them again.

They had all enjoyed their visit to the Daventrys, and a more relaxed atmosphere could be felt as they continued northwards. Giles's manner towards Annabelle was very nearly affable. Even Lady Ordway was impressed with the scenery before Matlock—the glens, the rippling, sparkling river, the rocks towering above them—and Annabelle was enraptured. They spent a very comfortable night in Bakewell, and set off in good spirits on the last stage of their journey. However, as they drove into the courtyard of a charming inn, not far from Avenell, a shadow fell over the company.

It was a beautiful afternoon, and the ladies had till then been very content with their day. But ever since midday, Giles had been growing steadily more taciturn. By the time they drew up at the inn, his face was grimmer than ever. Annabelle badly wanted to reassure him, give him support for the unpleasant task before him, but she dared not. Instead she concentrated on the scenery and did her best to distract him. She met with little success.

Lady Ordway whispered, 'Try not to worry, Anna. Giles was very short with you just now, I know, but he cannot be looking forward to this visit to his father. Their estrangement must give him pain.'

Annabelle did not know how to reply. She knew, more than Lady Ordway, how difficult it was going to be at Avenell. There was no easy way for Giles to break the news about his stepmother's death, whatever Lord Stanton's reaction might be. She knew, too, that she must say nothing of it to Lady Ordway. It was for Giles to tell her. She sighed and said, 'We must just wait until we see him tomorrow, Aunt Laura.'

After Giles had seen them comfortably settled in their rooms, he rode off to Avenell. Annabelle stood at her window and watched him go—he looked like a man riding to a wake. Then she turned back sadly into the room.

As the walls and towers of Avenell came into view Giles's heart grew ever heavier. It was the scene of so many happy childhood memories, all overshadowed by the nightmare of what had followed, when his stepmother had usurped his beloved mother's place. And now he had come to tell his father that the usurper was dead. The drive rose steeply from the road and Giles dismounted as usual and left his horse at the lodge. He walked up the winding carriageway, through hedges and trees, deep in thought.

As a child he had felt bewildered, hurt at the change in his life. He had regarded himself as an exile, forced to live among comparative strangers while his father filled his home with strangers. Later, when he was old enough to understand what had happened, he had become contemptuous of his father's doting fondness for Venetia Stanton. With increasing frustration, unable to do anything to prevent it, he had been forced to hear of the dissipation of Stanton wealth, the mortgage and loss of Stanton lands, to see his mother's jewellery given away—all to keep this woman happy and at his father's side. He had felt no sympathy, only scorn for an ailing old man left alone when the money, and Venetia, were gone.

Looking back now, Giles realised that Lord Stanton had long since regretted that catastrophic marriage, but Stanton arrogance and Stanton pride had prevented him from admitting it. It had not been surprising that his father had responded to his criticisms not with regret, but with fury, and that father and son had fallen out, comprehensively. The world was mistaken when it attributed Lord Stanton's resentment to Giles's efforts to buy back and own the Stanton lands his father had so stupidly lost. The roots of their estrangement lay in those unfilial expressions of contempt, in the arrogant lack of tolerance shown by his only son.

Older now, and wiser, Giles understood for the first time how his father had felt. He now knew what it was to despise a woman for what she had done in the past, what she was likely to do in the future, to know her to be a liar and a cheat, but still, in spite of everything, to remain fascinated. Since meeting Rosabelle Ordway he had been drawn himself into this honey-trap. He had seen Rosabelle enchanting the Daventrys, cultivating the children, pretending to take an interest in poor Daventry's schemes, laughing with Selina...

He had watched her apparently artless delight in the beauties of nature on their journey, her solicitude for his aunt. He could remember the sincerity in those deep blue eyes as she swore she had no idea who Selder was... And in spite of all he knew about her, he still had to exercise the greatest possible control not to seek her out, to coax her to smile at him, talk to him, laugh with him. In danger of such a spell himself, he could at last understand his father's infatuation with Venetia Stanton, and feel ashamed that he had been so unforgiving.

He had reached the gatehouse, its ancient tower guarding

the entrance to Avenell. He paused, then strode across the courtyard to the massive oak door which opened on to the Great Hall.

He was met at the door by an elderly valet who, on the few occasions such services were required, acted as both footman and butler.

'Good evening, Howells. How are you?'

'Very fit, master Giles, very fit. Lord Stanton is waiting in the little parlour. If I may mention it, we've been looking forward all day to this moment.'

Giles permitted himself an ironic smile. 'You're kind to say so. Is my father well, too?'

'Fair. But he hasn't his old strength. He doesn't stir much out of his chair nowadays.'

'I need to talk to him. Is he well enough for that?'

Howells stopped and gave Giles a worried look.

'He's well enough for a talk. It…it… Forgive me, master Giles, but is that all it would be? The last time…'

'I know, I know. The last time I tried to have a talk with him there was an almighty row, and we parted on very bad terms. You needn't be so careful in mentioning it, Howells. God knows, the shouting was so immoderate that most of Derbyshire must have known the Stantons had fallen out again! Very embarrassing for all concerned.'

'It's not that. After you left, he was really ill, master Giles. Very distressed was Lord Stanton. And he's not getting any younger. I'm not sure that another…talk like the last would be good for him.'

'I intend this one to be different, Howells.'

'I'm very glad to hear you say so.' Howells led the way into a small passage and opened a door to the side. 'We've put you in your old set of rooms, sir. Would you like anything to eat?'

'Not now, though I might have something later. But a tankard of ale wouldn't come amiss. I'll have it in the little parlour with my father. I'll only be a minute or two.'

'Very well, sir. I'll be waiting for you.'

Minutes later Giles entered the passageway leading to Lord Stanton's rooms to find Howells waiting there, as he had promised. Howells opened the door to the little parlour, went in and said quietly,

'Colonel Stanton, my lord.'

Chapter Eleven

Giles bent his head as he entered. The Stantons were a tall race, and the Tudor members of the family who had redesigned the south range had forgotten to allow for it. But the low door led into a beautiful room. It was spacious—'little' only by comparison with Avenell's state reception rooms—and panelled throughout in silver-grey wood. At the end of the room surprisingly large mullioned windows overlooked the terraces falling down to the valley below. Giles could remember hearing, on summer evenings in the past when the windows had been open, the sound of water swirling round the boulders in the river, and splashing against its banks. But now the windows were shut, and though it was still quite light outside, the curtains were half drawn against the evening sun. There was a large wing chair by the fireplace, and a table by it.

'Since you're here, you'd better come in, hadn't you? You've taken your time. We've been expecting you this past hour or more.'

'I'm sorry, sir. I had to see that Lady Ordway and her daughter-in-law were comfortably settled.'

'They're at the Stanton Arms, I suppose.'

'Yes.'

'Hmm.'

Howells came in with a tankard of ale and some wine for his master, which he put on the table. He poured the wine, then left the room, giving Giles a significant look as he went. The interruption gave Giles time to marshal his thoughts. The sight of his father, a gaunt figure huddled in his chair, dark eyes sunk deep in their sockets, had affected him more than he was willing to admit.

'How are you, sir? Howells seemed to think you were not altogether the thing.'

'Howells is an old woman. You needn't concern yourself about me, sir. I don't suppose for a minute you're here to enquire about my health. You've more important things to see to, no doubt.'

'No, Father. This time I've come to see you. I'd like to talk to you.'

'Hmm. Would you? I'm not sure I'm fit enough for that.'

Giles took a breath and said resolutely, 'Father, things have happened recently which…which have caused me to think again about the past. I…I have come to regret some of the things that I have said and done. I'd like you to forgive me for them.'

Lord Stanton sat up and stared at his son. 'Well, I'm damned! This is a change of heart! What the devil has caused this turnaround?'

'Several things. But before we go any further, I have…' Giles paused. He could not in all honesty call his news bad. 'I have some news for you, which I hope will not be too much of a shock. Venetia has died.'

'Who?'

'Venetia, Father. Your ex-wife.'

'Has she, indeed?' Lord Stanton sat in silence for several minutes, a number of expressions chasing one another across his face—a frown, a look of sadness, and finally one of relief.

'So she's gone. I suppose you've come to congratulate me on my loss.'

'No. Though I'd be a hypocrite if I expressed any sorrow for it,' Giles responded, silently conscious all the same of regret for the manner in which Venetia had died.

'Hmm.' There was a slight pause while Lord Stanton looked away. Still not looking at his son, he said eventually, 'You're right, of course. I lost my head over her and regretted it ever after. I was a fool.'

'You may have been a fool, sir, but it was at least a human failing. I was far too critical of your behaviour. I forgot the respect I owed you. And I should have understood your situation better.'

Giles kept his gaze steady, as his father shot him a fierce look, as if suspecting him of irony. Then Lord Stanton looked away again. 'How could you?' he said. 'You were a child.'

'I meant later. I didn't think ill of you when I was a child. I loved you and I loved my home, and I was deeply unhappy when you sent me away. Especially as at the time I couldn't understand why.'

Another fierce look, then a rueful nod, as if to acknowledge the justice of Giles's remark. 'The thing was, Giles…oh, damn it, I discovered I'd made a mistake very soon. Of course I did! But I wasn't going to acknowledge it. I was determined to live with it. And that meant countenancing her friends and putting up with their ways. But I wasn't going to have you corrupted by them. I *had* to send you away.'

'I understand that now.'

'You do? Hmm.'

'And I'd like us to bury the past. It seems a suitable moment to do it. Could you do that, Father? Will you forgive my harsh words the last time we met?'

His father was clearly having a struggle with Stanton pride. 'So you admit you were at fault, do you?' he said gruffly.

'I do. Freely.'

'You were damned impertinent, sir. Not just on that occasion, either.'

'I was angry. But I shouldn't have expressed myself so immoderately.' Giles met Lord Stanton's glare this time with a hint of affectionate amusement. 'We both have a temper, sir.'

'Very well, very well. I daresay there were faults on both sides. How long are you staying?'

Taking this to mean that his apology was accepted, Giles sat down and relaxed.

'As I told you in my letter, I'm escorting Aunt Laura to Buxton.'

'Hmm. And she's at present at the Stanton Arms? With her boy's widow?'

'Yes. I thought it might be too much for the household here…'

'I've never heard such nonsense! Bring them to Avenell! Howells is perfectly capable of seeing that they're comfortably accommodated. That woman—what's her name? Dunnock! She can sort out the rooms tomorrow. Glad of something to do, I daresay. Tell her to get some help in if she needs it.'

To Giles's astonishment, Lord Stanton's eyes had suddenly brightened, his voice was clearer and stronger, and he was sitting upright, impatience and energy in every line. The elderly invalid had vanished. Was that all it had needed to cause this transformation? A reconciliation with his son? Giles was moved, suddenly overcome by a feeling of humility, which was as rare as it was unexpected. He took a moment to recover his normal voice.

Then he said mildly, 'There's quite a party of us. Aunt Laura has her own maid and manservant. We travelled in my own carriage, and with our own horses, so there's a coachman and two grooms. And Goss, of course.'

'Good God! What a household! Too high in the instep to

travel like ordinary mortals, eh? Post horses not good enough
for you?'

'It wasn't that, sir. But that's a tale for tomorrow.'

'Well, Avenell's big enough, heaven knows. Tell Howells.
He'll deal with it all.'

'It's very good of you, Father.'

'Nonsense! It's a poor day for Avenell when the guests of
the Stantons have to put up at the local inn! Fetch them tomorrow as soon as the ladies are up.'

'Thank you, sir. I will. Now, tell me truly, how you are?'

Giles and his father talked in unusual harmony for some
time. Lord Stanton had clearly long wished for a reconciliation, but was too stiff-necked ever to have asked for one before it was offered. But now that barrier was overcome, father
and son both felt the need to make up for lost time. More
wine and ale were called for, and it was late before Giles
finally bade his father goodnight. He left him planning how
to entertain his guests, and harrassing poor Howells by issuing
all sorts of conflicting orders.

When Giles set off from Avenell the morning was bright
and fresh and glimpses of sunlight sparkling on water could
be caught between the lush foliage on the river bank. He
paused before riding down into the valley and gazed about
him. He was surrounded by a landscape—his landscape—of
sun and shadows, hills, moorland and meadows, rocks and
rivers—green and grey, purple and brown. It stretched for
miles in every direction, gleaming in the morning sunlight.
He listened with contentment to the sound of water rushing
down from the hills in a thousand tiny waterfalls, forcing its
way through narrow channels, past huge rocks, rippling over
the pebbles of the river bed.

For so many years he had returned here with feelings of
loss and resentment, an alien in his own country. Even own-
ership of the land had not brought back a sense of belonging.

He had sought compensation, won rewards on foreign soils, but they had only ever at best been a poor substitute for Derbyshire and Avenell. Now, his estrangement from his father ended, things had changed—miraculously so—and once again he felt he belonged. Nothing could blunt this feeling of joy, of satisfaction in this reunion with his roots, and in his happiness he was ready to reconsider his other problems with a more open mind. Chief among them was the question of his feelings towards Rosàbelle Ordway.

At Woburn Rosabelle had asked him for a truce, and he had agreed to it. It would have been inconvenient, to say the least, if they had continued their journey in an atmosphere of open antipathy and distrust. But till now, though he had adopted a more friendly attitude, he had not actually felt more kindly towards her. She had remained the woman who had betrayed his cousin and had lied outright to protect herself afterwards. He had still suspected her of setting out quite deliberately to attract him, and, though he had kept it well hidden, he had still resented her power over him, despised himself for his own weakness.

But suddenly such thoughts seemed unworthy. Rosabelle Ordway might be the villain he had thought her—but this morning it suddenly seemed less likely. All his instincts were against it. The full story of her association with Falkirk had yet to be revealed, and there might well be an explanation which could clear her. One thing was certain. Rosabelle Ordway seemed to have reached a part of him which no other woman ever had. Surely that must mean something? Perhaps he should trust his instincts after all?

But then a small cloud crossed the sun, and Giles gave a frown. He had seen a good few men go to the wall because they followed their instincts rather than their heads, his father for one of them. Damn all women! Life would be so much less complicated without them. Perhaps, until the Falkirk business was resolved, it would be wiser not to let Rosabelle

Ordway gain the complete hold on his life and his emotions
that instinct told him she could. But he could surely allow
himself to enjoy her company without any grave danger,
couldn't he?

Lady Ordway and Annabelle had got up early, too. The inn
was right on the river and Lady Ordway had not been able
to sleep for the noise made by the water.

'I never have been a devotee of the countryside, Anna. I
find it very noisy. Town life always suited me very well.'

'Aunt Laura! The world goes into the country for peace
and solitude! How can you say it is noisy?'

'The world is mistaken, Anna dear. That river is extremely
loud! And I'll swear that forty or fifty birds never stopped
shouting to each other outside my window this morning. For
a while I even thought one of the cows was in the bedchamber
with me! I do so wish we had gone to Bath!'

'But even from the little I've seen of it, Derbyshire is beautiful!' Annabelle looked out of the window. 'Ah! Here's
Giles. I wonder how he got on?'

'He looks remarkably cheerful.'

As Giles came in through the arch, he looked up and saw
them, and his face lit up in a smile. Annabelle's heart turned
over. If only, she thought, oh, if only he would always look
at me like that! For a moment she was lost in a dream where
she and Giles... Reality took over, however, and with a wry
look, she followed Lady Ordway sedately down to the coffee
room.

'Good morning, Giles. Did you sleep well?'

'Very well, Aunt Laura.' They exchanged greetings—'the
niceties of polite conversation', thought Annabelle ironically—and then Giles issued an invitation from his father to
stay at Avenell for the next day or two.

'How kind,' said Lady Ordway. 'Er...how far is Avenell
from the river, Giles?'

'Quite a way above it. But I thought you'd been there before?'

'Once. A very long time ago. I can't remember much about it.'

'Avenell stands on a hillside a hundred and fifty feet or more above the river valley. Why do you want to know?'

'Aunt Laura was kept awake all night by the sounds of the river, Giles,' said Annabelle, her eyes full of amusement. 'She finds the country very noisy.'

'I shall see you are put in one of the rooms at the back, Aunt Laura,' promised Giles. He grew grave. 'But there's something I have to tell you before we leave for Avenell. Shall we go into the garden?'

As they walked along the paths of a pretty little garden at the back, Giles gave Lady Ordway the news of Venetia Stanton's death, though without any unnecessary detail.

'But, Giles,' she protested, 'we cannot possibly intrude on Lord Stanton at this time!'

'He wants you to come. Say you will, Aunt Laura! Your rooms in Buxton are not yet available—they have been reserved from the weekend. It would please my father—and me—immensely, if you would agree to spend the rest of the week at Avenell. I think you must know what an act of hypocrisy it would be for him to pretend he is distressed at Venetia's death. They were divorced some years ago, as you know. And…it would mean a lot to me.'

Lady Ordway was eventually persuaded to consent, and they set off about an hour later. Though the steep winding drive up to Avenell gave her some qualms, and though she was not at all happy when the carriage rumbled over the ancient drawbridge, they arrived perfectly sound at the door of the Great Hall.

Lord Stanton was at the door to greet them.

'My dear Lady Ordway,' he said. 'Laura! This is a delightful honour. It must be twenty-five years since we last met.'

'More than that, Lord Stanton. It was not long after I married Sir John.' She allowed herself to be ushered in and gazed
round doubtfully. 'Avenell hasn't changed... This hall is so
large! All that stone! It must be impossible to heat—and the
draughts...'

'We only use the Great Hall on state occasions, Laura. The
South Wing is very cosy. Come, I'll conduct you myself to
meet Mrs Dunnock. Howells has gone to see to the disposi-
tion of your staff and luggage. All of it.'

'All of it! It's barely enough to keep us decently clothed!
As for the sheets and other things... Giles sent the van off to
Bath, Lionel!'

'Did he, indeed? I wonder why? Well, you won't need
household stuff at Avenell, Laura. And I believe some boxes
arrived for you here yesterday. Mrs Dunnock will show you
to your rooms, and then we'll meet in the Little Parlour.
You'll find that more to your taste.'

'I remember it. A sadly low ceiling. But the views were
quite nice. If you like the country, that is...' Her voice died
as Lord Stanton escorted her out of the Hall and along the
passage.

Annabelle and Giles were left alone in the Great Hall.

'She's tired, Giles,' said Annabelle. 'She didn't sleep last
night, and though you've looked after our comfort on the
journey wonderfully well, it has taken a lot out of her. She
really needs to stay in one place for more than a few days.'

He smiled at her. 'Don't worry. I'm not offended, and neither is my father.'

'You've...you're on better terms with him again?'

'I can't think why I waited so long. Venetia's death provided me with an excuse... No, excuse isn't the right word.
Gave me the impetus. But I shouldn't have needed one.'

'I think relationships with one's parents are often difficult. My own father ignores my existence most of the time.'

'That's not altogether surprising, is it?'

'I beg your pardon?'

'Well, surely you've lived with Aunt Laura for most of your life? You don't see him often.'

'What? Oh, no! No, I don't. Er…perhaps I should see what is happening to Aunt Laura?'

'I expect you'd like to see your room, too. I hope you like the sound of running water, Rosabelle. I expect they've given you the Blue Bedchamber, and that overlooks the river.'

The subject of Annabelle's father was forgotten, much to her relief. Though she did not claim, even to herself, that she had been honest with Giles, she had always tried to avoid telling him an outright lie. Sooner or later she was bound to be faced with the problem, but the longer that moment could be postponed the happier she would be. Perhaps at Buxton, when they were settled for some weeks, she could find a way of ending the imposture and telling him the full truth at last. But not yet. Not here at Avenell.

The day after their arrival Giles rode over to Buxton to take a look at the rooms which had been reserved for them and to have a talk with Gregson, who was waiting there until they came. He came back just in time for dinner. Mrs Dunnock, excited by the opportunity to show her mettle to these London visitors, had produced an excellent meal, and, to accompany it, Howells had brought up some very good wines from the cellar.

But after the table had been cleared for dessert, and the company was sitting replete and relaxed, Giles informed them that Buxton was suffering from an outbreak of summer influenza.

Lord Stanton said instantly, 'You must stay here till the worst of the epidemic is over, Laura.'

'We couldn't so impose on you!'

'Don't be foolish—I'd enjoy your company. And I can't allow you to expose yourself and that lovely young creature to infection! No, I insist. Another two weeks—the worst of it will have passed by then.'

Lady Ordway looked helplessly at Annabelle.

'I think it's extremely kind of Lord Stanton to invite us to stay longer, Aunt Laura. He's right. It would be foolish to risk catching such a very unpleasant disease, when you have come all this way for your health! The waters of Buxton will keep. And you couldn't ask for a more beautiful place to stay.'

'You like Avenell, d'ye?' asked Lord Stanton, enormously pleased with these words.

Annabelle, already after one day at her ease with him, smiled. 'I have no great experience of the world, sir. Till now I have only known Berkshire—and London, of course—but I can safely say that I have never seen a place which suits me more. Berkshire is beautiful, but it has nothing to compare with the splendour of Derbyshire. A gentle domestic cat compared with a mountain lion.'

'D'ye hear that, Giles? You seem to prefer Europe. Laura, I know, is more at home in London. But this young lady has more taste than the lot of you put together!' He shot a sly glance at them both. 'Except that she seems to have a liking for you!'

Annabelle gasped, but Giles was already speaking. Smiling lazily, he said, 'Father, I hate to disillusion you, but the young lady in question has been in Derbyshire for not much more than three days, and the road from Matlock to Avenell has so far been her sole experience of the county. I think we should pay tribute to her charming manners and desire to please, rather than her judgement.'

Annabelle responded with energy, 'I was perfectly sincere in my praise! But in spite of my natural desire to please Lord

Stanton, I cannot allow his partiality for his son to blind him.' She turned to her host. 'Though I am grateful to Colonel Stanton for his help and support in the last months, I must confess that I have not found it at all easy to like him. His life in the Army has encouraged an unfortunate tendency to order people about, which I find far from pleasing!'

'Rosa!' Lady Ordway was scandalised, but Annabelle stood her ground.

'I hope you will forgive my plain speaking, sir.'

'Of course I do! And I know exactly what you mean. A touch arrogant, is he?'

'High-handed, certainly.'

Lord Stanton was enjoying this exchange. 'But you're obviously a girl of spirit. You don't let yourself be overborne, I hope?'

'I try not to. But it can be very difficult for a mere female—'

'A mere female?' asked Giles. 'You underrate yourself, Rosabelle.'

Lady Ordway intervened. 'Lord Stanton, I don't know what you will be thinking of my goddaughter. She is not usually so forgetful of her manners. Giles has been very kind to us both. He is a dear boy.'

Having made her position clear to anyone who cared to notice, Annabelle was now prepared to enjoy herself. 'A "dear boy" was not how you thought of him when he changed our minds for us at a moment's notice and hauled us off to Buxton, Aunt Laura. Or am I wrong?'

'No…not exactly. Though he has since made up for it a little—he has at least seen to it that our boxes were diverted here to Avenell, though the rest of the things went on to Bath in the fourgon. I don't think I have yet thanked you for that, Giles,' she said, turning to him with a smile.

'Thanked him! When the confusion was all his doing! Really, Aunt Laura!'

Lord Stanton frowned. 'You must have had good reason for all this, Giles? I don't believe you're as arbitrary as this tale would suggest.'

Annabelle now regretted where her careless words had led her. Giles might not wish to tell his father the whole of what lay behind the change of plan. He would certainly not want to frighten Aunt Laura with it.

'I…I will allow that it was reasonable, sir. He had some… sad news which he wished to convey to you personally, I believe?'

'Ah, yes. Venetia. Quite true. Hmm. We will grant that he is a good son, Mrs Ordway.'

'Since we are all speaking frankly, I will contest that,' Giles said. 'But I intend to be a better one in the future, sir.'

'Very good, very good. Now, what plans do you have for entertaining the ladies, Giles?'

'You see me demoralised, sir. I hardly dare suggest a thing for fear of being called high-handed or arrogant,' Giles said with a perfectly straight face.

'How delightful to hear it!' said Annabelle sweetly. 'Well then, Giles, in that case, I shall take shameful advantage of this rare state of yours and, if Aunt Laura agrees, I shall ask you to take us to see more of your wonderful countryside. I shall then be able to converse with enough authority on Derbyshire and its attractions to satisfy even you.'

'I should be very pleased to show you anything you would like to see. Aunt Laura?'

'Yes. That would be very agreeable.'

'We shall all go,' said Lord Stanton. 'And I know exactly the place to make for. There's an excellent inn at Bradshaw— you remember it, Giles? The landlady there worked in our kitchens when she was a girl, and she's an excellent cook. We'll have a day's tour of the countryside, and stop for something to eat at the King's Head. How would you like that?'

It was settled that they should go on a tour of the district

the day after next. Lady Ordway felt she would like time to
settle in at Avenell before venturing on any expeditions.

The company broke up. Annabelle and Lady Ordway were
led through a warren of rooms by one of the maids, who was
to take Lily's place during Annabelle's stay at Avenell. She
had a strong Derbyshire accent, but turned out to be deft and
helpful. After she had gone Annabelle stood at the window
in her wrapper, listening to the sound of the river, and looking
out over the hills to the moorland beyond. She took a deep
breath. Whatever Giles may say, she felt an affinity with this
land, such as she had never before experienced. She was enchanted by the serene beauties of its valleys, or dales as they
were called, but there was more to it than that. Something
about the restless energy of its rivers and streams, the uncom-
promising strength of its rocks challenged her, appealed to
the rebel in her. She was eager to know more of it.

There was a tap at the door. She went over and opened it.

'Giles! Is something wrong?'

'No, no! I just thought you might prefer to have this tonight. When I was in Buxton today I called at the Receiving
Office and collected several letters which were waiting there.
I've only just managed to look through them. This one is for
you. I believe it's from your sister. Goodnight, Rosabelle.'

'I'm very obliged, Giles. It was kind of you to bring it.'

'So I'm not as bad as you painted me tonight?'

A smile broke over Annabelle's face and lit her eyes with
mischief. 'Not always, Giles. I even manage to like you sometimes. Goodnight.' She shut the door.

The candles burned low as Annabelle sat at the table reading her sister's letter. It made distressful reading. Rosabelle
was perplexed and unhappy. Her relationship with Philip
Winbolt had developed even more quickly than Lady Ordway
had hoped, and, though Mr Winbolt had not exactly declared

himself, he had made it clear that he was strongly attracted to her. And she knew herself to be in love, truly, deeply in love, for the first time in her life. But the gentleman was under the impression that she was Annabelle, of course. Though she had found it very hard, Rosabelle had been forced to put a stop to his overtures before they went too far.

At this point Annabelle lifted her eyes from the letter and slowly shook her head in despair. How could they have imagined, the two of them, that a simple exchange of places—just to give Rosabelle extra time for recovery—would lead to such heartache, not just for one, but for both! They had been foolishly irresponsible, and now they were paying the price. She took up the letter again...

The situation between Rosabelle and Mr Winbolt had come to a head on the very day that Annabelle's letter had arrived, telling her of the plan to go to Bath. Ashamed and unhappy, Rosabelle had seen the letter as a welcome release. She would go to Bath with her godmother, and hope that she would in time manage to forget Philip Winbolt. But now...! The decision to go to Buxton had changed everything. It would be impossible to keep the situation in limbo for seven or even eight weeks! She would simply not be able to sustain it!

Annabelle's heart gave a leap. If Rosabelle wanted her permission to reveal everything, she would give it without a second's hesitation. She wanted nothing more than to confess her real identity to Giles, while there was still time to repair the inevitable damage and perhaps to go on to a better understanding with him... She read on eagerly.

But to her intense disappointment this was not what Rosabelle wanted. On the contrary. She had consulted their father, and his advice had been to continue to see the Winbolts as before, without yet revealing her true identity. He had suggested that she should give Philip Winbolt time to get to know her so well that, when she eventually confessed her deception, he would understand and forgive her. And this

was what she had decided to do. But if Mr Winbolt was to
believe in her basic honesty, then it was obviously vital that
the changeover should remain a secret until Rosabelle herself
told him the truth. It would be disastrous if he heard it from
any other source. The letter ended with a disguised, but none-
theless passionate, plea to her sister to do nothing which
might jeopardise this plan.

Annabelle slowly folded the letter and put it away. In other
words, she had to remain Rosabelle Ordway until her sister's
situation had been cleared up. She must! Rosabelle's happiness was at stake. In the last few weeks she had learned so
much more about the life Rosabelle had led with Stephen
Ordway, how unhappy she had been. How could she possibly
refuse to help her now? From her knowledge of Philip
Winbolt he was sure to forgive gentle, vulnerable Rosabelle,
once he knew her. She sighed. Clarification of her own situation with Giles would just have to wait… And, to look on
the bright side, perhaps Giles, too, would understand and forgive Annabelle, once he knew her properly…

Chapter Twelve

The day of the expedition dawned bright and sunny. Lord Stanton's own barouche was harnessed up, and laden with the impedimenta which its owner thought necessary for the comfort and convenience of his guests. Lady Ordway was to travel in the barouche with Lord Stanton, but there had been a certain amount of discussion as to how Annabelle would go.

'Mrs Ordway will ride, of course,' said Lord Stanton decidedly. 'It's the only way to see the countryside to advantage.'

'It's quite a long round trip, Father,' said Giles. 'And Rosabelle is not accustomed to country riding. She is a town girl at heart.'

'Oh, no, I should love to ride!' Annabelle exclaimed. 'How fortunate that I have brought my riding dress with me!'

'It's not a canter in the Park, Rosabelle! It's hard country, and you would spend a good part of the day in the saddle.' Giles was quite firm. 'I really don't think—'

'If you do not wish me to accompany you, then there is no more to be said, Giles.' Annabelle looked at him with reproachful blue eyes. 'But after leading us all to believe that you were prepared to do anything we asked, I am disappointed…'

He looked as if he was about to deny her, but then he smiled and shrugged his shoulders. 'If you are determined to suffer, how can I refuse? I should be delighted to escort you.' He added kindly, 'You could always ride home in the carriage, if it proves too much for you.'

Annabelle thanked him meekly, secretly swearing to herself she would ride all the way there and all the way back, if it killed her! She caught Giles's gaze and lifted her chin defiantly. From the grin on his face he had guessed what she had been thinking.

It was settled that Lord Stanton's carriage would take the road to the village of Bradshaw, while Giles, Annabelle and a groom would ride over the moors. The two parties would meet in the King's Head, where Lord Stanton had already ordered a meal for them.

'You could show Mrs Ordway Blackhole cavern on the way, Giles. But you must promise not to hide from her!'

Giles laughed, and his father explained that he had taken Giles as a child to the cavern some miles before Bradshaw, and the boy had completely disappeared.

'Disappeared?' exclaimed Lady Ordway. 'But did you not keep a strict eye on him?'

'He wasn't out of my sight for more than thirty seconds, Laura! But don't worry—the little devil wasn't in any danger. He had slipped behind a crack in the rock and was hiding from us. He was completely invisible. He came out a few minutes later roaring with laughter. The only damage he suffered was the thrashing I gave him for the fright he had given us.'

'One of the few times—in my childhood—that I remember your being really angry with me, sir,' said Giles ruefully. 'We were usually good friends.'

'I was furious that you had frightened your mother so. You

were the apple of her eye.' Lord Stanton paused, lost in
thought. Then he sighed. 'Yes…you're right, Giles. Those
were happy times… And so is today. So, Mrs Ordway, don't
stand any nonsense from this villain.'

'I won't, Lord Stanton. I'll get him to show me the crack
first, and then I shall know where to look if he disappears.
Though I might just leave him there! He's not the apple of
my eye!'

'I think that is most unhandsome of you, Rosabelle. After
I have given in to you on all points, too.'

The party set off in laughter and mutual good humour.

Annabelle and Giles reached Blackhole cavern after one of
the most enjoyable rides she had ever known. They managed
to keep up a fair pace, except when Annabelle stopped to
exclaim over the view, or paused for a breath of the clean,
invigorating moorland air.

'It's like nothing I've ever seen or imagined, Giles! Those
weird shapes on the hills in the distance. What are they?'

'They're rocks eroded by the wind.'

'Sculpted by the wind, rather. Like strange, contorted monuments erected by a race of giants. And the sweep of the
moors all round—beautiful! I could stay here forever!'

'I doubt that. You're seeing the moors today in sunshine—
at their kindliest. They can be cruel, and very dangerous. I'd
rather contend with a battalion of crack French troops than
these moors in bad weather. But, as you say, on a day like
today they are…magnificent.' He looked round with an expression of supreme contentment. To Annabelle he looked
completely one with this powerful, beautiful landscape, and
a sudden feeling of desire ran through her veins so strongly,
that she had to restrain herself from touching him. She was
shocked and confused by its force, and turned her face away,
pretending to look at the hills in the other direction.

'Rosabelle, if we are to see the cavern before meeting the others, we must move more quickly.'

'What? Oh, yes! Lead on!'

If Giles found her more silent on the rest of the ride, he made no comment.

They reached the cavern in good time, in spite of Giles's warnings, and, leaving their horses in the care of the groom, they walked up a steep path to its mouth. Here they paid their fee, and followed the guide—an elderly, craggy man who talked in a dialect which sounded very strange to Annabelle's ears—into the hillside.

In truth, Blackhole cavern was an awesome place. Flares had been placed at each bend, and anywhere where the going was insecure, and the smoke from them curled upwards towards an invisible roof, veiled in a mysterious swathe of darkness. Their guide went on ahead, his flambeau gleaming on the wet surfaces of the cavern, the uneven flickering from its flames reflecting a thousand twinkling stars in the rocks around. At one point Giles took Annabelle's hand to help her down a slippery descent, and afterwards kept it in his. Once again she was astonished at her unruly body's response to his touch. She wanted to take the hand to her cheek, feel its warmth against her mouth… Shocked, she almost snatched her hand away, but controlled the impulse. Giles might well wonder what was wrong, and, on a more ordinary human level, she was grateful for the warmth of the contact. The cavern was impressively awesome, and she felt threatened by its dank atmosphere, stifled, even, by the pall of darkness pressing in on them from every direction…

Then they turned a corner and Annabelle stopped short, confronted by a fantastic sight. Numerous flares had been installed here, and their light was caught by a hundred…two hundred…more than she could count…luminous white shapes, chandeliers, long, cathedral-like structures, hanging down in graceful clusters.

'Giles!' breathed Annabelle. 'What *are* they?'

'Stalactites, mistress.' The guide had evidently mastered the word for the benefit of visitors and was proud of it.

'Stal-stalactites? Made by magic?'

'Nothing so sensational. Constant dropping of water over limestone, Rosabelle.'

'It's an amazing sight,' she breathed. 'Icicles of stone. What a strange, wonderful country this is, Giles! The monuments on the hillside, and now these... You have no need of art galleries—Nature does it all for you.' She gazed at the stalactites for a long while. There were hundreds of them, in all sizes, disappearing into the darkness at the back of the chamber. She shivered.

'You're cold!'

'I suppose I am. But it's not just that. I...I think I prefer to be above ground, Giles.'

'Then we shall go back. Come!' He shouted to the guide, and the little party set off back to the open air.

Not far from the entrance, where the daylight made things more visible, Giles said softly, 'Wait a moment. Look!'

He went over to the wall of the cavern and put his hand behind a fold in the rock. Annabelle followed. There was a small niche where Giles had put his hand, invisible to the casual observer.

'So that's where you hid?'

He nodded. 'I doubt I could get in now, though!' he added with a smile.

'For Heaven's sake, don't try, Giles! You would surely get stuck, even if you succeeded.'

The guide had missed them. He came back, apologising for having wandered on without them.

'I was just checkin' the gate. It's kept open in summer, but I like to check it now and then, just to see it's in workin' order. We 'ave to be careful, like! Look!' He took them beyond the narrow throat of the cavern just before the exit and showed them a rod set into the wall. He unhooked it and a metal gate, rather like a portcullis, descended from above, closing the cavern behind them. 'It's gradely, isn't it? The Duke 'ad that put there. We shut it in winter—we doan't want gypsies or the like winterin' 'ere.'

They showed suitable admiration for the Duke's arrangements, then Giles paid their fee, adding a small douceur. With relief, Annabelle breathed in the sunshine and sweet, fresh air.

'I'm sorry, Rosabelle. I wouldn't have taken you down there if I had known it would have such an effect.'

'No, no! I'm very glad you did! An extraordinary sight!' She took another deep breath, then smiled apologetically. 'You'll have to forgive me, Giles. I am a poor creature, and ashamed of myself. But thank you for taking me. I would not have missed it for the world.'

They walked down to the horses. Once again Giles seemed to find it necessary to support her with a hand under her elbow as they trod over the rougher places on the path. Annabelle was grateful. She had not had such a long ride since leaving Temperley, and the unaccustomed exercise, followed by the experiences in the cavern, had used up her reserves. Time enough later to keep a distance between them. For the moment, she enjoyed the feeling of Giles's protective hand under her arm.

Lord Stanton and Lady Ordway were waiting for them at the inn. 'There you are!' cried Lord Stanton. 'Our good landlady was only waiting till you came to serve our dinner—there's spatchcocked eel, cold fowl, mutton chops, pigeon, gooseberry pie, cheese cake, tarts, custards—'

'Stop, stop!' Annabelle protested, as the buxom landlady showed them into the parlour which had been set aside for them. She surveyed the feast laid out for them. 'I thought I was hungry, but I shall never do justice to such a splendid repast!'

'I shall. Mrs Gantry, how do you go on? I'll swear you're handsomer than ever!'

'Get away with you, master Giles! Pay your compliments to them as deserves them! And who is this young lady, might I ask?' She regarded Annabelle with a benevolent eye, clearly hoping that she was Master Giles's young lady.

'Hmm,' said Lord Stanton. 'You're off the mark, Bessie. This is Mrs Ordway, Lady Ordway's daughter-in-law.' Mrs Gantry was disappointed, but curtsied and assured Mrs Ordway with undiminished good humour that she was very welcome.

After the meal Lady Ordway announced her intention of taking a short rest. The landlady had put a bedchamber at her disposal, and she intended to spend an hour or so on the bed before they set off for Avenell again. Lord Stanton approved of the idea, and said that he would stay in the tap room and exchange a few words with Tom Gantry. Giles looked at Annabelle.

'Would you like to rest, Rosabelle?'

'No, thank you. But I am perfectly capable of keeping myself amused if you wish to be with your father.'

'Well, Giles?' asked Lord Stanton. 'Do you wish to listen to Tom and me chatting over old times, talking of people you never knew? Or…do you think you should look after your guest?'

Giles gave his father a level look. 'I think you'd be easier without me, sir. Tom is not a fan of the reforms I've introduced at High Kimber. I'm sure you'd be more comfortable making gloomy forecasts about the probable outcome, without my presence to bring reason into the argument.'

'Go along with you, Giles. Enjoy a pretty girl's company,

and forget us fogies. We don't like change, that's our trouble. Off with you!'

'Would you like a walk, Rosabelle? The path along the stream is comparatively shady.'

'Yes, I should. But can we not walk up to the moor?'

'Of course. I am at your disposal, as you said. But…without daring to dictate to you in the slightest…' He said this gravely, but with a twinkle in his eye that made Annabelle laugh. 'May I point out that there is little or no shade up there, and the sun is still high? I know your intrepid spirit too well to suppose you will drive back in the barouche, and this means that you have a long, energetic ride back. You might prefer to conserve your strength for that. The stream here would be a more restful walk—it isn't one of your placid Berkshire meanderers, but I think you'd like it. But…I merely place the facts before you. You must make up your own mind, of course.'

'Giles, you worry me. I hardly recognise you in this guise!' Annabelle laughed up at him. 'But I would not wish you to think me deaf to reasonable persuasion. I'd like to see your stream.'

They walked in companionable silence through the garden at the back of the inn, past dogs and chickens somnolent in the afternoon sun. A wicket gate opened on to the footpath which led down to the stream. Giles was right. There was shade here, and a cool, refreshing breeze.

'Giles, where or what is High Kimber?'

'It's a small estate a few miles across the moor from here. Tom Gantry was a gamekeeper and general factotum there when he was younger.'

'Stanton land?'

'Yes,' he said curtly. Then, more amiably, 'I'm sorry. Yes, it belongs to the Stanton estates. It was out of our hands for some years, but I managed to get it back. It's not an important part, though. The land there is not much use—some sheep, a few cattle. Before he…got rid of it, my father used it chiefly as a…a retreat, I suppose. There's some fishing, and shooting on the moors. The house is comfortable, but quite small.'

'So what are you doing that meets with such disapproval?'

'Trying different breeds of sheep. Getting rid of the cattle. Don't worry, my father and Tom will enjoy their chat, but they know things were not doing well at High Kimber. It's so remote that no one bothered with it until we took it over again. But the country round about is glorious.'

'I should like to see it.'

Giles's expression had been rather forbidding, but now it softened. 'Is there any corner of Derbyshire you would *not* like to see?' he asked with a smile.

'I suppose not. I love it all so far. It's so different from Berkshire.'

'And even more different from London.'

'What? Oh, yes!' The mention of London had brought a feeling of constraint into the conversation, and there was a pause. Then she went on, 'It seems so remote now—London Society, the balls, the receptions, and all the rest. Unreal.'

'And you now feel you'd like to reform. To live a more useful life?' There was more than a touch of scepticism in his voice. After a morning of such mutual enjoyment and harmony this took Annabelle by surprise, and she was hurt.

'I'm not certain that you're in a position to judge what my life has been, Giles,' she said steadily. 'I assure you it has been useful at times. And though I am far from claiming that I am perfect, I see no need for any drastic reform.' She moved away from him and stood on the edge of the bank, looking down into the water. 'Are there trout in this stream?'

'Rosabelle, if only—'

'You could believe me? Trust me?' She looked up at him, meeting his eyes frankly and fearlessly. 'Why don't you try,

Giles? What have you to lose? You were wrong about
Stephen. Perhaps you've been wrong about me, too.'

'How can I be? How can you justify your denial that you
knew Falkirk?'

'Oh, no! That's not what I meant. I'm suggesting you have
faith, Giles. Not that you should have your doubts explained
away. What value would there be in an explanation, however
convincing it might be? Unless you have confidence in me as
a person, you could never be *sure* it was the truth.'

'You ask a lot, Rosabelle.'

'I don't deny that.' Annabelle held her breath, as they
walked on in silence. Was it possible that she could persuade
Giles to listen to her?

'I don't know what to think about you,' he said almost
angrily. 'I've never before known anyone who has confused
me more. When it comes down to it, things like "trust" and
"faith" are matters for instinct, not reason. But with you my
instinct is so very much at war with my reason.' He stopped
abruptly, as if he regretted having said so much. Then he
shrugged and went on, 'The evidence, which you seem to
treat so lightly, is damnably convincing.'

'So it is.' Annabelle's tone was neutral, though her heart
sank. She had failed.

'But when I see you with my father, with the Daventrys,
with my friends...I can't understand how anyone so loving,
so concerned for others, could be the woman I first thought
you. A schemer, an unfaithful wife, Falkirk's mistress, a
greedy opportunist...'

'Pray go no further, Giles! You are making my head swell
with your compliments!' Annabelle said bitterly.

'I tell you, I now find it impossible to believe you have
been such a woman! My instinct tells me that much, if nothing else. I believe you are telling me the truth when you say
that you were never unfaithful to Stephen.'

'Giles! I...'

'But there is obviously a great deal more which you are hiding from me. And that is where my instinct advises me not to trust you.'

Annabelle felt a curious mixture of delight and disappointment at Giles's words. That he no longer believed Rosabelle to have been unfaithful was a huge step forward, but he was perfectly right not to trust her in everything. And when he did discover the truth, it was by no means certain that he would find it possible to forgive her. She was very serious as she said, 'Giles, I swear you will know the truth in time, and my hope is that you will understand. But I cannot tell you the whole yet.'

He looked disappointed. 'So trust is to be one way only?'

'My secrets involve someone else. Otherwise I would tell you instantly.'

He nodded. 'You sound as if you sincerely mean it. In that case I will try to manage without. It won't be easy.'

'I imagine not. I...I am sincere in my feelings for you, Giles.'

'Are you?' he asked with a return of his glinting, teasing smile. 'What a pity! You regard me as a tyrant, an unfeeling despot, rude, overbearing, arrogant... Is that enough?'

'You forgot "high-handed".'

'Ah, yes.' He took her hand. 'Do you really think so badly of me, Rosabelle?'

'Not...not always.' As usual, his touch was confusing her, making it difficult for her to think, even to breathe! He was lifting her chin with one finger, forcing her to look at him.

'Tell me one thing,' he said. 'When this is all over, when Falkirk has been dealt with and Stephen's unhappy story is buried with him, when the truth is at last out between us...' He paused.

'Yes?' Her voice was hardly more than a whisper.

'Could you like me better?'

'I...I think so.'

'Good!' He bent and kissed her, very gently. 'I'll wait till then. Meanwhile…we shall be friends. Real friends, not just enemies in a truce. What do you say?'

With an effort Annabelle pulled herself out of the dream his words had called up. 'I'd like that. And I swear you won't be sorry, Giles.'

The excursion to Bradshaw was the first of several equally delightful days spent in exploring the countryside. Lady Ordway accompanied them to Chatsworth, Haddon Hall, and the town of Bakewell, but she was not interested in spending time on the moors and in the dales. Giles and Annabelle were free to ride almost anywhere they chose, accompanied only by a groom. The original two weeks passed in a flash. Lord Stanton declared that their sojourn at Avenell was doing them far more good than any waters Buxton could provide, and pressed them to stay longer. Avenell was proving a pleasanter place than Lady Ordway had remembered, and though she demurred, she was easily overruled.

'Avenell is at its best in this weather, Aunt Laura. Why don't you enjoy it?' said Giles. 'I plan to go to London for a while at the end of August, and I could escort you to Buxton just before I leave.'

'London?' said Annabelle sharply.

'There are people I have to see, Rosabelle. But I won't be away for longer than I can help. And you'll have Gregson and the other two to look after you.'

So it was decided. Giles and Annabelle were free again to roam the moors in perfect weather and perfect harmony. They spent one whole day at High Kimber, and Annabelle was entranced by it. The house was old—as old as Temperley—but built to withstand the harsh climate, the icy winds, the hail and rain which, she was told, winter brought to the moors.

'And not only winter. You've been fortunate, Rosabelle. The weather has been so fine that you haven't any notion of what the moors can be like in a storm—even in summer. In that respect it's like Spain. A man can die of exposure if he's caught out on the moor for long.'

Giles talked to Annabelle freely of his experiences in Spain and elsewhere with the Army. She became surprisingly well acquainted with the foibles and virtues of the great of Europe—including even the great Duke himself. On one occasion she accused Giles of not liking him. It was towards the end of the fortnight and they had ridden up to the moors once again.

'Like him? I've never considered whether I like him or not. He's short-tempered, pig-headed, unreasonable, high-handed—all of the things you've called me—and more. But I would trust him more than any other man alive to pull us out of a mess—as he did at Waterloo. He's the greatest man I shall ever meet.'

'I should love to meet him. Though I am very much beneath his notice, I know,'

Giles gave a crack of laughter. 'He would make straight for you, Rosabelle! The Beau has a connoisseur's eye for the ladies. A beauty like you would be a prime target.'

'The Beau? Is that what you call him?'

'Not in his hearing.'

'I find it hard to believe he would even look at me! In competition with all the great ladies of Europe? You exaggerate, Giles!'

He grew serious. 'I think you're the loveliest thing I've ever seen. Even when you were ill and unhappy last Christmas I thought you had possibilities. But now...' He looked up at her. She was standing on a rock, the better to view the scenery. The wind was teasing her hair and blowing her riding habit against her body, outlining long, slender thighs and a tiny waist. The effort of climbing the rocks up to her vantage point had given colour to her cheeks, and an extra sparkle to her dark blue eyes.

'Rosa!' He held up his arms, and she laughed and bent down to be lifted off her rock and into his arms. For a moment they looked at one another.

'The groom,' she murmured.

'He can't see us. He's down behind the hill with the horses.' Giles's voice was uneven. 'Rosa, I promised myself I wouldn't kiss you again before everything was clear between us.'

'But I didn't promise not to kiss you, Giles,' Annabelle said softly. She put her arms round his neck and pulled his head down to hers...

After a minute or two Giles lifted his head enough to murmur, 'Rosabelle, my lovely rose...'

Annabelle felt a cold shiver run down her spine. Giles, misinterpreting her reaction, held her more closely, and started kissing her again. She responded to his caresses eagerly, in a feverish effort to drown her fears. But some of the magic had gone, and after another minute Giles said firmly, 'This will not do. This is not the way.' He put her gently, reluctantly, from him. 'After I come back from London—'

'Giles, are you going to London to find Falkirk?'

'To see what has been happening, yes.'

'Oh, Giles, take care! I couldn't bear it if... Take care!'

'Don't worry Rosabelle. I shall come back within ten days to Buxton, I promise. And if you are not already submerged in invitations to the balls and concerts there, I shall take delight in escorting you. But we won't have the freedom we have enjoyed here.'

'Nor could we anywhere else! Our London friends would be shocked at how much time we have spent alone together. I'm not sure that even Aunt Laura is aware of how much. It would be considered most improper by the *ton*.'

'Most reprehensible, I agree. Have you felt threatened by it?'

'Not in the slightest.' She looked at him shyly. 'I have enjoyed getting to know your country...and you, Giles.'

'Thank you. But it isn't over yet, Rosa. There are years more to come—once we have rid ourselves of the...burdens of the past.'

Annabelle was as anxious as Giles to bring an end to the deceits and burdens of the past, but the weeks at Avenell had been so idyllic that she left with regret. Who knew whether she would ever see Avenell again? One person was convinced she would. Lord Stanton had watched the growing friendship between his son and his younger guest with complete approval.

'I won't bid you too hearty a farewell, Mrs Ordway. You're welcome to come at any time. But I expect Giles will see to that, and I would be happy to see him do so. It's time he settled down.'

'But, Lord Stanton, there's nothing—'

He chuckled. 'Roses all over your cheeks! I've embarrassed you! But time will tell whether I'm right or not. Meanwhile— I might even pay a visit to Buxton. I've a fancy to see Laura Ordway's face when she is drinking those waters!'

The carriage was loaded, the grooms sprang away from the horses and they were off on the last stage of their journey.

The healthful properties of the water at Buxton were known to the Romans, but it had been a fairly obscure place in the north of England until just forty-odd years before. Then the fifth Duke of Devonshire, husband of the exquisitely lovely Georgiana, had commissioned one of his architects to design an ambitious group of buildings to house visitors to a modern watering place. This was the Crescent, and, as the carriage carrying the party from Avenell drew to a halt in front of their hotel, even Lady Ordway paid tribute to the success of his designs.

The Assembly Room and other public rooms were to be found in the Great Hotel, which stood at the eastern end of the graceful curve of stone. At the western end was another hotel, the St Ann's, which was almost as large. And in the centre of the Crescent were five sets of comfortable lodging houses. An arcade of shops under a covered walkway linked the two hotels.

Giles had reserved a suite of rooms in the St Ann's Hotel. 'I thought it would be quieter for you here, Aunt Laura. St Ann's Well is close by, too.'

'The rooms are very handsome, Giles. Thank you. I dare say it is not more than five minutes' walk to the Great Hotel.'

'Less than that,' said Giles.

'Or possibly much more—there are some delightful shops, I see, on the way,' Annabelle remarked with a smile at Lady Ordway.

Indeed, Buxton proved to be much more pleasant a place to stay than Lady Ordway had feared. The new buildings were commodious and comfortable, the shops in the Arcade could satisfy the most demanding tastes, and the company, though not quite as worldly and sophisticated as that to be found in London, Brighton or Bath, was sufficiently interesting to keep Lady Ordway happy. The day after they arrived Giles took them to the Great Hotel and introduced them to the Master of the Rooms. Under this worthy's benevolent eye they entered their names in the Subscription Book, and were introduced to a number of ladies and gentlemen, all of whom, as Lady Ordway later remarked, seemed to have a surprising elegance of mind, and dress.

'For you know, Giles, that I was very doubtful of what we should find here by way of company. I am very favourably impressed.'

Annabelle had been reading the Rules of the Ballroom. 'There are balls every Wednesday, Aunt Laura, and on Mondays and Fridays you can play cards—though I believe there's a card room, as well, isn't there, Giles?'

'Yes, there is. But I'm afraid that you'll have to ask the Master to introduce you to suitable partners for the next ball. I'm off to London as soon as I am sure you are comfortably settled.'

'Giles!'

'I'm sorry, Aunt Laura. I have urgent business there, but it shouldn't take too long.' He looked at Annabelle. 'I'll be back as quickly as I can.' But then he stopped. It was impossible to say anything more. Agreeable as Buxton was, it was too busy a place for anything but the briefest of private conversations. The freedom they had enjoyed on the moors was a thing of the past.

It was ironic that when their place of retreat was eventually betrayed to Falkirk, it was done quite unconsciously. And by someone with every reason to wish them well.

Chapter Thirteen

When Giles reached London he set about gathering information—though the city was very thin of society. Old Lord Banagher was holding on to life by a thread, and Falkirk must be expecting to hear that he had succeeded to the title at any moment. Gossip had it that the new Lord Banagher would waste no time in seeking a wife and settling down to enjoy his elevated position.

There was also news of Selder. One of Giles's old friends worked in the Navy Office and had been investigating Kingsley.

'I'm sorry, Gil. I know Kingsley was one of your cousin's closest friends, but he almost certainly killed himself because he knew he was about to be found out. He was giving information about shipping to a man called Selder—you've heard the name?'

'Yes, I have.' Giles hesitated, then said, 'I'm about to make an accusation which I cannot yet prove.'

'Dangerous work.'

'I'm sure it will go no further. Freddy, what would you say if I told you that Selder is another name for Julian Falkirk?'

'Falkirk!' But, after this first astonished exclamation,

Commander Halton fell silent. Then he said, 'You know, Gil, it wouldn't surprise me at all. It would fit in with one or two other things we've heard. Yes, Falkirk might well be the man, though, like everything else in this damned case, neither you nor I can prove anything. If, as I understand, Falkirk is about to move up in the world, you'd need impeccable evidence. He's acquired some powerful friends.'

'What sort of evidence?'

'Unimpeachable witnesses willing to swear to the link between Falkirk and Selder. And something which linked either, or both, to criminal activity. Preferably written. Good enough for a court of law, anyway. Listen, I'd be delighted to hear from you if you learn anything else. My friends would be more than grateful if we could nail the fellow. Everything seems to have gone quiet at the moment, so there's no chance of catching anyone red-handed.'

A letter to Giles from Charlie Fortescue gave a possible explanation for this lack of activity.

Dear Gil,

I have a small item of news for you. Da Costa has been found, but I'm afraid he will not be the source of information we had hoped for. He appears to have had a fatal disagreement with some of his friends here in Bristol. His body was fished out of the harbour two nights ago. If I hear any more I'll let you know.

I hope your other enquiries are meeting with more success than this.

Yours, Charlie

Falkirk didn't leave anything to chance, thought Giles grimly. Venetia, Stephen and Da Costa—all eliminated.

Possibly Kingsley, too. And Rosabelle? No, that was one death that Giles was not going to allow. Not while there was breath left in his body. He suddenly felt he could stay in the city no longer. He must get back to her, see that she was safe.

When Giles arrived in Buxton, the first person he encountered after a tediously slow journey was Gregson.

'Any sign of untoward interest in the ladies, Gregson?'

'None at all, sir. But they are generally admired. Very popular we are, sir.'

'Oh?'

'Her ladyship has made one or two friends among the gentry here—there's a sprinkling of older tabb— I mean older ladies, Colonel Stanton, sir. And Mrs Ordway is all the go with the younger ones. Out most days, she's been. I've had my work cut out to keep an eye on her.'

'I wouldn't have thought there'd be that many young men at Buxton.'

'Oh, it's not that many, Colonel! Just the one.'

Giles stopped. 'Indeed? Who's that?'

'Lord Monteith, sir. Very taken with Mrs Ordway, he is.'

'That young puppy!' The exclamation was out before Giles could stop it. But well aware of the impropriety of discussing such matters with Gregson, he went on with a frown, 'I'm glad to hear she has been kept amused. Is Lady Ordway well?'

Gregson failed to notice the warning signals. 'I don't think she likes the waters much, sir. But she's pleased as Punch at Mrs Ordway's success. Hearing wedding bells, I imagine.'

'Wedding bells? What rubbish is this? What the devil are you thinking of, Gregson? Don't let me hear any more damned stupid gossip about your betters!'

'Sir!' Gregson drew himself upright and looked suitably rebuked. Still frowning, Giles strode into the hotel and went up to his room.

'So that's the way of it!' said Gregson to himself. 'Well, well!'

By the time Giles entered the Assembly Room dancing had already begun. He had no eyes for the stately Corinthian columns, the handsome marble fireplaces, the magnificent ceiling decorated in the style of Mr Adam, though the room was generally accepted as one of the Crescent's chief splendours. What he saw was Lord Monteith leading Mrs Ordway down the room, with an air of triumph, while the rest of the world, it seemed to him, looked on in approval. Giles joined his aunt at the side of the ballroom and grimly prepared to wait for the end of the set.

'Giles! We had quite given you up! How nice to see you!' said Lady Ordway. 'Rosabelle is dancing with Lord Monteith. Such a handsome couple.' She looked fondly at the two on the floor. 'I must tell you that I have great hopes. He has been most particular in his attentions.'

Giles's eyes followed hers, admiring Rosabelle's graceful movements. 'And what about the lady?'

'Rosabelle? Well, Giles, it would be an excellent match, would it not? And she seems quite taken with him. Look at her!'

Giles's first reaction was one of angry protest, but then he looked again at the couple, and started to grin. Rosabelle was the very picture of a polite young lady enjoying herself at a ball, exchanging snippets of conversation with her partner, and accepting his obvious admiration with becoming modesty. Though it was understandable that the company at Buxton should be deceived by her expression of smiling interest, it did not deceive him for one instant. The poor girl was bored beyond measure.

Much cheered, Giles looked and wondered at his aunt's blindness. How could anyone who knew Rosabelle fail to see the signs, the total absence of everything which made her special? Her enchanting, heartwarmingly spontaneous smile, the confiding tilt of her head when she was intrigued, the eager readiness to take up the conversation again when the movement of the dance had interrupted it...

He relaxed and enquired of his aunt how she was enjoying life in the watering place, complimenting her on the obvious benefits of her regime.

'The waters must be doing me some good, Giles, for they are perfectly horrid to taste! But the climate here is excellent! Even on the hottest day there is always a breath of air—I suppose it is because Buxton lies so high.'

'I'm glad to hear it, Aunt Laura. Ah! The end of that interminable dance.'

Lord Monteith was leading Rosabelle off the floor. He was still talking to her, and she still maintained her air of courteous interest. But when she saw Giles she stopped dead, and the enchanting smile he had remembered illuminated her lovely face.

'Giles!'

If Giles had suffered the slightest pang of jealousy on hearing of Lord Monteith's pursuit of Rosabelle, it evaporated without trace in the spontaneous warmth of that smile. She recovered herself immediately, however, and continued so calmly with civil enquiries about his journey that, had he not known her better, he might have thought he had imagined it. Certainly Lady Ordway and Lord Monteith had not noticed anything. The latter spoke as soon as there was a gap in the conversation. He asked with the air of a man who was sure of his reply.

'Mrs Ordway, may I have the pleasure of the supper dance?'

'I'm afraid not, Monteith. Mrs Ordway should pay some attention to the head of the family, now that I have returned. Duty before pleasure, you know.'

Giles's words could not have been better chosen to appeal

to this dutiful young man. Lord Monteith nodded, bowed, and excused himself, promising to approach Mrs Ordway later.

'Really, Giles! How dare you dispose of my beau in that cavalier way! As if I owed you any duty!'

'No, but I recognise mine to you! And rescuing you from that pompous young ass is the least I could do. Do you care to dance?'

'You don't deserve that I should!'

'Good! I should much prefer to talk. Shall we sit down? I could fetch you both something to drink. What would you like, Aunt Laura?'

Lady Ordway was staring at Giles rather strangely, as if a new and startling idea had just occurred to her. 'I...I...think I shall have a word with Lady Skelmersholme, Giles. She is on her own at the moment. I am delighted to see you back. But I can talk to you tomorrow, after all. Excuse me.'

She moved away, nodding to this acquaintance and that as she went.

'Would you like to sit down, Rosabelle? Or shall we take a turn outside?'

'Please, I should love to walk! It's very hot in the room.'

'I think the weather must be changing. There's a sultry feel to the air.'

Giles and Annabelle went down the wide staircase and out across the gravelled forecourt to the Slopes beyond. They were not alone. The heat of the rooms had tempted others to take the air, and the Slopes were dotted with ladies in their pale ball gowns and gentlemen in evening dress. They strolled up the grassy incline. Annabelle was happy to remain silent, enjoying the faint breeze and the sounds of music which drifted across from the open windows of the Assembly Room.

'Aunt Laura looks well,' said Giles.

'She is enjoying herself.'

'And you? Have you been enjoying yourself, Rosabelle?'

'Of course.'

'If I may say so, you looked rather bored when I first saw you.'

'You may not say anything of the kind! I was not in the slightest bored! This is mere prejudice against Lord Monteith, who is a most estimable gentleman.'

'Oh, Rosabelle! You may deceive the rest, but you cannot deceive me.'

Her eyes flew to his, then dropped. 'I…Lord Monteith has been very kind while you have been away.'

'So I hear. I'm afraid you have been raising false hopes in the young man's breast.'

'What makes you think they are false?'

'You won't marry Monteith.' Once again her eyes flew up to meet his. What she saw there caused the delicate colour to rise in her cheeks. 'Not while I am alive,' he added, casually.

'Really, Giles! You always think you have the ordering of everything! Allow me to tell you that Lord Monteith is the epitome of every girl's dream—rich, eligible, personable…'

'But not for you. I know you too well.'

'Wha…what do you mean?'

'Tell me, if you can, that I'm wrong.'

'I shan't choose to tell you anything. But I shall soon begin to wish you had not come back if you are going to tease me. How was London?'

'Pretty empty. I saw some friends. Falkirk had not as yet come back from Bath.' He eyed her carefully. 'Rosabelle, how many people have you written to since being here?'

'Only my sister. Why do you ask?'

'I was wondering how Monteith knew you were here.'

Her tone was cooler as she said, 'I am aware that your opinion of me is low. But I do not write to gentlemen I hardly know, Giles. Lord Monteith is here with his great-aunt. We met by chance.'

'Good. Let us hope there's no one in London he would be likely to tell. What about your sister?'

'My sister?' As usual, Annabelle grew wary when her sister was mentioned. 'What about her?'

'Will she tell anyone where you are?'

'It's most unlikely. She lives very quietly at Temperley. Unless she says something to Mr Winbolt.'

'Winbolt?'

'Yes, m— her neighbour in Berkshire.'

'It's not a common name. Is that Philip Winbolt? Of the Second Dragoons? With a grandfather in Arlington Street?'

'I don't know about his army career, but he has a grand-father in Arlington Street, yes. Do you know him?'

'I should say I do! A great fellow. Gentleman Jack, we used to call him.'

'Really? Why was that? Was he…was he rather too much of a gentleman, then?' asked Annabelle carefully.

'As polite and neat a fellow as you ever met. You wouldn't think he would willingly offend a soul. But give him a horse, put a sword in his hand and an enemy to fight—my God, what a transformation! Rides like a whirlwind and fights like a demon. There isn't anyone I'd rather have by my side in a fix. Well, well, well. Gentleman Jack in Berkshire, eh? Your sister knows him, you say?'

'He's…he's a neighbour.'

'What did you think of him? You met him when you were at Temperley, surely?'

'Er…the Winbolts were away for the whole of the time. My sister seems to approve of him.'

'Very popular with the ladies, was Philip. But discreet. He won't talk. And if he did meet Falkirk in London, he'd have the chap's measure in no time. I think we're safe there.'

Annabelle forgot to mention Philip's sister, Emily, who was also in Rosabelle's confidence. And she could not possibly have known that Philip would take his sister to London at the point when Falkirk was scouring the capital for information about Rosabelle Ordway's present whereabouts, nor that Emily would be introduced to the future Lord Banagher, and find him a charming man, who shared her interest in the theatre. And that, in the course of their conversation, she would mention, quite harmlessly, that her friend's sister, Mrs Ordway, was taking the waters at Buxton.

But the result was dramatic.

Giles had hardly been back a week when Gregson told him that a stranger from London, a tall, good-looking fellow with blond hair, had arrived in Buxton and was making enquiries about a Mrs Rosabelle Ordway. Gregson, a lad Giles had always said was born to be hanged, had feigned ignorance, but had most obligingly offered to find out where the lady was staying and promised to bring the information the next day to the gentleman's hotel, the White Hart. This seemed to suit the newcomer—he seemed strangely reluctant to be seen abroad himself, and didn't seem to object to the delay. He was waiting for a friend to arrive, he said.

Within an hour of receiving this information, Giles had completed his arrangements. A surprised Annabelle and an absolutely outraged Lady Ordway had been bundled out of the hotel, and urged into Giles's travelling coach. Servants and luggage were bundled off, too. Annabelle noticed that not only were Goss and Gregson in close attendance, but two grooms were riding alongside. Giles was leaving nothing to chance.

'But, Giles, it is too bad of you! I don't understand! I don't understand at all! Where are you taking us? And why did you refuse to tell us before this?'

'To Avenell, Aunt Laura. To stay with my father again. And I didn't want anyone in the hotel to overhear.'

Annabelle looked at Giles with a slight frown. 'Falkirk?'

'Fraser is in Buxton. Somehow or other Falkirk has learned where we are.'

'Giles, before we go another mile I insist on knowing what is going on!' said Lady Ordway. She sounded most unusually angry. 'What do you mean by saying I shall be safe and comfortable? I was perfectly safe and comfortable at Buxton!'

Giles looked at a loss, but Annabelle nodded her head at him. 'It is better that you tell Aunt Laura, Giles. Being kept in the dark is far more nerve-racking than the truth, however unpalatable.'

'The hotel at Buxton was too public a place to be safe, Aunt Laura. Avenell was once a fortress, and it can be so again.'

'But why on earth should we need a fortress?'

Picking his words with care, Giles told his aunt of the serious threat Falkirk represented to Rosabelle's safety. 'Apart from two men who are his closest associates, Rosabelle is the one person left alive who can identify Falkirk with Selder, the man who, among other things, murdered Stephen. I have men looking for evidence to incriminate Falkirk, but until then Rosabelle must be kept safe.'

'But that's impossible! I think it is time I told—'

'Please don't bring Annabelle into this, Aunt Laura!' said Annabelle desperately. 'I know you feel she ought to be told, but we cannot at the moment consult her. I have every confidence in Giles. Leave Annabelle in peace at Temperley. You know she has other things on her mind.' She turned to Giles. 'I should have told you this when we were speaking of your friend, Mr Winbolt, Giles. My sister and Mr Winbolt are in a fair way to making a match of it.'

In spite of his worries Giles was intrigued. 'Gentleman Jack in love? And with your sister, Annabelle?'

'Exactly!' said Annabelle with a meaning look at Lady Ordway.

'When this is over, Rosabelle, I insist on meeting the lady! I'd like to see the girl who has caught Philip Winbolt at last.'

Annabelle smiled at him with the strange sadness Giles had noticed once before. 'You shall, Giles, you shall!' she said.

'Good God, what is all this?' was Lord Stanton's greeting as the two coaches with four outriders drew up outside the Great Hall. Giles had sent one of the grooms on ahead to warn his father, but his message had been brief. 'One two, three, four… Giles, what the devil is going on? Come in, come in, Laura, and you too, my dear Mrs Ordway! What a time to be arriving, you must be worn out. Come in!'

In the short time given him Howells had done wonders. The ladies' bedchambers had already been prepared, and a tray of refreshments was waiting on the table in the Little Parlour. Lady Ordway sank down on to a conveniently placed chair.

'Lionel, you must forgive us. I don't perfectly understand why we have come here in such haste, but I am sure it must be highly inconvenient.'

'You are talking nonsense, Laura! I am delighted to see you back here, though I am even more in the dark than you are! Where is that boy of mine? Howells, go and find Master Giles.'

'I'm here, Father.' Giles came in with the air of a man who has accomplished as much as he can.

'Tell me what this is all about. Don't think I'm not pleased to see you all again—I'm delighted! It was damned dull after you'd gone to Buxton, and in fact you've saved me the effort of joining you all there in a day or two. But what's this army you've brought with you, Giles? It's worthy of a prince of the blood at least! Delusions of grandeur, my boy! You'd better send some of them to the inn—there aren't enough decent rooms over the stables here.'

'They are soldiers. Or at least ex-soldiers, well used to

discomfort. And they can't go to the inn, because they're here
to do a job.'

'What the devil is all this, Giles?'

'And it's really all so unnecessary. If only Giles knew…'
began Lady Ordway.

'Aunt Laura, I think we ought to leave Giles to explain the
situation to Lord Stanton, don't you? I expect you'd like to
change after the journey. Please excuse us, Lord Stanton. You
are very kind to make us so welcome.'

Annabelle swept Lady Ordway off to her room without
allowing her to say any more. They found Wilson unpacking
her mistress's bags, sniffing at the manner in which the
clothes had been bundled up.

'I shall have to give several of your dresses a good press,
my lady. Such a rush we were in!'

'Of course you couldn't pack properly, Wilson. We left in
an indecent hurry, and I know who should bear the blame!
Annabelle, you have twice interrupted me when I was about
to tell Giles the truth, but it cannot go on. I can't let him
continue to take all these absurd precautions to protect you,
when they are not at all necessary! You must tell him you
are not Rosa! He will be angry, I know, but not half so angry
as he will be if you leave it much longer.'

'I can't, Aunt Laura! And you must keep quiet, too! Not
for my sake, but for Rosa's. Philip Winbolt isn't merely one
of Giles's acquaintances—they are old comrades in arms, and
great friends! If Giles discovers that his friend is being deceived, what is he most likely to do?'

After a moment Lady Ordway said slowly, 'He would write
and tell him so.'

'Exactly! Now read this letter. I didn't show it to you before—it is too unhappy and I didn't want to distress you.'
Annabelle handed Lady Ordway Rosabelle's desperate plea
to keep up the deception for a little longer.

'My poor Rosa!' said Lady Ordway, wiping her eye. 'Oh,

Annabelle, what a fix we are in! Why did I ever let you talk me into it?'

'I meant it for the best! But, Aunt Laura, I know Philip Winbolt. If Rosa is given her chance, I am sure he will forgive her. Rosa will have her happy end, you'll see. It will just take a little time.'

'Are you sure?'

'I am quite certain. And you'll like Mr Winbolt. He is perfect for her.'

'Well, then, I suppose…'

'And what is Colonel Stanton going to say?' asked Wilson grimly.

'Colonel Stanton has nothing to say to anyone! Miss Rosa and Mr Winbolt can settle their future without him!' said Annabelle sharply.

'But what about your future, Anna!' wailed Lady Ordway. 'I had begun to think… Oh, it is too bad!' She started to weep again.

'Don't cry, dearest Aunt Laura. I'm sure I could make Giles understand. Eventually. And if I don't…' Annabelle stopped.

Lady Ordway lifted her head and started to look more cheerful. 'There are other fish in the sea! That's quite true! Anna, that's very true! Lord Monteith was extremely attentive. And he is even more eligible than Giles. He'll be a Viscount one day.' This thought seemed to provide real consolation. She went on, 'I cannot like deceiving Lord Stanton while we are his guests, but I will say nothing more. It would be wonderful if Rosa could be really happy again. And, as you say, Giles is not the only possible husband for you.'

Annabelle was so shocked at her reaction to these words that she was silenced. She stared at Lady Ordway without really seeing her, all her energy concentrated on the effort not to burst out with an angry contradiction.

'Good. I'm glad,' she said at last. 'Excuse me, Aunt Laura.

I…I think I'll go and tidy myself up. We left in such a hurry… Excuse me.'

She made her escape.

But once back in her own room Annabelle dismissed the maid who had been waiting for her, sat down at the dressing table and stared into the looking glass. Lady Ordway's words had removed a veil from something she had really known all along. Aunt Laura was wrong. Giles Stanton *was* the only possible husband for her! What she felt for him went far beyond friendship, or physical attraction, or any of the other excuses she had found for hiding the truth from herself. She had indisputably fallen irrevocably in love with the man. Marriage to anyone else was out of the question. She gave a deep sigh of despair. What a senseless piece of idiocy! How could she have been so stupid?

She stared at the reflection in the looking glass. She could hardly believe she was looking at herself. Sad and pale, a lost, vulnerable look about the eyes…surely this was Rosabelle! The lips twisted in a wry grin. If it were, there would be no problem! Oh, how could this have happened? She had been immune to love for so long, so complacent in her ignorance of its irrational powers—how absurdly ironic that she should eventually fall in love with the man who had been so ready to condemn her sister! She had sworn to make him pay for it, but it now looked as if she was to be the one who would pay.

Rosabelle Ordway was not the liar and cheat he had thought her, but Annabelle Kelland was! He could despise her with some justification—and certainly never love her back. She watched a tear roll down the cheek of the face in the mirror… But then she lifted her chin defiantly. She was not Rosabelle Ordway, she was Annabelle Kelland and that stood for something, too. Annabelle was not going to give in without a battle!

She was sure that Giles felt something for her—otherwise why go to all this trouble to protect her? What if she told Giles before the matter went any further, while she was still at Avenell? He could hardly throw her out, and with time she might persuade him...but there was Rosa to think of...

She would write to Rosabelle! Perhaps her sister's affairs had progressed to the point where the secret could come out... That was it! She would write to Rosabelle immediately.

But after the letter was written and sealed, and Lord Stanton had franked it for her, Giles refused to let her dispatch it.

'Rosabelle, it would be madness to write from here!'

'It's to my sister, Giles! I must tell her where I am—she'll be worried! It must go!'

'I'm afraid I can't allow it. I don't know how Falkirk knew we were in Buxton, but I suspect your correspondence had something to do with it. No, the letter will have to wait till I have heard from London. It won't be long now. Trust me!'

A few days later she was sitting in the garden admiring the view when he came in search of her. She watched his lithe figure striding along the terrace against the background of Avenell's massive grey stone walls, and she once again felt the kinship between man and surroundings. This was undoubtedly Giles's heritage. There was an unconscious pride, arrogance almost, in his movements, and she could feel the presence of generations of Stantons walking along the walls with him. But the Stantons appeared to be marching into battle.

'What the devil do you mean by this?' Giles demanded as he reached her.

The sun was in Annabelle's eyes as she looked up. 'What is it?' she asked.

'A letter, Rosabelle! A letter you gave to Gregson to post in Bakewell!'

'That's my letter!' Annabelle jumped up and snatched it from him. 'How dare you take it!'

'You're lucky I didn't tear it up, you little vixen! What do you mean by going behind my back to one of my own men?'

'You said yesterday that Fraser must have gone back to London. There's surely no danger now. And since I couldn't get word to my sister any other way, I had to ask Gregson to take it. If you had been more reasonable—'

'Reasonable! God give me patience! Don't you realise that Falkirk has other men working for him? Fraser is bound to have left someone behind in case we turn up again! And I'd be willing to wager a considerable amount that his deputy has already conscripted half a dozen men or more to find out where we've gone. It won't be long before they do—Avenell is, after all, an obvious place to look—but there's no sense in making them a present of the information! You're a fool, Rosabelle!'

Annabelle was by now as angry as Giles. 'I suppose you pay Gregson to go running to you with reports on everything I do!' she said icily.

'Have you paid the slightest attention to what I've said? Of course Gregson reports to me. All my men are under orders to tell me everything. And you needn't look at me with that basilisk stare—perhaps you've forgotten that it's all for your benefit.'

'For *my* benefit? That's a joke! You're enjoying yourself enormously, Giles! Back to war. Heroes, all of you! Well, I'm not one of your men, and I'm not under your command, and I shall do as I please!'

'Try it! You'll find you won't get very far, my girl. And if you were one of my men you'd learn that it's wiser not to cross me!'

'You're a bully, Giles! I always suspected it, and now I know it for a fact.'

'Bully or not, I want no more of your childishly stupid

obstinacy. You can send your letter when I'm satisfied the danger is over. Not before.'

He strode off again before she could find suitable words to reply. She was fuming. The fact that she loved him did not blind her to his faults. He was an arrogant, high-handed oaf, and she wouldn't be able to live with herself if she allowed him to get the better of her. That letter had to go!

It took a few days for Annabelle to form a plan to outwit Giles, and another few before circumstances were favourable. But the day finally came when Giles had to go to High Kimber to see to some business there, and took Goss and Gregson with him. As soon as they were safely away Annabelle dressed in her riding habit, put her precious, franked letter in her side pocket, and went in search of another of Giles's men.

'Good morning, Challing! I'd like you to do something for me, if you please.'

'Can't be done, Mrs Ordway, ma'am. Colonel's orders,' said Challing promptly.

'Whatever do you think I am going to say? I wouldn't dream of asking you to disobey Colonel Stanton's orders. What a notion! No, it's just that I was thinking I would exercise my horse—within the park, of course. On the front lawn. I have Lord Stanton's permission, and if you were with me there could hardly be any danger, I think.'

'Well, er…'

'Good! Let's get the horses.'

They cantered and trotted happily enough for some time, Challing ever watchful. At last, when his attention was elsewhere, Annabelle's hat, encouraged by a jab from her whip, went sailing off in a breath of wind and landed on the ground. Hearing her cry of dismay, Challing leapt from his horse and ran after it. Annabelle gave both horses a crack of the whip and they galloped off down the lawn towards the fence. The mare took the fence easily, the brown cob less so. A few more yards and the cob gave up. Annabelle and the mare went racing off towards the drive at the bottom. Before poor Challing had even caught his mount, she was on the road to Bakewell. All she had to do now was to get her letter to the Receiving Office, ready for the London coach.

Chapter Fourteen

It was market day in Bakewell, and the town was full of people, stalls and carts. The Receiving Office, she knew, was on the other side of the square, and, feeling rather noticeable on her horse without a groom or a hat, she dismounted, and tied the mare to a post outside one of the inns. Then she turned to make her way through the crowds who swarmed around her, jostling and pushing. Suddenly she felt herself being caught and dragged behind the back of one of the booths. When she opened her mouth to scream a handkerchief was thrust over her mouth.

For a moment she struggled, then a voice said in her ear, 'If you move an inch more you'll get this knife between your ribs.'

Convinced that her last moments had come, Annabelle stiffened. She would not give in without a fight. But the voice went on, 'I won't kill you unless I have to. But you'd be surprised, Mrs Ordway, at how very easy it is, if you know your job, to slide a knife into just the right place. And I'm an expert. I hope you understand? Nod, if you do.'

Annabelle nodded.

'Good. Now, you're going to walk with me to the carriage. I'll remove the handkerchief, but, if you want to live, you

won't make the slightest sound.' His arm was still tight round
her and she could feel the point of the knife against her side.
A second man put a cloak round her shoulders and removed
the rag. She took several deep breaths as they moved into the
open square.

'Make way there, make way!' her captor called. 'Can't you
see the lady is feeling faint? Make way!'

Annabelle could hardly believe what was happening. The
sun still shone, the crowds still chattered and laughed all
around them, but she was inexorably led to a closed carriage
which was waiting on the edge of the square. When they
reached it, she was pushed inside. The door was shut and the
carriage moved off. Annabelle felt stifled.

'Please,' she whispered. 'Please…let go of me! I need
some air.'

'Let her go, Burrows,' said the other man. 'She can't do
anything now.'

Burrows shrugged and released Annabelle. She sank back
against the squabs and closed her eyes, fighting to overcome
a deadly faintness. The carriage rolled on.

'Cor! What a piece o' luck, Burrows! How did you know
she'd come to Bakewell?'

'I was on the watch. Fraser said she'd be at Avenell.'

Cautiously Annabelle opened her eyes and gazed at her
captors. They could not have presented a greater contrast.
Burrows was short and stocky with dark hair and close-set
eyes. The man opposite had a long melancholy face. She
would remember both of them. When she looked back she
saw that Burrows's eyes were on her.

'What do you want of me?'

'I don't want anything!' he said. 'I was told to find you,
that's all.'

'Not to…kill me?'

'No. You'd be dead if I had.'

'Then why?'

'Fraser wants to talk to you.'

'Do you know why?'

'You have something he's been told to find.'

Annabelle was about to argue with him, but again decided to hold her tongue. It might be that this was the reason she had not already suffered the same fate as Venetia Stanton. Not yet, at least. She sat back to consider her situation. That it was perilous she had no doubt. Falkirk and his gang were ruthless, so much was certain. It would be some time before Giles heard of her disappearance, though she was sure he would come looking for her as soon as he did.

But until he found her she was on her own. She rejected the thought that he might not find her at all. So what should she do? She decided that all she could do for the moment was try to find out where they were taking her. And, giving the impression of being even more passive and helpless than she actually felt, she lay back with her eyes half closed...

The air was sultry, and it became very hot in the carriage. Burrows opened one of the blinds. Annabelle guessed they were travelling in a northwesterly direction—certainly what shadows she saw suggested this. After what seemed like an age her vigilance was rewarded. They turned off at a place she thought she recognised. If she was right the road would begin to rise... Sure enough, the pace slowed down and the surface became rougher. The air was still heavy, but a few degrees cooler.

They were high up on the moors. Suddenly, in the distance she caught sight of the strangely shaped stones she had seen on that first ride with Giles—and many times since. They were on the road to Bradshaw! In her excitement she had grown less cautious. When Burrows saw her looking out, he promptly drew down the blind. Annabelle bit her lip. She had been careless. It was vital he shouldn't know that she knew where they were.

'Where are you taking me?' she asked, letting her voice tremble. 'It all looks so strange and desolate! Where are we?'

'Never you mind. Is there anything to eat, Cartwright?'

So the other man was called Cartwright. Something else to note.

Some sort of sausage and bread was produced, and a flagon of ale. Annabelle had no liking for it, but forced herself to eat and drink a little. She needed to keep her strength up.

After another age the carriage came to a stop and Cartwright opened the door.

'For God's sake! Are you sure this is the place?' he exclaimed. Burrows pushed Annabelle before him into Cartwright's arms.

'It'll do till Fraser gets back. No one's going to look for her here! The farm is deserted, and the fellow who looks after the cavern is away.'

'I wouldn't look for the devil himself here. A godforsaken country, this is.'

Annabelle looked around, taking care not to seem other than tired and dispirited. She had been right! The carriage was standing in front of the set of semi-derelict buildings at Blackhole cavern. The cavern itself was only a hundred yards away. And High Kimber was just six miles distant across the moor...

'Ah, there you are! Well met.' Burrows was greeting a third man who had just ridden up. 'See to the horses, will you! They can have an hour's rest, then I shall take the carriage to Buxton. You can keep Cartwright company—he's scared.'

'I am not! I just don't like the place.'

'Never mind that, get the girl into the house. I'll bring the rest of the things in. Make sure you tie her up!'

'Oh, come on, Burrows, there's no need for that! Where would she run to up here?'

Burrows shrugged his shoulders. 'As you please.'

Annabelle allowed herself to be hustled into the house, her

mind busy with plans. There were now two points in her favour—she was free to run, and she knew where she was. How could she turn them to her advantage? She needed a horse…and time.

They had something else to eat, then Burrows and the driver of the carriage got up to go. 'I'll be back in the morning with Fraser. Don't damage our prize, Cartwright. She's to be delivered whole. You'd better see what you can do about the window, though. It looks as if there might be a storm before long. Till tomorrow, then.'

Burrows and the coachman went out, and some time later Annabelle heard the sound of the carriage being driven off. She wondered what time it was. The light was fading, but that might be because of the clouds which were massing towards the west, covering the sun.

'I'd better look for something to cover the window. We don't want our sleeping beauty's bedchamber to get wet, do we?' said the newcomer with a leer.

Cartwright said laconically, 'Touch her and you're a dead man tomorrow. She's prime meat, she is. Reserved for the chief.'

'Come on, then. Come and help me get this window sorted.'

Cartwright cast a glance at Annabelle. She was sitting on the ground, her back to the wall, the very picture of hopeless dejection.

'There might be something round the back…'

Annabelle got softly to her feet. She crept to the window and saw the men busy with a pile of ancient wood and what looked like old cloths. Picking up her skirts, she ran to the door, then scrambled desperately up the path towards the cavern. She heard shouts behind her and looked back. Cartwright and the other man were at the bottom of the slope. She was discovered. Waving her arms, she gave a terrified scream and plunged past the narrow throat into Blackhole cavern. But once out of sight her demeanour changed surprisingly. She moved purposefully along the side of the cavern feeling for the small irregularity which would tell her she had reached her goal…

When the men came storming through Annabelle was safely hidden in Giles's niche. 'The girl's a fool! There's no way out, and she could kill herself in here!' Cartwright was worried. His voice sent echoes all round.

'Are you sure? There's nothing at the other end?'

'There can't be! It goes into the hillside—doesn't it?'

'Well, she's not here, and, if there's no way out, then she must be further down. Come on!'

'Wait!'

Annabelle's heart gave a leap. She held her breath.

'What is it?'

'Go slowly! We don't want her slipping past us. You go on ahead and I'll follow.'

Breathing as shallowly as she could, Annabelle waited while the sounds of the men's footsteps faded into the depths of the cavern. She counted ten to make sure, then crept out of her shelter and made for the gate. Her hands were shaking so much that it took precious minutes to unfasten the hook, but she managed it, and the gate shut with an impressive clang. By the time the men came running back, Annabelle was at the bottom of the path, and racing for the stable. Here she saddled up the third man's horse and galloped off.

After a while she slowed the horse down. There was no sense in risking a fall in strange country, and though it was still only afternoon, heavy clouds in front of the sun were darkening the sky. The light was very poor. She was safe enough. The men would not get out of the cavern till someone came to release them, and High Kimber was a mere six miles away. All she had to do was to head in the right direction and hope that the storm would hold off till she reached it.

* * *

After half an hour Annabelle began to realise that a ride in full daylight with Giles leading the way had prepared her ill for the journey she was now attempting. The path was elusive, crossed with sheep tracks and old drainage ditches. Snatches of rain were making it slippy. Boulders could be avoided easily enough, but there were smaller stones and rocks which were difficult to see in the half-light, and she was often forced to dismount. But she kept the horse's nose pointed in the direction of High Kimber and plodded on, comforting herself with the thought that every step took her further away from danger.

Then the storm, which had been rumbling for some time, suddenly broke overhead with a spectacular flash of lightning, followed immediately by a loud clap of thunder. Annabelle's horse reared up in terror, so suddenly that she had no time to save herself. She fell, hitting her head on something hard…

It was the rain which brought her round. She lay for a moment, thankful for its refreshing coolness on her aching head. Then, as consciousness returned, she stirred and made an effort to sit up, but as soon as she put her hand to the ground an excruciating pain shot up her right arm. Sick and dizzy, she paused before attempting anything further. But she soon began to realise that she was in some danger. The rain was no longer a friend, it was fairly beating down, no longer refreshingly cool, but soaking through her riding habit, heavy and chilling.

She must stand up. There was no sign of the horse, but a cluster of rocks could just be seen through the curtain of rain. If she could get to those she might find some shelter for a while. With infinite care she took first one step then another, supporting her injured right arm with her left. By the time she had reached the rocks she was exhausted. She sank down and huddled under an outcrop, grateful for shelter from the storm, however slight.

Here she sat in a daze, forcing herself to think, in spite of
the throbbing of her head and the pain in her arm. She was
very cold. She dared not stay here for very long. Giles had
said that many had died of exposure on the moors, and she
could believe it. Though the thought of setting off again into
the full force of the storm appalled her, she knew she must...
This would not do! Annabelle Kelland was made of sterner
stuff than this.

Slowly, painfully, taking one step at a time she made her
way along the path. She knew another fall would finish her,
so she looked for and found a stick and, holding it in her left
hand, used it to test the ground ahead. There was no idea of
time, nor any thought to spare for her aches and pains. Her
whole being was concentrated on progressing towards High
Kimber.

After a while the rain eased, then stopped and the evening
sun came out again. The going became easier, and the path
started to descend. Surprisingly, this was more difficult to
manage, and each jolt as she dug her stick into the ground
for support sent more pain shooting through her head and
arm. She was barely conscious by the time she reached a
farmhouse on the edge of the moor, and only vaguely heard
the barking of the dogs as she went up to its door.

'Well, dang me! Whatever's this? A gipsy, by God! Get
off with you, before I let the dogs loose!' said an angry voice.
Annabelle could just make out a substantial form outlined in
the doorway against the light of a kitchen fire.

'Please!' Annabelle croaked. 'High Kimber.'

'What is it, Pa?' Another figure joined the first. A child's
voice.

'A gipsy woman.'

'Let me see... That's not a gipsy, Pa! Look at her dress—
it's soaked through, but it's a decent riding habit. She's hurt!
Let her in!'

The farmer took hold of Annabelle's arm as she staggered. The pain was so intense that she fainted.

The first thing she became aware of was the smell of lavender, scenting the sheets in which she lay. She opened her eyes. Giles's face hovered over hers.

'I wish you *were* here!' she said fretfully.

'I am. What did you think I was? A hallucination? I assure you I am not.'

'How did you find me? Where am I?'

'Burton sent for me. I've brought you to High Kimber.'

'That's good,' Annabelle said. His face drifted away again. 'No!' she cried in panic. 'Don't go away! Please don't leave me!'

'I won't go, I promise.' His voice, deep, calm, firm, penetrated the shadows surrounding her. 'Don't be afraid, Rosabelle. I shall stay with you.'

The next time she became conscious she could hear Giles in discussion with someone else.

'I cannot advise it,' said the stranger's voice. 'I understand the difficulties, but she really ought not to be moved again.'

'In that case we shall make do. I can have her mother-in-law fetched tomorrow, and my housekeeper will soon be back for tonight. Are you going to set her arm now?'

'The sooner the better. In case there are…complications.'

'Complications? What do you mean?'

The doctor came to the bed and saw that Annabelle's eyes were open. 'Mrs Ordway, you have broken your arm just above the wrist. The break is not a bad one, but it must be set. Do you feel you could allow me to set it?'

Annabelle looked at Giles, who nodded. 'Do it!' she whispered. 'Giles will help me.'

'Drink this first. You'll feel better,' said Giles, putting a glass to her lips. The liquid was bitter and she would have rejected it, but Giles held her firmly until it was all gone. Then he and the doctor waited quietly until Annabelle gave a sleepy smile.

'Much better,' she said vaguely.

The laudanum was not quite strong enough to dull all the pain that followed, though it helped. But by the time the doctor drew back and said, 'Excellent!' Annabelle had had enough. She was still clutching Giles's hand desperately when the time came for the doctor to leave, and Goss was fetched to see him out.

'Thank you,' she said, her voice a mere thread of sound.

'I'll call again tomorrow, Mrs Ordway. I can't stay now— I was only in the neighbourhood to deal with an accident at Beckin, and I must get back there. Sleep as much as you can.' His voice dropped. 'If she is restless, tell Mrs Brough to give her some of this. There's more than she will need there, but it's better to be safe. I'm not sure what time I'll come tomorrow.'

'Thank you.'

The doctor went and they were alone.

'Giles.'

'Yes?'

'I was so stupid.'

'I know. Challing caught me just before I was about to set off back to Avenell. Then Burton came. Falkirk found you, I take it.'

'It was a man called Burrows, but they talked about Fraser, too. They took me to Blackhole cavern. Wasn't that strange?'

'Very.'

'I'm sorry, Giles.'

'Try not to talk, Rosabelle. You can tell me another time what happened.'

He sat quietly, waiting for the drug to take effect again, only removing his hand when her fingers relaxed. Goss came silently back into the room and waited by the door.

Giles went over to him. 'Where the devil is Mrs Brough?'

'I don't know, sir. Gregson went some time ago. They ought to be back by now. But it's a terrible night.'

'Try to see what's happening, Goss. I'll stay here.'

It was some time before Goss returned, and when he did his expression was gloomy. He waited at the door till Giles joined him outside.

'Bad news, Colonel. The storm has washed away most of the bridges. There's floods all round. No one will get here tonight.'

'What about Doctor Bryne?'

'He must have just got across before the Kimber bridge went. I didn't see any sign of his gig.'

'Hell and damnation! You mean we're stranded?'

'Yes, sir. Sorry, sir.'

'Why the devil did Mrs Brough have to visit her daughter tonight of all the nights in the year? I shouldn't have let her go.'

'It seemed reasonable at the time, Colonel. You planning to go back to Avenell and stay with Lord Stanton for a while, like.'

'Yes. Well, Goss, it looks as if we're on our own for the present. Let us hope that the complications Doctor Bryne mentioned don't materialise. Tonight at least.'

'What might they be?'

'He didn't say, but I suspect fever. Mrs Ordway was very wet and cold for a good while. If she came across the moor… It seems incredible, but that's what she said she did. It's very exposed up there.' Giles was silent for a moment. 'Check our food supplies, Goss. I know you're a dab at catering. Mrs Ordway may feel like something when she wakes—and I wouldn't mind a bite myself. Burton might have some milk and a few eggs if there isn't enough here.'

'Excuse, sir, but mightn't it be a good idea to get the farmer's wife to come for the night?'

'It would be an excellent idea if he had one, Goss. But Mrs Burton died two years ago, and so far Burton has not replaced her.'

'I see. Difficult. Right, sir! So it's back to Spanish days, aye, sir?'

'It looks as if we might be grateful for the things we learned there if we're stranded for long, my old friend!'

Both he and Goss ate their fill before the invalid woke, and it was as well. Far from wanting anything to eat, she was in a high fever, tossing and turning in spite of the splint on her lower arm. It needed both Goss and Giles to hold her while Giles administered the draught the doctor had left behind, and even then she was still very restless for some time. She eventually fell into another heavy sleep. The two men looked at one another grimly.

'Complications,' said Giles. Goss said nothing, but set about tidying the sick room while his master sat in thought. 'We might have an hour or two before Mrs Ordway wakes again, but she will need someone with her all the time. It ought to be a woman, but that's impossible. Damn Mrs Brough! Help me to fetch the big armchair in from next door. We'll put it over in the corner by the window. I can sit in that.'

This they did, and Goss fetched some cushions and blankets. 'What the devil are those for, Goss?'

'You might find you can snatch a few winks, Colonel.'

'I don't want to sleep, damn you!'

'Beg your pardon, sir, but we don't know yet what we're in for. Mrs Ordway don't look too clever to me. What if the others don't get through tomorrow? You're going to need all the rest you can get.'

'Of course they'll get through! They have to! Doctor Bryne, too!'

'You haven't seen the rivers, sir.'

Goss's gloomy forebodings were to be fully justified. Another storm the same night put an end to any hopes of the flood waters subsiding.

But by morning the state of the rivers was the least of Giles's worries. There was no doubt in his mind that Rosabelle was dangerously ill. She couldn't stop shivering, though her skin was dry and hot. She was delirious, too, frantically calling out her own name, together with her sister's or that of Lady Ordway. Then she would cry out for him in a cracked, dry voice, which no drink could soothe. She was clearly in distress, complaining of pains in her head, bringing her arms up to hold it, and crying out when the broken arm protested.

He gave her as much as he dared of the doctor's draught, bathed her forehead, talked to her gently, soothing and comforting her as much as he could. It was a hard, long night. In the morning Goss was sent out to view the state of the rivers and came back with no good news. They were, if anything, higher than ever. He brought with him a couple of chickens and some eggs, however, and later in the morning produced a warm broth which he proposed to feed to Mrs Ordway.

'Leave her to me, Colonel. There's a plate of eggs for you in the dining room, and Mr Burton handed in a loaf of bread and some butter from his farm. There's some milk, as well. You need to have a wash and shave and a bit of a rest. Mrs Ordway will be safe enough with me—I'm an old hand at nursing, you know that.'

Giles went without much ado—he knew Goss's skills better than most. But he could not stay away long. Before Goss had managed to persuade Annabelle to take more than a mouthful of the broth he was back again, anxiously feeling her pulse and bathing the burning forehead. For the rest of the day he hardly left the room, tending the invalid with a skill and a

patience which would have astonished anyone other than his
friends from the Spanish wars.

The next day was no better, nor the next. He and Goss
developed a routine, taking it in turns to sit with the patient,
though Giles spent longer with her, and Goss did the cooking.
On the fourth day there was a slight improvement in the
weather, and on the fifth they were able to reach the next
farm across a corner of the moor, and to get a message sent
out to Avenell. The farmer's wife, though busy herself, agreed
to come in for a few hours during the day to do some nursing.

But the roads remained too dangerous, and the moor too
treacherous to go any further. Another day brought Gregson,
but before he could go back to Avenell with news of the
invalid, the rain started again and the river was impossible
for anyone to cross. It was perhaps as well, for the news
would not have been good. The fever had hardly abated in
the six days since it had first started. Goss was looking worried and Giles himself was almost desperate.

In the evening Goss brought in a lamp and set it over by
the window next to the armchair. 'How is Mrs Ordway, sir?'

'I don't know, Goss. I don't know! She's so still! Oh God,
Goss! I've been in many a tight corner before, but never one
like this. I feel so damned helpless!'

Goss nodded, then said, 'I'll sit here for a bit, sir, shall I?
How about a bit of fresh air for yourself before it's dark?'

'No, I'll stay here. You go.'

'I don't think I will, sir, if you don't mind. I'll stay within
call.' Goss made sure that water, medicine, some barley water
and the lamp were within reach, then went quietly out. Giles
stood by the bed. Annabelle was flushed again, turning her
head restlessly from side to side.

'Giles,' she murmured. 'Giles.'

'I'm here. What do you want? Are you in pain?'

'No. Goss gave me something… But I'm so hot… Giles…I didn't mean it.'

'What didn't you mean, my Rosabelle?'

'I'm not your Rosabelle!' Suddenly she was struggling to sit up, and though Giles tried to make her lie down again, she clung to him with her good hand and wouldn't let him go. Her eyes bright with fever, she said hoarsely, 'I'm not your Rosabelle, I don't want to be Rosabelle any more! She's a liar and a cheat and you'll never forgive her. Never.' Giles put his arm round her and held her close. He could feel the heat of her body burning through the thick calico of the night-gown they had found for her.

'Hush, Rosa, my love. Forget the past. We're different people now from what we were. It will sort itself out, you'll see. But you must stay quiet and rest!'

'Will it? Will it?'

'Of course it will!'

'I don't believe you!' she cried. 'I've lost you and it's all my fault. Stupid, stupid me!' Her head turned away from him against his chest and she started sobbing. Nothing he could do would console her. But when he tried to lay her back against the pillows and cover her up she put her hand out again.

'Don't go! Stay by me! Don't hate me, Giles, stay with me just a bit longer.'

'Rosa, I—'

'*Please*, Giles!' He felt her pulse—it was racing, and her breathing was rapid and shallow. She was trembling violently.

'Let me bathe your face and hands. You're very hot.'

'No! I'm cold, and I want you to keep me warm!'

Giles gave in. He lay down on the covers beside her and carefully took her into his arms, smoothing her hair from her forehead, and holding her like a child close to him. The attack lasted for a while longer, then she grew still. Eventually she gave a sigh of contentment.

'That's better,' she said. 'That's…better…'

Chapter Fifteen

When Giles woke the next morning he wondered where he was for the moment. It wasn't the first time he had woken up with a woman in his bed, but never before with a barrier of bedclothes between them. What the devil…? Then he remembered. He looked at Rosabelle. She was breathing regularly, and her skin was cool and moist. Her hair was a dark tangle of gold on the pillow, and Mrs Brough's nightgown, made for a more ample figure, had slipped from her shoulder to reveal the soft curves of her bosom. Giles felt somewhat light-headed himself. He bent to kiss the hollow which lay so enticingly between her breasts… When he raised his head, he saw that Rosabelle was awake. He felt himself flushing dark red, and pulled the edges of the nightgown together.

'I…I…forgive me!'

'Dear Giles. For what? Saving my life?'

'I didn't mean…'

'I know you didn't.' She took hold of his hand and held it to her cheek. 'And if I weren't so stupidly feeble I'd show you that I forgive you. But I can hear Goss coming and I think you should be somewhere else when he comes in.'

Giles jumped off the bed, and by the time Goss entered he was in the chair by the window. Goss took one quick glance at the hollow in the covers on the bed and then studiously avoided it with his eyes.

'Good morning, Colonel. Breakfast is ready. How is Mrs Ordway?'

'I think I'm almost myself again, Goss. Have I been a great nuisance?'

'Good morning, ma'am. Not at all, ma'am. A privilege to serve you. I can see you're better. Would you like some breakfast?'

'I think I would. In fact, I am starving! But I should like to get up first. Could you send Mrs Brough in?'

'Well, now. I'm afraid Mrs Brough ain't here, ma'am. There's only the Colonel and myself until the woman comes in from the farm.'

'What? But who…?' Annabelle went scarlet. Without a word Giles got to his feet and lifted her off the bed. He wrapped her in a blanket, and carried her to the dressing room. He told her to wait, then went out and returned in a minute or two with a towel and a clean nightgown.

'Will you be safe on your own?'

'Thank you, yes. Giles?'

'Yes?'

'What happened to Mrs Brough?'

'She hasn't been able to get here. We've been cut off by floods.'

'I see. Who…who has been looking after me?'

'One of the farmers' wives.'

'All the time?'

'No. Goss and I have done a small amount. But don't worry. I've behaved impeccably. Till this morning.' He went and Annabelle looked round her. Warm water had been put into a washbasin on the stand, and a towel was waiting beside it. A commode chair was nearby. It took some time to get used to managing with only one hand, but she succeeded, and in twenty minutes she was ready again. She took a step to the door, and nearly fell. In answer to her call, Giles came to carry her through to the bedchamber. In her absence someone had changed the bedlinen. Her eyes filled with tears.

'How kind you both are!' she said.

He smiled down at her. 'Come, Rosabelle! This won't do. Tears were allowed when you were not yourself, but now you have recovered your wits and must behave sensibly.'

'Er…how long was I out of my wits, Giles?'

'It's nearly a week now. The longest week of my life.'

'It must have been. I can think of few things more tedious. I'm sorry, Giles.'

He settled her down on the bed and drew the clothes up around her. 'It wasn't exactly tedious. Well, now. Breakfast? Mrs Whatever comes in about half an hour. She has to attend to her own chores first.'

After another day the river was low enough for Mrs Brough to return, and for Gregson to ride back to Avenell. There was no excuse now for the unusual arrangements which had been in force while they had been completely cut off, and Giles's visits to the sick room were strictly conventional. On one of them he produced a tattered, indecipherable rag of paper.

'It's yours, I believe. The famous letter. Mrs Brough found it in the pocket of your riding dress. I'm afraid you'll have to write it again, Rosabelle.' He handed it to her. 'Was it so important? You nearly died for it.'

'No…it wasn't important,' said Annabelle, smoothing it out mechanically.

'So it was just that you couldn't bear what you saw as my arrogance. Is that it? If so, I'm sorry. More sorry than I can well say.'

'Don't! It wasn't that. Not…not exactly. It's true that I wanted to tell my sister that I was safe, but there was something else. Something I needed to ask her.'

'Rosa, I've had my suspicions for some time. If I ask you something, will you tell me the truth?'

Annabelle stared at him. If Giles challenged her here and now, she would have to tell him, whatever it meant to Rosabelle. She nodded.

'Is your sister Annabelle at the root of your reluctance to confide in me? I've decided that she is the only person you would defend at such expense to yourself. Am I right? Annabelle is somehow involved with Selder, and you are protecting her.'

'Wha…what makes you think that?'

'One of Selder's contacts was at Woolhampton. You remarked yourself how near it was to Temperley. Annabelle could have met him in Berkshire. You have sworn to me that you did not have an affair with Selder, and I am absolutely convinced of your integrity, your basic honesty. But there is *something* about him which you know and are concealing. It must concern your sister.'

'Giles, I…'

'You know, if Annabelle *is* involved, I would find it difficult to forgive her. She has caused you so much trouble.'

'My sister is innocent, Giles!'

'Is she? I hope so. Philip Winbolt is a good friend of mine. We neither of us enjoy being deceived.'

'No. No, of course you don't. That's very natural,' Annabelle said wanly. 'Giles, my head is aching…I can't think very clearly at the moment. Would you excuse me? You will have your answer soon, I promise.'

'I'm a brute, hectoring you like this. You're still very weak. I'm sorry. Tomorrow we shall go back to Avenell—I've thought of a way we can manage it. Rest now. The journey will make some demands on you. We'll discuss your family affairs when you're stronger.' He took her hand and kissed it, then went out.

Annabelle walked to the bed, threw herself down on it and

buried her head in the pillows. She was filled with black despair. There was to be no happy end, not for herself, and not for poor Rosabelle. Bitter tears soaked the pillow, and sobs racked her slender body...

'Why, Mrs Ordway, whatever's wrong? My poor lady! Colonel Stanton, Colonel Stanton!' Mrs Brough hurried out of the room, and came back with Giles.

'Rosabelle! My dearest girl! Oh, God!' He came to the bed and tried to take Annabelle in his arms.

'Leave me alone!' she cried wildly. 'Leave me alone!'

'Mrs Brough, fetch some of Doctor Bryne's draught, if you please. Mrs Ordway is ill again.'

With a doubtful look at her master the housekeeper went away.

'Rosabelle! Listen to me! You must be calm. This is not doing you any good at all. Forget what we talked about if that is what has upset you. We won't mention it again. Only be calm, my love!'

Mrs Brough came back with the medicine.

'Here, drink this,' he said. 'It will make you feel better.'

'I don't want your medicines! I want to be well, to go back to London! To Temperley!'

'You can't go anywhere till you are strong enough. You've been very ill, Rosa. Dangerously ill. Now be a good girl and take the sedative.'

'Give it to me, Colonel Stanton. I'll see she drinks it.' Mrs Brough took the glass from Giles. 'Don't worry, sir!' she added as she looked at his face. 'Mrs Ordway will be as right as rain soon. She's bound to have these fits of depression for a while. She must take it slowly, that's all. You can't hurry these things.'

'No,' he said heavily. 'No, I was a fool. But I'd like to get her back closer to civilisation, Mrs Brough.'

'So you shall, so you shall, sir. But perhaps not tomorrow.'

* * *

In the event it was another two days before Doctor Bryne agreed to let Annabelle make the journey to Avenell, and then only because Giles insisted. Every care was taken, but when she was finally put to bed in Avenell she was exhausted.

'Rosa! What happened to you? Oh, look at her—she's a wraith.' Lady Ordway hovered anxiously as Giles carried her in.

'Aunt Laura, it's so…so comforting to see you…' Annabelle's voice wavered, and Giles intervened.

'She needs as much rest as possible. I'll get my father's doctor to have a look at her tomorrow, but Doctor Bryne said rest was the most important part of the cure. Rest and good food.'

Rest and good food was what Annabelle had in plenty in the next few weeks. Mrs Dunnock produced no end of tempting dishes, and Lord Stanton brought some delicacy or other every time he visited her. The weather, having had its fling, smiled on them, and the countryside glowed red and gold in the autumnal sunshine. As she grew stronger Annabelle spent a little time each day in the garden, and fell in love all over again with Avenell and the country round it. Giles treated her with gentle consideration, never once putting pressure on her or referring to their conversation about her sister. It was Annabelle who finally broached the subject.

'Giles, I still owe you an explanation.'

'It can wait, Rosa.'

'I want to go to Temperley soon. I must talk to my sister. Then…then I'd like you to meet her. I think you'll understand then what it was all about.'

'I have some news for you. Falkirk seems to have made the acquaintance of the Winbolts. He has been to Shearings. It seems he went to Emily Winbolt's birthday party a few weeks ago.'

'Falkirk!'

'Yes. But he's back in London now.'

'I must go back!' said Annabelle, getting agitated. 'I must see my sister.'

'I'll take you and Aunt Laura back to London as soon as the doctor says you may go. It won't be long now. Everything is in readiness.'

'Please, Giles, please make it soon!'

He took her hands and held them in a warm clasp. 'I will. I have every reason to clear this affair up as soon as possible. Then…'

'We shall have no secrets,' said Annabelle, trying to keep the sadness out of her voice.

The journey southwards, though not as leisurely as the one to the north, had to be taken in easier stages than Annabelle wished. She was desperate to see Rosabelle. It was no longer a simple matter of ending their charade. If Falkirk knew the Winbolts, then her sister was in exactly the same danger from him as she herself had been—and with more reason! She was not an easy travelling companion. She resisted all the efforts of Giles and Lady Ordway to keep their travelling stages short, and sat in fretful silence when the state of the roads forced them into a more moderate pace.

Her companions made allowance for the fact that she was still weaker than she would admit from her illness and bore with her patiently. But on the last day, when they were expecting to reach Temperley by nightfall, early November fog in the Thames Valley reduced their progress to a snail's pace.

'I'm afraid we are going to have to stop for the night here,' said Giles, as they crawled into Wallingford.

This was the last straw for poor Annabelle. 'No!' she cried. 'It's not yet three o'clock! We can still get to Temperley.'

'Look outside, Rosa! The fog is thicker than ever. I am not going to risk being stranded for the night in some Godforsaken village, with no respectable inn, or anywhere to put the horses. Wallingford has the merit of providing at least two comfortable places to stay.'

'But I must get to Temperley! We've already wasted so much time. You promised!'

Lady Ordway intervened. 'Rosa dear, you are being unreasonable. I am sure Giles is right. And I confess, I am quite weary myself. This fog is very enervating.'

Annabelle looked at her and was ashamed. Wrapped up in her own problems, she had failed to notice how exhausted Lady Ordway was. 'I'm sorry, Aunt Laura. Of course we shall put up for the night here. But I warn you, I shall want to set off in very good time tomorrow!'

'At dawn, if you insist,' said Giles. 'And if the weather permits.'

But when she went into Lady Ordway's bedchamber the next morning she was greeted with bad news.

'Her ladyship had a very bad night, Miss Rosabelle,' said Wilson. 'She isn't fit to travel.'

'Be quiet, Wilson! I'm sorry, Anna,' said Lady Ordway weakly. 'I shall be perfectly well in a little while. I won't keep you back, I promise.'

'Aunt Laura, I am ashamed of myself. There's no question of your getting up before you feel well enough! Does Giles know?'

'Not yet.'

'Then I shall tell him.' Annabelle went to seek Giles.

When she told him the news, he looked serious. 'Another delay. And I wouldn't place any reliance on the weather. The mist may well fall again. It is most unfortunate.'

'Do you have to be so pessimistic?' cried Annabelle, distraught. 'Yes, it is unfortunate, to say the least! But what can we do? However badly I want to see my sister, I cannot risk Aunt Laura's health. I'll let you know as soon as Wilson and

I can judge it is safe to travel.' She hurried away again before disgracing herself by bursting into tears.

A few minutes later Giles appeared outside Lady Ordway's room. 'Rosabelle, may I speak to you?' Annabelle came out of the room, shutting the door quietly behind her. 'How is Aunt Laura?'

'She's asleep. Apparently she was awake most of the night, and Wilson thinks sleep may be all she needs. With any luck we should be able to set off in two or three hours.'

'I have a better idea. You and Goss could ride on ahead to Temperley, and I shall bring Aunt Laura as soon as she is ready to leave.'

'But I can't leave Aunt Laura!'

'Wilson and I are perfectly capable. There hasn't been a sign of Falkirk or anyone else since we left the north, so I think it would be quite safe as long as you have Goss as an escort. He's very resourceful.'

Annabelle looked at him doubtfully. She was strongly tempted. Not only would she arrive earlier at Temperley, but the scheme had another, unexpected, advantage, which Giles could not appreciate. She would be able to talk to Rosabelle before he met them together for the first time.

'Thank you, Giles. I'll do as you suggest.'

'But...' He smiled ruefully. 'You will take care? You are not yet fully yourself, you know. I don't want all my good work undone.'

Annabelle was overcome with a sudden rush of feeling. She loved this man so much. Why was she so desperate to reach Temperley and all that that meant? 'Giles,' she whispered. 'Oh, Giles!'

He put his arms round her. 'You'll be safe with Goss,' he said. 'I wouldn't risk it if I thought there was any danger.'

'It's not that. I...I just want you to know how...how grateful I am.'

'Grateful?' he asked, smiling down at her. 'Is that all? I'm not looking for gratitude, Rosabelle.'

Annabelle took his face in her hands. 'Have faith in me, Giles. Have faith. Please.' She kissed him. The kiss deepened, and would have been deeper still but for a chambermaid who came hurrying round the corner of the stairs and stopped dead when she saw them.

'Oh! 'Scuse me, sir, 'scuse me, ma'am!' She disappeared.

Covered in confusion, Annabelle muttered something about changing and whisked herself into her room.

Within quarter of an hour she and Goss were trotting off along the road southwards in the direction of Temperley.

But at Temperley they met with a severe setback. After the first excited greetings Becky told Annabelle that her sister was not there, but in London.

'In London! Oh, no! It can't be so!' cried Annabelle in despair.

'Well, I'm afraid it is. Miss Rosa was in such a tumult, Miss Belle. Mr Winbolt just swept her off her feet. Here one day and gone the next. She was worried about you, though. Why didn't you write?'

'Never mind that now, Becky. What am I to do?'

'Your papa is here, Miss Belle.'

'I haven't time to see him now. I'll have to leave you again. Get John to saddle up some fresh horses. Becky, you'll hear everything in due course, but for now just do as I tell you! There isn't a moment to lose.'

Annabelle sought out Goss, who was on his way back from the stables. 'Goss, we've got to go back. I must intercept Colonel Stanton. My sister is in London. There is no point in his coming here.'

Goss took some persuading that it was not better to stay where they were to wait for the rest of the party. 'The Colonel would want me to make sure you didn't wear yourself out, ma'am, beggin' your pardon,' he said stiffly.

'I can't sit still, Goss! If we are to reach London tonight we must not waste a moment before finding Colonel Stanton and the rest of the party! Please do as I say!' Though still unreconciled, Goss went all the same to find John and the horses, and soon, without any further delay, they were retracing their steps to the accompaniment of his *sotto voce* remarks.

When Giles and Lady Ordway eventually arrived at Temperley they were disconcerted to find that they were not expected.

'Miss Belle was here earlier in the day, my lady, but she never said anything about your ladyship and Colonel Stanton. In fact, she hardly said anything at all. She was in a terrible state when she heard that her sister was in London with Mr Winbolt, and left straight away. I thought she had gone to find you, but perhaps she went to London?'

Giles was looking very grim. 'You may be sure of it.' He turned to Lady Ordway. 'I must follow her, of course. Do you mind if I leave you here, Aunt Laura?'

'No, of course not, Giles. I have Mrs Bostock to look after me, and Wilson will help. Tell me, Mrs Bostock, is your master well enough to receive visitors?'

'Of course, my lady! And I'll see about a room for your ladyship straight away.'

Lady Ordway looked anxiously at Giles. 'What has happened to Rosabelle, Giles?'

'I expect she decided to make for London, as Mrs Bostock suggested. Try not to worry, Aunt Laura. I'll find her. And Goss is with her, don't forget. If I leave straight away, I might even catch up with her. Will you make my excuses to Mr Kelland?'

Calling Gregson, he wasted no more time on ceremony, but set off in pursuit.

Not long after leaving Temperley, Annabelle and Goss became aware that they were being followed.

'It's probably nothing, Mrs Ordway, but we won't take any risks. Don't slow down, not for anything. Keep going.'

Annabelle snatched a quick look behind. The figure was gaining.

'Faster, Mrs Ordway! And keep low in the saddle! Faster!' Goss drew a pistol from the holster at his side as they galloped on at a breakneck speed. They seemed to be making some headway, but as they joined the road at the end of Harden Lane another horse and rider appeared. Was it rescue or more threat? As they drew rapidly nearer Annabelle instinctively started to pull up.

'No, Mrs Ordway! Don't slow down...' But Goss was forced to rein in, too. He fired back towards their pursuer, but as they both turned and made to take up their former pace, the rider in front joined in. There was a shot, a cry from Goss and he fell to the ground. Annabelle wheeled round and chased back to where he lay. Goss was clutching his side, but he gasped, 'For God's sake, don't stop, Mrs Ordway. Get away while you can!'

It was too late. The first man was upon them, and the second came riding up immediately after. Annabelle dug her spurs into her horse. It reared, then galloped madly off towards the high road. For a moment it looked as if the ruse might succeed. The two men, taken by surprise, were slow to give chase. But they soon recovered and their powerful horses quickly overtook Annabelle's mount. There was a struggle, then all three riders came to a halt. Annabelle recognised one of the men. It was Cartwright— he had been in the coach at Bakewell.

'Fraser will crow,' said the other. 'He said they'd come back to Berkshire. And lo and behold, here they are!'

'Don't waste time,' said Cartwright. 'This is a public place. Take her to the carriage. And this time we'll make sure she doesn't get away! Tie her up.'

They pulled her from the horse and started to bind her wrists. Aware that protest would be useless she bore it stoically, though the pressure on her newly healed arm was exquisitely painful. But when they started to lead her away, she could not keep silent.

'What about Goss?' she cried.

'Who's he?'

'My groom. You can't leave him there to die!'

'Can't we? Who's goin' to stop us? You?'

'But…but he'll bleed to death!'

'What a shame,' said Cartwright. 'We'll send a wreath. Come on!'

'You mustn't leave him, I won't let you. I won't go!' Annabelle kicked and shouted with all her might. Someone must hear her, they must! Goss must not be left. For a short while they tried to hold her by force, but when she still screamed and scratched, Cartwright swore, then hit her on the head. While she was still dizzy with the pain they tied her feet together and put a gag over her mouth. Then the other man, the bigger of the two, hoisted her up like a sack, and threw her over the saddle. Annabelle was not aware of anything that followed. She was unconscious.

She became dimly aware of sounds of the high road, the toll gates, the inns, other travellers. Once or twice the motion of the carriage stopped and she guessed the horses were being changed. She had no idea of the time, though the light seemed to be fading more quickly than she would have expected. Later she saw that the fog of the previous night had returned. After what seemed like an eternity the carriage rolled in through some gates which clanged shut behind them, and came to a halt. She was carried in to a building which smelt of stale beer and worse, and deposited on a settle in the corner of a dingy room.

'She looks pretty sick.' It was Cartwright's voice. 'The bruise looks nasty, too. I hope Fraser doesn't think we've been too rough.'

'Not him. As long as she can talk that'll be enough. And what else were we to do? She's a wildcat, that one. Look at my hand! And I'll swear my shins are black and blue.'

'All the same, I'll get something for her to lie on.' Cartwright went away and came back with a rough blanket. 'Hold her up a minute.'

'Water!' croaked Annabelle.

'There's some in the old bar,' ordered Cartwright, who seemed to be in charge. 'Get it!' He held a pewter drinking vessel to her lips and she drank thirstily. The water was surprisingly fresh. Then he put a bowl of water down beside her, and untied her hands and feet. 'You can drink that if you need any more. We're going now, but Fraser's coming later. If you'll take my advice you won't try any tricks on Fraser. We've treated you like a baby compared with what he would do. We only hurt by way of business. He enjoys it.'

They left her, and Annabelle was left to her own dismal thoughts. She had no idea where she might be, though she suspected it was somewhere in London. Her physical state was pathetic—her head was throbbing, she still felt very dizzy, and there was a distinct possibility that she might be sick. She looked round. The room was lit by an evil-smelling lamp in the corner. Its dim light revealed a heavy iron door and bare stone walls, though the room appeared to be dry and free of rats. Opposite her was a barred window. She got up and walked over to it.

The window looked out on to a yard surrounded by high walls, dimly visible in the fog. No possibility of escape there

even if she were able to attempt it. She went back to her
makeshift bed and sank down, with nothing to do but ponder
her situation. She prayed desperately that Goss had been
found before it was too late. She wondered where Giles was
and what he was doing. She asked herself if she would ever
have a chance to tell him how much she loved him? And how
sorry she was? The chance seemed at present to be remote.

Weak tears rolled down her cheeks, but she wiped them
away fiercely. Fraser was not going to find her like this! She
wet her handkerchief and wiped her face. The cold water
refreshed her, and brought a return of her natural spirit.
Whatever her situation, she could do nothing about it at the
moment. It would be wise to conserve her energies for what
was to come. She made what preparations she could, lay
down and composed herself for sleep.

Meanwhile, Giles was riding as fast as he dared to London.
The fog came down just beyond Hounslow Heath, but his
pace barely faltered. Gregson, riding behind him, sent up
many fervent prayers for their safe arrival, though with little
real hope. But they pressed on, and towards nine o'clock they
finally came to a halt in Arlington Street. Gregson waited with
the horses while Giles hammered on the door. As soon as it
was opened he stepped past the footman and went into the
hall.

'I wish to speak to Mr Winbolt. The affair is urgent,' he
said curtly to the butler. 'Colonel Stanton.'

'The family are still at dinner, sir.'

'It doesn't matter. Tell your master I am here, damn you!'

The servant was shocked, but assessed the situation pretty
well. 'Very well, Colonel. I will see what I can do.' He made
for a door on the right. Giles heard voices, and he was prepared to swear that one of them was Rosabelle's! He pushed
past the butler.

'Excuse me for breaking in on you like this, Philip—' He

stopped dead. A pleasant scene met his gaze—three young people round the top end of a large mahogany dining table, the remains of a meal, candlelight reflecting on the richly coloured wood, the silver and glassware. Giles had eyes for none of this. On Philip Winbolt's right sat Rosabelle.

For a moment he was light-headed with joy. All the way to London he had held back his fears, forced himself to concentrate on the road before him, pushed to the back of his mind pictures of Rosabelle in Falkirk's power, the horror at what Falkirk might do to her. The relief at seeing her here, safe in London, was almost overpowering, and he, who had faced battalions of the enemy without a tremor, who had defied death in a dozen different countries, was as weak as a woman at the sight of her. It was no longer possible to deceive himself about his feelings for Rosabelle Ordway. She was everything to him!

His first impulse was to take her in his arms and hold her, just to hold her until the tumult of his feelings died down, till he was convinced that she was truly here, and truly safe. But then before he realised what was happening his relief turned to a fury which was as violent as it was sudden. How dare she subject him—and the others—to such fear, such unmanly weakness? How could she be so thoughtless, so cruel!

'Rosabelle! So you *are* here! What the devil do you think you've been doing?' He took hold of her, beside himself with rage, uncertain whether he wanted to shake her, or kiss her senseless. Then he became aware that Philip was beside him, had put a restraining hand on him, was trying to tell him that Rosabelle was betrothed to him, Philip Winbolt!

Giles began to feel that he had gone mad. He had somehow strayed into a lunatic asylum, and was the latest inmate. And now Rosabelle was speaking and he couldn't make any sense of it.

'Are you saying that you've brought my sister to London,

Giles? Oh, how could you? After all my warnings and letters…'

Warnings, letters? Reproaches because he had brought her
sister to London? What the hell did she mean? He hadn't even
seen her sister! And what was this nonsense about a betrothal?
It was Annabelle Kelland who was to marry Philip. Rosabelle
was his! He appealed to her to tell Winbolt the truth. But
Rosabelle remained silent, staring at him as if she had been
struck dumb, as if he was a madman.

They must be drunk! That was it! He began again, patiently
explaining, to go over the events of the last six months.
Rosabelle might be mad or incapable, but Philip would listen
sensibly. But Philip's face grew graver and graver. And
Rosabelle appeared to be perfectly sober. A nameless fear
started to grow in Giles. There was some mystery here to
which he did not have the key. But when Philip Winbolt
finally spoke it was all made horribly, hideously clear.

'Giles, I…I don't know how to tell you this. I can see that
you have been as deceived as I was. You obviously don't
know that the Kelland sisters are identical twins. This—' he
took Rosabelle's hand '—this is Rosabelle Ordway, who
changed places with her sister at Easter, and has been in
Berkshire and London ever since. The lady with you in the
North was Annabelle Kelland.'

Giles looked blankly at his friend. What nonsense was this?
Of course this was Rosabelle! His Rosabelle. But then, as he
looked more closely, the woman standing by Philip Winbolt
was suddenly no longer so familiar. She might be Rosabelle's
double, but there was something, a faint air, an aura, which
told him that this was not the woman he loved. And, for the
first time, the truth began to penetrate. The woman at present
standing next to Philip was indeed Stephen's widow, the
woman he had met on first coming to London. She was not
the Rosabelle he had known for the last six months, the
Rosabelle he had fallen so desperately in love with.

He stared unseeingly at them all while his tired brain absorbed what he had been told. Twins, yes. He had known that. But identical twins? No, that had never been mentioned, not by anyone. Not even Aunt Laura, though she must have known. They had all used the startling likeness to trick him. With bitter recognition he realised that his 'Rosabelle' did not exist. Had never existed. Annabelle Kelland had played him like a fish. It was ironic, truly, bitterly ironic, that all the suspicions, all his instinctive distrust of her, which had taken so long to overcome, had always been justified, right from the beginning.

Chapter Sixteen

For a moment he was filled with an intensely corroding sense of disillusion which blotted out every other feeling. Annabelle Kelland was false, as her sister had been false, as his stepmother had been false, as all the women he had ever known had been false. But then, as the shock faded, fear took its place. If this woman before him was not the one who had left Wallingford that morning to go to Temperley…

'But in that case, where is Annabelle now?' he demanded.

They all started as the butler came into the room. 'Forgive me, sir, but there's an individual at the back demanding to see Colonel Stanton. I thought it best to let you know straight away. He has ridden from Berkshire, sir.'

'Bring him in, Maynard.'

They waited tensely to see what this arrival might mean.

'John Bostock!' All three recognised the exhausted man who now entered the room.

'Colonel Stanton, sir, they found Goss, your man. He's been wounded. He says that he and Miss Belle were set upon shortly after they left Temperley by two men. They shot Goss and…and they carried Miss Belle off with them.'

'Falkirk's work!'

Philip Winbolt said, 'Maynard, fetch Stokes and Jenkins.

Hurry! Where are you going, Giles! Wait! This needs planning.'

'You don't realise, Winbolt. Falkirk is quite ruthless. There isn't a moment to lose. I must find her.'

'Where would you begin to look?'

'I have men in London, who've been keeping a watch on Falkirk. They might have some news... Gregson knows where they can be found. Bostock, you're done in. Find Gregson for me—he'll be in the stables. Then find somewhere you can rest.'

'Go to the kitchens, Bostock,' said Philip. 'They'll give you something there.'

'Bostock!' said Giles. 'Tell me first. Is...is Goss badly hurt?'

'He'll live, sir.'

'Thank God! Right, tell Gregson to come here, then go to the kitchen.'

'Beg your pardon, sir. But if Miss Annabelle is in danger I'd rather be up and about.'

'Get some food into you first, Bostock! It may be a long night.'

Emily got up from the table and said quietly, 'I'll see to him.' She took Bostock out of the room.

Gregson, Stokes and Jenkins were dispatched to find Giles's men, and while they waited Giles was made to eat something while Philip filled him in on their side of the story. But when the men eventually came their information was negative. Falkirk had not been seen in London for some days.

Giles sat down suddenly with his head in his hands.

Philip said, 'Giles, this isn't any good. Unless we alarm Falkirk unduly, I am sure Annabelle is safe for the moment.'

'But she's been in his hands since this morning! I'll go mad if I don't *do* something, Philip.'

'Remember what you told me at Badajoz? You have to

know the terrain before you attack. It was good advice then, and it's good advice now. Believe me, Giles, Annabelle is safe for tonight. Though Falkirk has searched the house in Upper Brook Street, he has failed to find his papers. He's desperate to have them in his hands, and his only hope is to get Annabelle to show him where they are. She's safe for tonight.'

'But Annabelle doesn't know anything about the papers, damn you!'

'We know that. But he doesn't.'

Giles turned to Rosabelle. 'Did Stephen say *nothing* before he died?'

'He was delirious,' she said miserably 'He could only think of money. He said again and again that his bank account had failed him, after all. He said it over and over.'

'No, no!' Giles exclaimed. 'It's where he hid the papers. Why didn't I think of it before?'

'But—' said Rosabelle.

'Where?' said Philip.

'I'll show you. Tomorrow. But first we must find Falkirk. I'll swear he's somewhere in London.'

'I think I could flush him out,' said Rosabelle. 'They keep an eye on this house, I know they do. If I were to take a walk out in the open street, it's very likely Falkirk would have me followed. I feel certain that he keeps a watch on us all, and he wants both Anna and me—he said so.'

Giles was of the opinion that this was far too dangerous a plan, but he kept silent. This was for Philip to decide. To his relief Philip put his foot down, and they set themselves to finding an alternative. It was clear that Philip had been as busy as he himself had been in his pursuit of Falkirk, and he had a fleeting regret that they had not been able to coordinate their efforts before. He and Philip had always been a formidable combination.

They decided that Burrows might be the key and spent

some time discussing how to set about finding him and what
to do when they did. Burrows was loyal, but he might be
intimidated. One thing led to another and the candles burnt
low. Giles hardly noticed Rosabelle's departure for bed. After
her initial offer to act as a decoy she had hardly joined in
their discussions at all. She seemed quite subdued, more like
the woman he had first met at Upper Brook Street—as, of
course, she was. How could he have ever mistaken one sister
for the other? His heart lurched as he thought of his lovely,
spirited, laughing Rosabelle in Falkirk's hands. But after a
moment it settled back to a steady, resentful beat. Annabelle
Kelland must be rescued, of course. But after that he would
forget her.

They left early the next morning, taking Gregson and
Jenkins with them. Giles's men were deployed all round
London, listening, looking, questioning yet again for any clue
to Annabelle Kelland's whereabouts. Philip's information on
Burrows proved to be sound, and they soon tracked him
down. At first he was more afraid of Falkirk than he was of
them, and reluctant to talk. But after a while it was gradually
borne in on him that these two officers and English gentlemen
could be every bit as ruthless as Falkirk, and much more
inventive. Moreover, between them, they seemed to have
gathered enough evidence to hang him. So in the end Burrows
recognised defeat and began to talk. At the same time reports
started to come in from Giles's men of a deserted tavern on
the edge of town where strange things had been happening
the night before.

But before any action could be taken on it, Philip's Bow
Street Runner, Barnaby Stokes, came racing up to them, puff-
ing and blowing with a message which was at first incom-
prehensible. When he finally managed to make himself understood, Giles was astounded and Philip was beside himself
with a mixture of worry and rage. Timid little Rosabelle

Ordway had ignored their advice and put herself into the lion's mouth in an effort to save her sister! She had the gall to assure them, through Barnaby Stokes, that she would bring Falkirk to Upper Brook Street within the hour.

'Why the devil didn't you stop her?' Philip asked fiercely.

'Couldn't be done, Mr Winbolt. Very obstinate, the lady was.'

'But I engaged you to guard her, damn you!'

Giles, seeing that Philip wanted nothing more than to throttle Stokes, said brusquely, 'How long ago did you leave her, Mr Stokes?'

'About forty minutes ago, Colonel.'

'Then we have no time to lose. Bring Burrows along with you. Gregson will give you a hand.'

They went through the streets of London at a pace which made no allowance for the fog which had descended once again, and were at the Upper Brook Street house within ten minutes. Here they took Burrows up to the little antechamber next to the drawing room. The man was a miserable wreck and he was unlikely to give them any more trouble.

'Gregson, take the carriage out of sight, and stay with it. Jenkins, Stokes, stay with Burrows until we call you. Understood?' Giles's voice was calm but brisk, his anxieties submerged in the need for action.

'And make sure you keep him quiet,' Philip added grimly. 'I don't mind what means you use as long as he remains conscious. We must leave the door open a crack, Giles.' Giles nodded. They needed to be able to judge the moment to strike.

They waited in silence. Presently they heard the sounds of arrival, footsteps on the stairs…

'I…I can't see!' Rosabelle's voice came clearly through the door, and both men heaved a sigh of relief.

A few murmurs, and the sound of shutters being opened. Then there was a long interval while Rosabelle obviously played for time, hesitating between one side and the other of the ornate mantelpiece. Her acting was perfect—it was impossible to guess that she really had no idea where to look. Finally they heard her say, 'I think this might be it. That cherub there. His head turns.'

Giles looked appalled. He knelt down and peered through the crack. He held up his hand in a signal to Philip. They waited.

'You have to press it in a certain way. It's no good hammering it.'

'You do it!' This was unmistakably Falkirk's voice!

There was a gasp from Rosabelle and a shout of triumph from Falkirk. Giles whispered, 'Quickly, Philip! Now!'

They burst through the door and threw themselves at the two men bending in front of the mantelpiece. Giles saw that Philip was already tackling Falkirk and went for Fraser...

In later years, when their wives were not there to remonstrate, Philip and Giles were wont to reminisce about the minutes that followed with a certain amount of pride. The fight was hard and dirty. From the tactics used it would have been impossible to judge who were the virtuous and who were the villains. There were no rules, other than the need to survive, and Giles and Philip used without a qualm every trick they had learned in the lowest taverns on the waterfronts of Spain and France.

In a short while Fraser was unconscious and, with Falkirk firmly in Philip's grasp, Burrows was brought in. After one quick glance to check on Annabelle Kelland, Giles concentrated on dealing with Falkirk. He made sure the man was disarmed, drew his gun and held it steadily pointing at Falkirk's heart. 'Right, you can let him go. What's that you've got there, Jenkins?'

'A stiletto, sir.'

'I should have used that thing on you, when I had the chance,' Falkirk said viciously.

'Instead of on a woman who was bound hand and foot.'

This was Rosabelle speaking. 'He held it to Anna's throat in
the carriage on the way here. He drew blood.'

Giles stole another glance at Annabelle Kelland. She was
holding on to her chair, white as a sheet, and he now saw
there was a red mark on her throat and a large bruise on her
head. He turned back with a snarl towards Falkirk, but the
man had taken advantage of his momentary lapse of attention.
Before Giles could stop him he had swept something up from
the floor and thrust it into Burrows in one fluid motion.
Burrows was dead before he reached the ground, his throat
pierced.

Giles hardly noticed what was happening. He was bent over
Annabelle, examining the slender thread of scarlet at the base
of her throat. She was pale and trembling. A cold and deadly
rage took hold of him. He turned on Falkirk, and, if the others
had not been there, he would have killed him on the spot,
with his bare hands.

But it was not necessary. Barnaby Stokes, suddenly a mag-
isterial figure, was arresting Falkirk. What the combined efforts of Lloyds, the Navy Office, Giles Stanton and all his
men, Philip Winbolt and all his had failed to do, had been
accomplished for them by Falkirk himself. Selder's previous
crimes were no longer relevant. Falkirk was being arrested
for the murder of one of his own accomplices.

Giles left them to it. He went back to where Annabelle was
being comforted by her sister. They stared at one another in
silence till Rosabelle left them and returned to Philip.

Annabelle found it impossible to divine what Giles might
be thinking. His gaze was concerned, but impersonal, almost
as if she was someone he had found hurt in the street. She
said wryly, 'I said you would meet Annabelle soon, Giles.'

His mouth twisted, but he did not reply. She sighed and
looked towards Philip and Rosabelle. Her sister appeared to

be faring no better. Philip Winbolt's voice was as cool as she had ever heard it.

'Though what you thought you might do with only my paper knife to protect you I cannot imagine,' he said evenly.

Annabelle roused herself. 'Don't!' she said with such vigour that her throat hurt. Giles would have stopped her talking but she ignored him. 'She cut my ropes with it so that we could join together to keep Falkirk's coachman out of the room. You'd have been outnumbered otherwise. Don't talk to Rosabelle like that!'

'Annabelle, you must save your voice!' said Giles, putting his hand over her lips. Tears filled her eyes. His touch was so familiar, so gentle. But his eyes were as cool as Philip's voice. 'The sooner you can rest, the better.'

She pulled her face away from his hand. 'I want to know something first,' she protested. 'What and where are these wretched papers?'

She watched as Giles went over to the merry little cherub on the right hand side of the mantelpiece. He pressed something and slid it to one side. When his hand reappeared it held a slender packet of papers.

'Here,' he said. 'Stephen's bank account. He used…he used to keep his pocket money here when he was a child.' His gaze held hers as he waved the bundle in front of them all.

'But that was the very place I… Oh, heavens!' said Rosabelle.

'Exactly so,' said Philip curtly. 'You took an enormous risk, Rosa. How long do you think you would have lived after Falkirk got his papers?'

Annabelle didn't hear the rest of what he said. Giles's eyes were boring into her, accusing her… She pulled herself together.

'I shall go mad,' she said as forcefully as she could. 'I've been chased, carried off, frightened half to death, rescued, beaten on the head and imprisoned, had my throat cut—well, nearly—and all for the sake of that wretched bundle of papers. What are they?'

'You mustn't talk, Annabelle,' said Giles.

'Really? Well, silence me by telling me what I want to know.'

'It seems to be a confession signed by Kingsley.'

'Kingsley?'

'Ah! And here's a letter signed by Falkirk, thanking Kingsley for his information, and telling him it will be put to good use. He even calls himself Selder in it! Exactly what we wanted. It would have been enough to deliver Falkirk into the hands of the authorities.'

'Stephen's revenge,' said Rosabelle. Her voice was sad. 'And his death warrant.'

These were the last words Annabelle could hear. The strain of the previous twenty-four hours was catching up with her. With relief she heard the sound of a carriage arriving. She hardly noticed as Giles swung her into his arms and carried her out like a baby. She was dimly aware of a crowd of people on the doorstep, but only later was she told that this was an escort to remove Falkirk and Fraser, and take them into custody.

In all the bustle of their arrival at Arlington Street Annabelle was aware that Giles was at her side constantly. She was desperate to talk to him, but they were never alone for long enough for her to attempt to breach the impenetrable wall which had come between them. He was patient, gentle, courteous—all the things he had not been when they had first met. But she had felt closer to him then, for all the accusations and taunts, than she did now, when he was being so considerate. Before he left he came in to see her, his face still inscrutable. She wanted to shout, to rage at him, anything to breach that calm, stony facade. But the drugs she had been given were working and, halfway through an incoherent speech, she fell asleep.

When she woke the next morning her first thought was that she would see Giles. He must come again to see how she was, surely? He must listen to her, he must understand, and…if he knew how much she loved him he was sure to forgive her! Wouldn't he? She insisted on getting up. It would never do if he came and she was unable to see him. Rules of propriety might be relaxed for one day, but there would be no excuse for him to visit her bedroom a second time. She must be downstairs to receive him properly.

When she came down there was such an atmosphere of happy anticipation that she was not at all surprised to hear that Rosabelle was to marry Philip Winbolt at Christmas. Anxious not to spoil Rosabelle's joy she hid her own anxieties and exerted herself to seem cheerful and eager to join in the plans that were already being made. Only once did she falter, when Rosabelle asked her about a possible second wedding. She meant Annabelle's to Giles, of course, and the question almost overset her. She kept her composure, however, and managed to turn it off with a joke. For the rest of that day throughout all the chatter and laughter, she never once stopped listening for his arrival, but though there was much coming and going, not one of the visitors had the firm tread, the deep voice that she sought.

She went to bed that night, wondering if she would ever see Giles Stanton again.

Word soon got around that lovely young Mrs Ordway was back in London after her journey to the North, and the next day flowers arrived from Richard Pettifer, and Captain Wainwright, and another huge bouquet from Major Dabney. Annabelle found it difficult to laugh when Rosabelle, Emily and Philip teased her on her success with London Society, to keep smiling when every card was eagerly perused for the one name which she wanted to see, but which was never there. Lord Monteith called, but Annabelle asked Emily to deal with him, pleading that she was not strong enough for visitors.

Then, ironically, the caller she had longed for came just as Lord Monteith was leaving. Fortunately, Maynard assumed he had come to see Philip and asked him to wait in the library while he saw Lord Monteith out. On his return Giles asked to see Miss Kelland; with a fatherly smile, Maynard showed him into the small parlour where Annabelle sat. After he had gone there was a short silence in the room. Giles did not sit down, but gazed round at the many floral offerings.

'Still as popular, I see. But do your admirers know who you really are, Miss Kelland?'

'Miss Kelland, Giles?'

'I understand that is your name. Or am I wrong? Again.'

'Giles, don't…don't be angry with me. Surely after all we have been through, you could call me by my given name? My true given name.'

'Very well. But, before you go any further, *Annabelle*, I ought to warn you. I am not very interested in excuses or expressions of contrition.'

'But I *am* sorry, Giles. And I hope you will forgive me.'

'Well now, I do find that a trifle difficult. In fact, I would rather forget the matter altogether and talk of other things. Tell me, am I right in thinking your sister and Philip Winbolt intend to marry? Have they set a date?'

'Christmas,' said Annabelle miserably. 'Giles—'

'No, *Annabelle*. I came this morning to make sure you had recovered. Nothing more.'

'But this is absurd! I was wrong, I know, to deceive you as I did, but my intentions were good! Do you mean to tell me that you are rejecting me, and everything I had to offer you, everything we have meant to each other, merely because I wanted to help my sister?'

'Everything you had to offer me! What was that? You demanded everything, *Annabelle*! And you gave me nothing.'

'What demands did I make?' she cried indignantly.

'You demanded faith. I gave that to you. You demanded trust. I gave you that, too. You had my respect. You even had something I had never bestowed on any woman before. You had my love. And what did you give in return?

'I loved you! I love you!'

'Oh, spare me that! You gave me neither respect, nor faith, nor trust. And I don't believe for a moment that you know what love is. Tell me, did you love me when you were lying through your teeth about your name, about your marriage to Stephen, your relationship with Selder? Did you respect me when you were laughing every time I called you Rosabelle? What sort of love is it that can't trust me with a secret as trivial as yours? Even when you were ill you kept it up—' He stopped.

'It wasn't trivial! I came to London convinced you were a monster! Rosabelle was ill, do you hear me? Ill! And all because of your unreasonable, cruel suspicions. I wanted to punish you for your treatment of her, your threats, the way you bullied her, reducing her to a shadow, a wraith…'

'And so you did!'

'Giles, you cannot believe that of me! That I would go to such lengths to punish you. No, you cannot believe it! You are not so ungenerous. You must have some remnant of feeling—'

'*Annabelle*, apart from relief that you have escaped without permanent injury from Falkirk and his companions, I assure you I feel nothing for you. For myself I am also relieved. I was in great danger of making a disastrous mistake. Greater danger than I have ever been in my life before.'

'By that you mean marriage to me, I suppose? You reject any thought of love I may have for you?'

'I can think of nothing more repellent. It is as I have always thought. A woman's love is a trap. Women are fickle, full of self-interest and better not taken at all seriously. In fact, the whole business is tedious.'

By now Annabelle was so angry that she forgot all her good resolutions. She had confessed her deepest feelings to this man, and he had called them repellent! She had spent months agonising over her deception of him, and in the end he had dismissed her torments as trivial. She should have been warned. A man who had treated Rosabelle so harshly would never understand, never forgive. It was a waste of time to think him capable of it.

'I am sure,' she said with dangerous calm, 'that I would not wish to cause you any further tedium.'

'Annabelle—'

'Forgive me, Colonel Stanton, if I say that I would much rather not see you again. In view of the very disobliging sentiments you have just expressed, I have no doubt that this will hardly distress you.'

'Annabelle—'

Rosabelle came into the room at that point and stopped short. She looked from one to the other and said in some embarrassment, ' I thought I'd find Philip and Emily here. Forgive me.' She made to go out.

'Pray do not feel you have to go, Rosa. Colonel Stanton was just leaving.'

'Annabelle—'

'If you do not leave this room, sir, then I will.'

'In that case, there is no more to be said. Goodbye, Miss Kelland.' He turned and gave a brief bow in Rosabelle's direction. 'Rosabelle,' and strode out.

For a moment there was complete silence in the room. Annabelle felt that if she moved or spoke she would shatter into tiny pieces, and it would be impossible to put her together again. Rosabelle tried to pacify her, but it was no use. Annabelle could not even bear to hear Giles Stanton's name. From that day on, whenever Giles Stanton's name was mentioned she simply withdrew into a private world of her own until the subject was dropped. But she could not control her dreams. Night after night, after days of cheerful activity, Annabelle would wake suddenly with her pillows wet, and tears rolling down her cheeks.

For the next few weeks Annabelle concentrated on Rosabelle's affairs and the preparations for the wedding. Having seen 'Gentleman Jack' in action, Annabelle respected him a great deal more, and if anything could cause the pain in her heart to ease a trifle it was the sight of Rosabelle's happy daze, and Philip Winbolt's devotion. She also found she had much in common with Emily Winbolt, which was as well, for the lovers tended to live in a delightful world of their own which shut out ordinary practicalities like mealtimes, appointments with mantua makers and the like. She and Emily rescued many a potential disaster, and in doing so cemented a firm friendship.

In the middle of December they all left London in an impressive convoy of carriages and wagons, and descended on Temperley. Here the activity, if anything, intensified. It had been decided that the wedding would take place on New Year's Eve, and the preparations for this, together with a traditional Christmas of the old sort which was to precede it, occupied most of Annabelle's time. She laughed and joked as gaily as the rest, teased Rosabelle and Philip, kept Lady Ordway amused, ran the household and flattered herself that she kept her constant heartache hidden from the rest of the world. Of Giles she had heard nothing.

Then one day, when they were making a list of guests,

Rosabelle asked almost too casually, 'Is there…is there any-one else you would wish to invite, Anna?'

Annabelle ignored this opening. 'I don't think so,' she said, equally casually. 'You've mentioned all the local people who should come. And there certainly isn't anyone else.'

She saw Rosabelle looking at her with such concern in her eyes that she almost broke down. 'Dearest Anna, are you well?'

'Of course I am! Pray don't worry about me, Rosa. I shall soon come about.' She knew she was speaking too brusquely, but it was as much as she could do to reply at all. The longing for Giles did not seem to weaken. If anything, it seemed to grow with each day that passed. So she threw herself with even greater enthusiasm into every detail for Christmas and the wedding and tried to bury all feeling under an avalanche of work.

Giles had left London as soon as the business with Falkirk and the rest had been completed. He had to leave town, oth-erwise the temptation to call on the Winbolts was too strong. Before he knew it he would be begging Annabelle Kelland to forgive him, besottedly swearing devotion and all the rest of the inanities that men fall into when they are haunted by the hurt in two dark blue eyes, the particular lift of a delicately proud chin, the brightness of golden hair, barely hiding a dark bruise…and other, more intimate memories. The lines of a slender figure, tossing restlessly in the room at High Kimber, the frantic voice seeking reassurance, protection, the hands clutching him, refusing to release him… He could feel them still. They were round his heart squeezing it till it ached… Enough of that! Let Philip Winbolt choose to marry if he wished! Such folly was not for him, and to be sure of it he would remove himself from temptation and retire to Avenell.

But as a relief from his thoughts the journey was not a

success. He was foolish enough to call on the Daventrys, and had difficulty in parrying their eager questions.

'So Gentleman Jack Winbolt is to marry Mrs Ordway! We were so surprised when we saw it in the *London Gazette*! He's a fortunate man—we thought her charming.'

'You've met her?'

Selina Daventry opened her eyes wide in astonishment. 'Well, of course we have! You brought her here yourself not six months ago, Giles! In fact, James and I were certain you would end up marrying her yourself. It just shows how mistaken one can be.'

Giles looked helplessly from one to the other. James and Selina were old friends of Philip's as well. It could lead to all sorts of complications if he left it. He said curtly, 'Things…aren't quite as they seem. The…the lady who was with me in July was, in fact, Mrs Ordway's identical twin, Miss Annabelle Kelland.'

The Daventrys looked astonished. 'I suppose there was a reason for this hoax,' said Captain Daventry, his voice carefully neutral.

'Oh, absolve me from blame. I was as taken in as you. But I'm sorry you were subjected to it.'

'But, Giles, how dreadful! Was it just…just a joke?'

'No, Selina. She had a reason.'

'I can think of few reasons which would justify such a deception,' said James's mother austerely.

'Miss Kelland took her sister's place in London so that Mrs Ordway could have time to recover from an illness at the family home in Berkshire.'

'Mrs Ordway seems to have recovered to some purpose if she is to marry Philip Winbolt,' said the elder Mrs Daventry, unappeased. 'He must be one of the best catches in London. But I still don't understand the need for pretence.'

Giles started to agree, then stopped. He had never before

really considered Annabelle's words. Had Rosabelle really been so frightened of him? Had he been such an ogre?

'After all,' said Selina Daventry. 'It's not as if you were an ogre. If Lady Ordway needed a companion, you would surely have accepted a substitute.'

Would he? Or would he have sent Annabelle back with a flea in her ear? Demanded that Rosabelle return to London, as she had promised? Having observed the sisters' fierce loyalty to each other, he could imagine that Annabelle would not have risked it. He said slowly, 'Whatever the truth of the matter, I owe you all an apology, I know. But try not to judge Annabelle Kelland too harshly. You know how close your own twins are, Selina. Miss Kelland was doing the best she could for her sister—other considerations took second place. I...I'm sorry you were deceived, but I don't suppose you will meet her again. Don't think too badly of Miss Kelland.'

'I won't,' said Selina Daventry. 'I liked her.'

But after Giles had departed for Avenell she said to her spouse, 'Not meet her again, indeed! I'll wager what you like she'll be visiting us within the year. Probably on her bridal journey to Avenell, too!'

Chapter Seventeen

Giles's journey to Derbyshire was overshadowed by memories of that other journey earlier in the year. Annabelle's voice was constantly in his ear, fragments of their conversations, the sound of her laughter, her spirited responses. It was no better when he reached Avenell. His father's greeting was warm, if a little surprised, and he exerted himself to entertain him. But Avenell, too, was full of Annabelle. He was haunted by memories—of riding about the countryside with her, her cheeks rosy with exercise, her hair blown by the wind, of her flight over the moor to High Kimber, of the desperate hours when he thought she would die, and of the courage and gaiety that were such an essential part of her.

One night they were sitting in the south dining room, the heavy curtains drawn against the biting winds outside, and a huge fire burning in the hearth.

'Well, I thought I was glad to see you, Giles, but you're no better than a wet week. What's wrong?' said Lord Stanton eventually. 'And what have you done with that charming girl? Is she the trouble? The last time I saw you together I thought you were in a fair way to making a match of it.'

'So did I, Father,' said Giles, turning his glass round between his fingers. 'But I was wrong.'

'Refused you, did she? I'm surprised. She showed every sign of being in love.'

'Father, I'd like to tell you what happened. May I?'

Giles left nothing out, from his cruel suspicions of Rosabelle Ordway, through his slow discovery of the truth about Stephen and the final defeat of Falkirk, to the last bitter quarrel with Annabelle. By the time he had finished the only light in the room came from the fire. The candles had guttered long since.

'Hmm. A curious history. What do you propose to do now?'

'What do you mean?'

'You've told me the facts. But what do you feel? Do you still condemn Annabelle Kelland for being a woman? Oh, don't look at me like that, Giles! It seems to me that that is your chief grievance. And I'm sorry for it. I had hoped that Venetia's death and our reconciliation had wiped that particular slate clean. But you're being absurd, you know. You wouldn't love this Annabelle as you do if she wasn't a woman. And a damned attractive one.'

'She may be attractive, but she lied to me, father.'

'Her reason for doing so may not seem adequate to you. But have you considered how important it was to her to protect her sister? Surely loyalty is a rare and laudable virtue? If she can be so loyal to her sister, is it not likely that she would be as loyal to a husband.'

'Why didn't she confide in me?'

'Ah! There we have it! The canker at the heart.'

'What is that?'

'You can forgive your own lack of faith in her. What you cannot forgive is her lack of faith in you!'

'What nonsense!'

'And,' his father went on, 'you are wrong. She trusted you with her life. She gave you her love. But she couldn't, or wouldn't, risk her sister's happiness. That wasn't hers to risk.

Think about it, Giles. I've made some mistakes in my life and spent many lonely years as a result. I don't want you to go the same way.'

For the next few days the debate raged furiously in Giles's mind. For so many years he had lived with the assumption that women were not to be trusted. Was he in danger of losing the one woman who could rescue him from loneliness, who could give him more happiness than he had ever imagined? Had he resented the fact that she had put her sister's happiness before his?

Then two letters arrived. One was from Rosabelle. It was an invitation to the wedding at Temperley.

I do not need to tell you how pleased we would be if you could come, Giles. And I think I may also speak for Annabelle. I sometimes worry about her. Though she is always busy and cheerful, something of her old spirit seems to have vanished. Can it be that her experiences in the north and afterwards have left a mark? Some of them were certainly unpleasant. Perhaps if you came you could help her to put them into the right perspective? Of course, if you feel you cannot, then we shall try to understand. Forgive me if I seem to be interfering in matters which do not concern me—my excuse is that Annabelle's health and happiness are a matter of deep concern for all those who love her. And Philip and I are so happy that we want the world to be happy, too...

The second was from Lady Ordway. She thanked him for his efforts on behalf of her family, and gave a vivid description of the preparations for the wedding. It ended thus:

With Rosa's permission, I have enclosed a page from one of her letters written to Anna at Avenell. Anna has forgotten she left it with me, and I have not consulted

her before sending it to you. You might condemn me for
this, I suppose, but I thought it might explain Anna's
reticence, which must have seemed unreasonable, or
even sly, to you. She is the dearest girl, Giles. Do not
judge her harshly.

Giles unfolded the page. It was an affecting plea from
Rosabelle for her sister's continued silence on the matter of
their changed identity. Only a monster could have ignored it.
He mind up his mind, and went to his father straight away.

'You were right, sir. I was at fault, and I intend to rectify
it immediately. It means my leaving you alone for a month
or two—unless you wish to come with me... But the journey
would be too much for you at this time of year.'

'What rubbish is this? I like that Kelland girl, and I'd like
to make sure that you don't make a mess of it this time! Too
much for me, indeed!'

Giles could see that his father's mind was made up, so,
apart from warning him that they would be travelling as
quickly as circumstances permitted, he said no more. They
set off more or less straight away without attempting to inform anyone at Temperley, since he meant to be there before
any mail could reach them. Unfortunately the weather did not
smile on them. England was swept with a series of storms
which delayed any traveller foolhardy enough to attempt such
a long journey in winter. Others gave up and took shelter in
the various inns, but the Stantons pressed on gamely to
London. Here they stopped briefly, then set off again along
the Bath Road.

Now that Giles had made up his mind, he was determined
to arrive at Temperley before Christmas, and any delay was
intolerable. It was a severe setback when they arrived at
Reading on Christmas Eve to find that a heavy snowfall had
blocked the road further west. But undeterred, he left his father and the carriage in the care of Goss at the inn, and, taking

a single bag, set off alone on foot. He trudged through the snow, hearing church bells, and snatches of song from the villages, but never meeting a soul. Once or twice he wondered if he had lost his way, but then a signpost would loom up and he would rub it clear to confirm that he was still on course.

After what seemed hours, he saw the dark bulk of Temperley ahead. One of the church clocks had struck midnight an hour or more before, and he wondered if anyone would still be up, but he took heart when he saw lights in the windows. Feeling a curious mixture of exhaustion, apprehension, and elation, he knocked on the huge oak door. After a moment it opened cautiously to reveal the substantial figure of Mrs Bostock.

'Miss Kelland?' he asked.

'Well, I don't know, I'm sure...'

'It's all right, Becky. Let Colonel Stanton in.' Annabelle's voice. Brushing the snow from his shoulders, Giles stepped into the hall. The candles were still burning in the sconces, and in their light he could see greenery wound round the bannisters of a wide oak staircase and arching over the top of the stairs. The warm, intoxicating smell of spices and apples, mulled wine and baking filled his nostrils. But he took in very little of this familiar Christmas scene. His eyes were fixed on a figure halfway up the stairs. She held a branched candlestick in her hand and the light gleamed in the dark gold of her hair.

'Annabelle! Oh God, I'd forgotten how lovely you are! Annabelle, I've been such a fool. Can you forgive me?'

The candlestick wavered in Annabelle's hand and Giles leapt up the stairs to take it from her. Holding it high, he put his other arm round her to steady her...

'Let me take that, Giles.' It was Philip, carefully removing the candlestick from his grasp. 'I don't want to interfere, but you'll manage better without.'

He could have been on the moon for all the notice taken of him. With a smile he slipped past the twined figures on the stairs and ushered the Bostocks back into the kitchen, where they set to preparing something to sustain the traveller.

'Giles! Oh, Giles, I thought you'd never come.'

'I came to my senses. And then I couldn't keep away. Say it's not too late, Annabelle.'

'I love you, Giles.'

'I don't deserve this,' he said with an unsteady laugh, as she wound her arms round his neck…

'Giles, you're soaking! You don't mean to say you've *walked*…'

'No other way to get here. I've left my father with Goss and the carriage in the inn at Reading. They'll follow in the morning, when it's light.'

'You're mad!'

'No, Annabelle. I'm sane. Truly in my right senses for the first time in my life. Marry me?'

'Oh yes, I will. I will!'

'There's room for another wedding at the church on New Year's Eve,' said a helpful voice above them. 'And everything's prepared.'

'The guest list will be much the same, too,' added another.

They looked up. Framed in the greenery along the landing was a motley collection of nightcaps and laughing faces. Rosabelle was smiling down at them, a grinning Emily at her side. Leaning over the balustrade on the other side was Lady Ordway, nodding benignly. Mr Kelland was emerging from his room in a magnificent brocade bedgown, and from the gallery round the corner came the tapping of Lord Winbolt's stick, and a voice demanding to know what was going on.

Philip came back into the hall. 'It's not a bad suggestion. Can it be done?'

Giles smiled complacently. 'A good soldier, Philip…'

'Is always prepared. I take it that the licence is under all those capes? If you're staying, old fellow, I think you should remove some of your outer garments. There's a bit of a puddle on the stairs.'

'Well, if that's all settled I'll be off back to bed,' said Mr Kelland. 'You can see me in the morning to ask my permission, Stanton. I might even give it.'

'And I'll be off, too. Oh, Giles, I'm so *happy* for you both,' said Lady Ordway as she went back to her room. 'Wilson! Wilson!'

Emily went off to satisfy her grandfather's curiosity, and Rosabelle passed the two on the stairs, murmuring that she would find Becky to do some mopping up. Philip went with her.

'Giles!' said Annabelle, smiling her enchanting smile. 'Oh Giles! Do you really love *me*, Annabelle?'

Giles had removed his greatcoat. He gathered her up into his arms and kissed her like a man who has been starving. 'I worship every last inch of you,' he whispered. 'And after High Kimber, I do know what I'm talking about. I've been haunted for weeks by it.'

'Giles!' Annabelle tried to look shocked, but she was too happy. A smile kept breaking through. 'Happy Christmas, Giles!'

'Happy Christmas, my heart,' he said. 'A happy, happy Christmas.'

Epilogue

'Past three a clock, and a cold and frosty morning:
Past three a clock: good morrow, masters all!'

The carol singers were on their way home. Almost too happy and excited to sleep, Annabelle lay listening to their voices fading into the distance. She could hear Rosabelle and Emily breathing quietly beside her in the darkness. The curtains were not completely closed, and in the blackness outside gleamed a brilliant star. It was Christmas Day—and such a day as she had not dreamt of just twenty-four hours before. Giles was here. He had come, after all, to be with her, and in just a short week they would be married. There would be a lot to do, but this special day would be spent rejoicing, giving her family and friends a chance to get to know the man she loved so dearly. Darling, dearest Giles... Annabelle at last fell asleep.

Temperley had in the past been famous for its hospitality, but this Christmas feast exceeded everything that had gone before. Half the women from the estate had been at work for weeks in the kitchens and stillrooms preparing for the celebrations, and their menfolk, too, had been drawn in to help with the heavy work. And now the house was full of bustle and happy anticipation as the maids and kitchen staff approached the climax of their labours.

In the parlour the Kellands, Ordways and Winbolts were in the middle of making their guests welcome when Annabelle came in, flushed and excited.

'Giles! Giles! Come quickly—look!'

She dragged Giles through the hall. A large sled, drawn by two sturdy horses, and jingling merrily, was drawing up at the door. In the driving seat was Goss, and behind him, swathed in furs and rugs, was Lord Stanton. Others had followed Giles out, eager to see what was causing such excitement, and the sled was soon surrounded by a laughing crowd, congratulating the new arrival on his courage in braving the weather. Lord Stanton disengaged himself and barely had time to raise an eyebrow at his son and receive a nod by way of reply before Annabelle swept him off into the house to meet her father. Giles was left with Goss.

'You're a genius, Goss! How did you find the sled?'

'Spanish ways, Colonel. I commandeered it, you might say. It cost a bit, though.'

'Never mind! I'm glad to see you both safely here! I've been getting myself engaged since I last saw you, my friend. Are you going to wish me well?'

'I can't say I'm surprised, Colonel! And yes, I do wish you every happiness, both of you. A nicer young lady than Miss Kelland you couldn't wish to meet.'

Lord Stanton was taken to his room where he took off his wrappings and was led downstairs and introduced. He received a warm welcome, though some of the less well-informed visitors wondered why he had been invited. They were to learn. After a while, Mr Kelland clapped his hands and addressed the assembly thus:

'My friends, may I have your attention?' A silence fell. 'Thank you. I am a man of few words, so you will not have

long to wait for your dinner. But I must do two things. I must
welcome you all...heartily...to the first true Christmas at
Temperley for many a long year. And second, I have to tell
you... Where are you, Rosa? And Winbolt? Come here, both
of you! That my daughter Rosabelle is to marry Mr Winbolt
on New Year's Day.'

'God bless us, we know that!' cried someone in the crowd.
'We've all got our wedding clothes ready and waiting!'

'But what you don't know, Will Darby,' said Mr Kelland
with a triumphant smile, 'what you don't know, and what I
am happy to tell you all, is that...where's that other daughter
of mine? And Stanton? Come on my other side! That
Annabelle, here, is to marry Colonel Stanton at the same ceremony!'

A moment of astonishment and then congratulations and
cheers filled the room. The twins stood on either side of their
father, each holding the hand of her betrothed, shyly acknowl-
edging the good wishes of their friends. It was a very pretty
picture. The three men were dressed in the conventional garb
for the country—buff breeches, Giles in a dark green coat,
Mr Kelland in black and Philip in chestnut brown. The girls,
in contrast, wore vivid Christmas colours—Annabelle in red,
and Rosabelle in green.

'Gad, sir!' exclaimed Lord Stanton. 'I don't think I've ever
seen a more striking sight! How the devil *do* you tell those
girls apart? If one wasn't wearing red and t'other green, I'd
think I was seeing double!'

Giles looked down at Annabelle, then smiled at his father.

'I can tell,' he said confidently. 'Now.'

The sound of a pipe and tabour, and a group of singers and
dancers caused a diversion.

> 'The boar's head in hand bear we,
> Bedecked with bays and rosemary;
> And we pray, you masters, merry be
> And seat you in the hall!'

The company joined in the old carol and followed the dancers into the Great Hall. The huge chamber was normally divided into two by screens, put in by an earlier Kelland whose wife had complained of the impossibility of heating the place. But these had been drawn aside and a number of long tables, covered with stiff damask cloths, and decorated with ivy and boughs of evergreen, filled the space. Along the side near the kitchens were serving tables laden with tongue, game pies, plates of venison, beef and duck, jellies, fruits and syllabubs, all laid out to tempt the eye as well as the palate. Flagons of ale, lemonade, and bottles of wine invited the thirsty to partake, and as soon as they were all seated eager hands started to serve them.

Then to a roll of the drum and a shrill call from the pipe, John Bostock paraded in, carrying a boar's head on an enormous dish. Applause greeted him, applause which grew louder, then turned to laughter when they saw that, in addition to the traditional rosemary and bay, the boar wore a bridal wreath and veil on its fearsome head.

The feast was memorable. Lady Ordway was heard to say to Lord Winbolt that life in the country might have its compensations, and Lord Stanton, looking none the worse for his journey, swore he hadn't enjoyed himself so much in years, though he was still damned if he could tell the difference between the Kelland twins!

'Still—as long as Giles can, I suppose it doesn't matter. He seems sure enough.'

'He does, doesn't he?' said Emily thoughtfully. 'Philip is just the same. I wonder how they do it?' Then she turned the subject and asked about Buxton.

But when the feasting was nearly over, and Giles and Philip were being taken round the tables to have a word with the guests, Emily could be seen having a private word with Mr Kelland. He smiled indulgently and nodded, whereupon Emily collected the twins and bore them off upstairs.

After a while a roll on the drum stopped the buzz of conversation, and everyone looked up to see Miss Winbolt, dressed in a tall hat and carrying a wand, standing on the half landing of the stairs.

'My Lords, Ladies and Gentlemen!' she called in an impressively deep voice. Another drum roll. 'I beg your indulgence for a few moments, for an ancient ceremony which cannot be delayed! For...

> By ancient law, or so they say,
> Each Kelland daughter this very day
> Must choose a Lord whose rule will extend
> From this day forth, till Twelfth Night's end.
> To rule us all, both saints and devils,
> The Lords to be called—the Kings of the Revels!
> Come, Queen in Red, who'll be your choice?
> Then, Emerald Queen, we'll hear your voice!'

Emily bowed to laughing applause, then turned and held up her wand. Annabelle and Rosabelle, looking like the very spirit of Christmas in their red and green dresses, appeared at the top of the stairs, and slowly descended. Each wore a glittering paper crown on her head, and carried a golden sceptre in her hand. Emily silenced the enthusiastic cheers from the assembled company with a wave of her wand. 'Let the Red Queen speak!'

The Red Queen raised her sceptre and pointed it at Giles. 'I command you to approach, sir!' she said. Giles had a smile in his eyes as he came up to her, kissed her hand and took his place at her side.

Then Emily bade the Emerald Queen to choose, and, to no one's surprise, she pointed her sceptre at Philip, who joined the other on the stairs, with the same ceremony, and much the same smile as Giles.

Then the Red Queen took Giles's hand and looked lovingly into his eyes.

> 'Husband-to-be, our troth is plighted.
> Swear that we'll stay forever united.
> To reign together forever more
> In accordance with our ancient lore.'

Giles hesitated. 'I've done many things in my time, but I've never been foolhardy enough to attempt impromptu verse. Still, if Mr Winbolt will help…' He raised an eyebrow at Philip. Encouraged by a nod, he cleared his throat and said, 'Let me see…' Then, after a moment's thought, he said,

> 'Oh loveliest lady, beauty divine!
> Alas! I can never be consort of thine…'

He paused. Philip, stepping forward to take the Red Queen by the hand, said,

> 'Tho' now you wear red, and in spite of your wiles,
> Rosa can hoax neither Philip nor Giles…'

Giles smiled and bowed to Philip. 'Thank you, my friend! Just what I needed!' He went on,

> 'That minx over there, who is now wearing green,
> Is really my Anna, my heart's only queen!'

The dignity of the two Queens was quite spoiled, as Philip and Giles, grinning broadly, unceremoniously claimed their true brides, and the hall was swept with more shouts of laughter and applause.

'Well, I declare!' said Lord Stanton delightedly. 'What a pair, eh, Kelland? What a pair! What a family! All the same, Giles, don't stand for any nonsense. You ought to punish the girls.'

'A forfeit, a forfeit!' called someone in the crowd.

'What shall it be, Annabelle?' said Giles with a mock frown. 'Philip, how shall we punish these brats?'

'A kiss, a kiss!' shouted someone else.

Giles gave a sweeping bow. 'Just what I was about to suggest myself, Will Darby. Thank you!'

With a laugh and a blush Annabelle and Rosabelle submitted gracefully to their fate. It was difficult to judge who was enjoying the 'punishment' more—the brides, the bridegrooms or the assembled company. But the applause finally died away, and the lovers drew apart as music was heard outside.

'It's the wassailers again,' said Annabelle. 'Listen!' They listened for a moment, and then softly joined in the chorus.

Love and joy come to you,
And to you your wassail too,
And God bless you, and send you
A Happy New Year,
And send you
A HAPPY NEW YEAR!

* * * * *

MILLS & BOON®

*Makes
any time
special*

**Enjoy a romantic novel from
Mills & Boon®**

Presents™ *Enchanted*™ *Temptation*®

Historical Romance™ *Medical Romance*™

We are giving away a year's supply of Mills & Boon® books to the five lucky winners of our latest competition. Simply match the six film stars to the films in which they appeared, complete the coupon overleaf and send this entire page to us by 30th June 1999. The first five correct entries will each win a year's subscription to the Mills & Boon series of their choice. What could be easier?

CABARET	__	GONE WITH THE WIND	__
ROCKY	__	SMOKEY & THE BANDIT	__
PRETTY WOMAN	__	GHOST	__

C8L

Please turn over for details of how to enter ➔

HOW TO ENTER

There are six famous faces and a list of six films overleaf. Each of the famous faces starred in one of the films listed and all you have to do is match them up!

As you match each one, write the number of the actor or actress who starred in each film in the space provided. When you have matched them all, fill in the coupon below, pop this page in an envelope and post it today. Don't forget you could win a year's supply of Mills & Boon® books—you don't even need to pay for a stamp!

Mills & Boon Hollywood Heroes Competition
FREEPOST CN81, Croydon, Surrey, CR9 3WZ
EIRE readers: (please affix stamp) PO Box 4546, Dublin 24.

Please tick the series you would like to receive if you
are one of the lucky winners

Presents™ ❏ Enchanted™ ❏ Historical Romance™ ❏

Medical Romance™ ❏ Temptation® ❏

Are you a Reader Service™ subscriber?   Yes ❏   No ❏

Ms/Mrs/Miss/Mr ....Initials ....
                                              (BLOCK CAPITALS PLEASE)
Surname..
Address ....

....

....Postcode...........................

(I am over 18 years of age)   C8L

Closing date for entries is 30th June 1999. One entry per household. Free subscriptions are for four books per month. Competition open to residents of the UK and Ireland only. As a result of this application, you may receive further offers from Harlequin Mills & Boon and other carefully selected companies. If you would prefer not to share in this opportunity please write to The Data Manager at the address shown above.

Mills & Boon is a registered trademark of
Harlequin Mills & Boon Ltd.